A moment later, we joined Sam in the atrium. My sister looked first at me, then at Sam. Her mental wheels were turning, and I didn't trust their direction. She smiled sweetly. "I'm sure looking forward to this dinner."

"We'll lock up," I said. Theft wasn't a problem in Wilfred. Murder, yes. Robbery, not so much. But after the recent goings-on, I wasn't taking chances. "Hold my coat, please." I handed it to Jean while I dug for my keys in my purse. As Jean pulled her hands from her pockets, something fluttered to the floor.

"What's this?" She knelt to retrieve a sheet of paper torn from a small spiral-bound tablet. "This isn't mine."

I was all too aware of Sam leaning over my shoulder to look at the note. "Don't touch that," he said with enough authority that Jean yanked back her hand.

"No," I whispered. "Please." I didn't need to read the note to know what it said.

*READY*, it read in block letters. Next to the word was a taped list of workshop participants cut from a program, with a jagged black line through Jean's name.

Jean swallowed. "That's our agenda from yesterday."

Maybe the murders weren't my business before, but they definitely were now . . .

Books by Angela M. Sanders

BAIT AND WITCH

SEVEN-YEAR WITCH

WITCH AND FAMOUS

WITCH UPON A STAR

Published by Kensington Publishing Corp.

A WITCH WAY LIBRARIAN MYSTERY

# Witch Upon a Star

## Angela M. Sanders

Kensington Publishing Corp.
www.kensingtonbooks.com

KENSINGTON BOOKS are published by

Kensington Publishing Corp.
119 West 40th Street
New York, NY 10018

All Kensington titles, imprints, and distributed lines are available at special quantity discounts for bulk purchases for sales promotion, premiums, fund-raising, educational, or institutional use.

Special book excerpts or customized printings can also be created to fit specific needs. For details, write or phone the office of the Kensington Sales Manager: Attn.: Sales Department. Kensington Publishing Corp., 119 West 40th Street, New York, NY 10018. Phone: 1-800-221-2647.

The K and Teapot logo is a trademark of Kensington Publishing Corp.

First Printing: June 2023
ISBN: 978-1-4967-4091-5

ISBN: 978-1-4967-4092-2 (ebook)

10 9 8 7 6 5 4 3 2 1

Printed in the United States of America

To the animals—mine and those of my friends—who have inspired places and characters in this series: Kirby, Buffy, Thor, Sailor, Bitsy, Squeaky, and Sylvia. We're so lucky to have you in our lives.

# CHAPTER ONE

I shivered in the parking lot of Darla's café. Heavy-bellied clouds, threatening snow, blocked any hint of the new moon. Tomorrow, at the café's grand reopening, the lot would be full, but tonight it was nothing but frosty gravel—and me. Waiting for my sister.

Mom had given me firm instructions about Jean. "Watch her carefully. That outfit is a cult, I know it. Your sister is too gullible. What kind of workshop leader is named Cookie, anyway?"

"Mom," I'd told her, "It's only a workshop. How much trouble can she get into?"

"That's what your father said when she went to camp. Remember? She came home with a broken arm and three kittens."

"She was twelve. It wasn't her fault her bunk-mate got homesick and climbed a tree to hide." Jean had crawled up to convince her things were going to be okay. The kittens I couldn't account for, except that Jean's heart was so soft that during rainstorms she'd circle the block, lifting earthworms from the sidewalk so they wouldn't get trampled.

"And no talk about magic," had been Mom's last warning. "On no account are you to tell your sister you're a witch. She already feels like she'll never catch up to you and Toni."

Headlights appeared down the road that bisected town. The lights grew nearer, and my breath quickened. At last, the shuttle bus pulled into the parking lot, crunching gravel as it braked and opened its doors.

"Jean!" I enveloped my little sister in a hug before her feet even hit the ground.

"Josie," she said, her laughter steaming the December night air. "I thought I'd never get here."

Duke was at the wheel. "You have everything?" Driving the retreat's shuttle bus was part of his portfolio of side hustles as the town's jack-of-all-trades. I made out the shapes of a few other people in the bus's darkened interior.

Jean lifted her duffel bag. "Right here. Thanks, Duke."

The shuttle bus's doors closed with a pneumatic whoosh, and the bus circled the parking lot to disappear up the access road to the retreat center.

"It's so good to see you. Let me carry that." I swung Jean's duffel over my arm and leaned back to take her in. Despite Mom's warnings, she didn't look like the soon-to-be victim of a life coaching workshop scam. Her strawberry blond waves gleamed in the parking lot's mercury vapor lamp.

She smiled, her upper lip slightly thicker than her lower, giving her the air of a friendly cherub.

Jean examined me in return. "You look different."

"In a good way, I hope?"

"Yes. Like someone turned up your dimmer switch. Not that I can see much right now." She glanced at the dark café and storefronts across the road. "Where do you live?"

"There. A five-minute walk." I pointed up the hill to the Victorian mansion that housed the library and my apartment. Only its tower showed above the cottonwoods along the river.

Arm in arm, we climbed the road to cross the stone bridge over the Kirby River. We took a right through a copse of fir trees. In the clearing, dotted with oaks, squatted a solid house with a wide porch.

"Is that it?" Jean asked.

"That's Big House. The library's straight ahead."

Across the lawn on the other side of Big House lay the caretaker's cottage and, finally, the library, as prim and upright as a turn-of-the-century duchess. Lights shone from my top-floor apartment in the former servants' quarters.

"Who lives in Big House?" Jean asked. She turned her head toward me, her breath hanging in the air. She'd sensed something, probably my unrequited crush on Sam, Big House's owner and the town sheriff.

It was going too far to say my sisters and I could read each other's minds, but we had an unusual connection. Years ago, my older sister Toni was in a car accident. Both Jean and I ran to the living room window from our separate corners of the house before the phone even jangled with news of it. Fortunately, Toni wasn't badly hurt. All the same, we'd known.

"Sam Wilfred, the town's sheriff, lives there," I said as nonchalantly as I could and added quickly, before she pressed for details, "That's the library, straight ahead."

Jean shifted her attention and inhaled sharply. "Oh, I love it."

A circular driveway fronted a porch, trimmed in gingerbread fretwork, with a square tower rising above it. The mansion was built from an Italianate Revival pattern in a book of house plans I'd found in the bottom drawer of a desk. When I'd opened the drawer, the book shouted "ta-da!" and flipped open to the library's floor plan.

We took the side entrance to the former servants' staircase.

"I'll give you the full tour tomorrow. You must be exhausted. Let's get you to bed."

Inside, the library's warmth brought out the scent of wood and books. We climbed to the third floor, and I unlocked the door to my apartment. Before entering, Jean leaned over the wooden railing to gaze into the atrium. The stained glass–windowed cupola glowed with dull reds and blues.

On the two floors below us, open doorways showed books. Thousands of books, from romance novels and cookbooks to car repair manuals and art history tomes. They filled the air with centuries of story and knowledge, and they whispered greetings to me, a whoosh of voices only I could hear.

This was my home and my favorite place in the world.

"Something has changed about you." Jean peeled off her coat, a vintage princess-cut jacket with a daisy-patterned lining and bell sleeves. She culled her wardrobe from thrift stores, yet had more style than found on the racks of Beverly Hills boutiques. If I did the same, I'd look like I'd spent the night under a bridge.

"What do you mean?" I asked.

She laid her coat over the Eastlake sofa that would be her bed for the week. "For instance, this. Your old apartment in DC was beige and boring. Your books were the only interesting part of it. But this . . . Look."

She ran a finger through the fringe on the embroidered piano shawl over the sofa's back before taking in the thrifted portraits of anonymous women I'd hung here and there. A mid-century lamp glowed from next to a heavy marble bust of a woman I'd decided was Emily Dickinson. The faint scent of incense and woodsmoke clung to the air.

"Things have changed since then." That was an understatement.

Jean yawned. I squeezed her once again in a big hug. My baby sister was here at last. I glanced at the clock. It was way too late to call Mom, three hours ahead on the East Coast.

Once again, Jean guessed my thoughts. "Mom asked you to check up on me, didn't she?"

It wouldn't be any use to deny it. "You know how she worries."

"Josie, promise me. You have to trust me. I know

everyone thinks I'm not capable of doing anything on my own, but I am. Okay?"

It was too late to argue—too late in the day and too late to persuade Jean not to attend the workshop. At least she was here. I could hang out with her for a week.

"I know Mom thinks this workshop's a scam and I'll lose my money for nothing, but she's wrong," Jean added. "Life coaching is huge. This certification will change my life."

"I don't know. I—"

"Don't worry," she said. "You'll see. I've got this."

I woke to the series of booms and rattles of the furnace kicking in. Within minutes, warm air coursed through my apartment. I threw back the down comforter and nosed my feet into my slippers. The old furnace, converted decades ago from one fed by sawdust, had its quirks. Lyndon, the library's caretaker, had told me where to find instructions on resetting it if it misbehaved while he was on his honeymoon in England with Roz. So far, I hadn't had to use them.

"Josie?" Jean called from the adjoining living room.

Rodney, my cat, blinked sleepily and stretched. After a few licks to make sure his fur was as luxurious as always, he jumped from the bed to follow me.

Still on the sofa, Jean clasped her hands behind her head and smiled. Rodney leapt up beside her and purred as Jean stroked his head. "You didn't tell me you had a cat. A black one, too."

"He was here when I moved in. He sort of adopted me." I dropped into the armchair across from her. "You look happy."

"Why shouldn't I be? I get to see you. Plus, the workshop. Today is the first day of the rest of my life, you know."

I hesitated before speaking. "Is that something your coaching guru says?"

"No, dummy. It's a cliché." She sat, and Rodney jumped to the back of the couch.

I smiled. Sisters.

"What's this?" Jean held up a boxed set of CDs of Verdi's *La Traviata*. "I didn't know you liked opera. I don't remember you listening to music at all, actually."

"A friend lent it to me." Sam. In return, I was guiding him through the classics of vintage crime novels. He was turning into a diehard Raymond Chandler fan.

"A friend?"

"He's introducing me to opera. The music is great, but you should hear some of the stories that go with them."

"*He's* teaching you?" She sat straighter. "A man?"

"Never mind," I said quickly. "Anyway, the library's closed today, so I have lots of time for you. I thought I'd show you around town this morning, then we could pick up something for dinner. I'll walk you to the retreat center at noon."

"What are you going to do while I'm at the workshop?"

"Today's the café's grand reopening."

"Wow," Jean said. "You Wilfredians really know how to party."

"It's a huge deal." Rodney jumped from the couch and trotted down the hall, probably headed toward his food dish. "The café's more than a breakfast spot. It's the community center. Last spring a flood closed it down. It needed a total rehab." I went to the window to pull back the curtains. A light was on in Big House. Sam must be preparing a bottle for Nicky. Over the bluff, orange morning sun illuminated the mist rising from the river. I turned to Jean, quilts still piled on her lap. "Let's talk about you. Tell me about the workshop."

Her face animated with excitement. "I'm going to be a wellness coach. It's a big deal. I make a little investment now in the certification program, and I can earn hundreds of thousands a year, like Cookie does."

Mom's warning rang in my ears. "Come to the kitchen and tell me more."

Jean, in men's red flannel pajamas, followed me to the landing, where I silently bid good morning to the books. She stopped again at the banister to take in the view, brighter now with day breaking.

"This place is paradise," Jean said. She pointed to the full-length oil portrait hanging above the atrium's main entrance. "Who's that? She's gorgeous, if a little intense looking. Love the flapper dress."

"Marilyn Wilfred, the library's founder."

"She has a black cat, too." Jean pointed to Rodney's double, forever immortalized at her feet.

"Weird, huh?" I'd done a double take the first time I'd noticed it. Now almost nothing about the library surprised me. "Come on. I bought green tea just for you." In the kitchen, Jean settled into the banquette while I put water on. "So, what is a wellness coach?"

"Someone who helps other people achieve their best health."

"Like yoga?" Jean was a yoga teacher.

"That, and nutrition and meditation. A coach meets with clients regularly and puts them on a plan."

"And that makes you rich?"

"Cookie's model has several parts. Besides meeting one-on-one, people can buy monthly subscriptions to her coaching club and pay for online workshops. I could do the same. It builds up. You should see how Cookie lives—she gives lectures throughout the world. She's a huge inspiration."

"What does the workshop get you? Coaching doesn't sound like anything you couldn't figure out on your own."

"Oh," Jean said. "Cookie really knows how to build a coaching business. She does podcasts, is super-active on social media, has a membership program—everything. I've been following her for months."

*Cookie Masterson,* a periodical whispered. *Celebrity coach, multimillionaire.*

"How much does this Cookie Masterson charge you?" I asked.

"Have you been talking to Mom?"

"Of course. She's happy we're spending time together," I hedged.

Jean pressed her lips together. "The workshop's a bargain when you consider the money I'll be making once I'm certified as a life coach. Plus, I got a discount for staying with you instead of at the retreat center."

"In other words, the tuition put you in debt, and you don't want to tell me." I might be the middle sibling, but I was still Jean's big sister.

She studied the table's wooden top. "I used Grandma's inheritance." She shifted her gaze to me. "But it'll pay off. It will. Cookie almost never does small workshops like this. Usually she takes over convention centers. I was really lucky to get in."

I pulled my coffee mug near. "It doesn't sound like the retreat is about wellness at all."

"No," Jean said, her excitement returning. "It's about Cookie's special coaching method called Ready-Set-Go."

"Ready-Set-Go," I repeated, doubt in my voice. Grandma's money was going into something kindergartners recited on the playground?

"Yes. She talks about it in her podcasts. She has millions of followers. She was on *Good Morning, Hollywood.*"

Rodney stuck a paw in his water dish and splashed some on the linoleum. I still didn't understand why that was so fun for him.

"You're really excited about this, aren't you?"

"I am." She tugged the sleeve of my chenille bathrobe. "Mom thinks I'm making a mistake. She had one of her *premonitions*"—Jean said this in a voice meant to belittle it—"and tried to convince me to stay home. You'll support me, won't you?" When I didn't respond right away, she added, "I know what I'm doing. I've dreamed about this for a long time. It's what I'm meant to do with my life."

"I see." I returned to the table and held my mug between my palms.

"You have books. You've been settled on your path your whole life. Toni's a doctor. She's helping tons of people, plus she has a family. All I have is a part-time job teaching yoga at the community center. I want to do more than that. I want to help regular people be the best they can. It's in me, Josie. It's what I'm meant to do."

Although she didn't know it, magic flowed through Jean's blood. Her magic might be less potent than mine, but she was a healer, just like Toni. And like Grandma, who shared the star-shaped birthmark on my shoulder as well as the heightened power of my own magic. Besides, who was I to judge how Jean spent her money? I'd blown Grandma's inheritance—modest as it was—to escape to Wilfred a year earlier. Maybe this was what Jean needed to grow into her full self.

"I get it, I really do. Now, drink up. We have lots to do before the workshop starts."

I understood Jean's desire to be a wellness coach, but it didn't mean I trusted this Ready-Set-Go scheme. Mom's premonitions had been on target more than once.

# CHAPTER TWO

I waved an arm over the view. "This is Wilfred." From the bridge crossing the Kirby River, Jean and I surveyed the town. To the right of the lazy highway running through Wilfred spread a few square blocks of modest houses, some with wood-smoke drifting from their chimneys. Stately Douglas fir trees rose here and there.

"It must feel strange to live in such a tiny town after DC," Jean said.

"It was—at first. Everyone knows your business, and it's a drive if you want decent sushi. Now, I love it. Maybe I can't buy aspirin without someone asking about my health later that afternoon, but I also feel they care for me. People have each other's backs here."

It was true. Wilfred felt like an extended family, complete with crazy uncles and nosy aunts. Over the year-plus I'd lived here, I'd considered returning to the East Coast, but the fresh air, gorgeous countryside, and most of all, friendly neighbors kept me in town. In Wilfred's library, I'd found my home.

Jean pointed to what looked like a treehouse. "What's that?"

"Mrs. Littlewood's bird-watching platform. That's the church spire just beyond it."

*Spire* might have been too ambitious a word. The church was barely larger than the Grange Hall, and its spire was a wooden cupola. The pastor served the entire county, and as a result, we had services only once a month.

"That's where the shuttle bus let me off." Jean pointed toward the café on the highway's left.

"Exactly." I looked forward to the café's reopening, not only for the food, but because the library's kitchen had become Wilfred's replacement town square. It was a full-time job keeping the beer out and feet off the table. "The trailer park behind it is called the Magnolia Rolling Estates. Beyond that is the meadow. See how the river curves? You can just about make out the retreat center on the other side."

Looking at the log building in the distance, Jean's eyes lit up. "Cookie's there right now."

"I hope you're not going to be disappointed," I couldn't help but say.

She shot me a warning glance. "We already talked about this."

"Fine." I nearly sighed, then realized I was starting to sound like Mom. "Let's go to the grocery store and pick up a few things for dinner. Are you still vegan?"

"No, but I don't take gluten or nightshade vegetables, and I eat raw food only, especially macrobiotic. Do you have a juicer?"

"Seriously? There's no way I—"

"Kidding! I try to stay away from too much sugar and red meat, but that's it."

A few minutes later, we pushed open the door to the PO Grocery, named because it had taken over the shuttered post office when the mill had closed. The word *Wilfred* and our zip code still studded the wall in bronze letters above the dairy case. Elvis's "Viva Las Vegas" played quietly over the store's sound system.

"Let's make soup." All I'd have to do is unpack my grocery sack, and a dozen cookbooks would shoulder for attention to suggest recipes. We were loading our basket with butternut squash and kale when a man's forceful voice prickled the hair on my arms.

"Leave him alone."

Onion in hand, I glanced at Jean. The voice came from the aisle behind us, on the other side of a pet food display. In the background, Elvis's baritone continued to praise Vegas.

"Calm down. I'm simply—" began a woman's voice, with an earnest Midwestern accent.

"I saw you last night at the airport. It's not right."

The woman's boots shuffled on the linoleum. "I don't even know you. Leave me alone or I'll call the police."

"This is your last warning," the low, smooth voice said as the store's soundtrack shifted to Mac Davis warning "baby" not to get hooked on him.

"You don't want to find out what happens when you don't do as you're told."

My breath caught in my throat. Jean crept to the shelf and stealthily parted cans of chicken pâté cat food. We knelt in front of the opening but, thanks to an inconveniently placed bag of maxi-pads, couldn't make out more than the midsection of a man's zip-up green jacket. A woman's hand, still red from the cold outside, lifted in a "stop" motion. Silver gleamed from her ring finger. Both people were strangers to Wilfred.

Jean and I shared a glance, and our thoughts raced into each other's minds. *Should we step in?* I wondered. *No. Wait just a moment,* I read in her eyes.

"What do you want? Money?" the woman said.

"I told you what I want. Lay off."

"Keep your voice down." The woman's head swiveled, and we ducked. "It's not that easy. We'll talk about it later."

Both people shuffled, and Jean and I hurried to the vegetable display to study the mushroom bin as if we hadn't heard a thing. At the ding of the front door's bell, Jean darted around the aisle for a clear view of the exit. "He's still here," she mouthed.

I strolled to the snack aisle and pretended to debate the merits of gummy bears versus Junior Mints, all the while keeping an eye on the man. To my surprise, he pulled a cellophane-wrapped bundle of red roses from the bucket near the cash register, paid for them, and left.

The cashier picked up her crossword puzzle. "Are you going to buy those, or not?" she asked me.

"No, thank you. I'll stick to vegetables." I returned the gummy bears to the shelf and hurried back to Jean. "Did you recognize them? Are they with the retreat?" I asked under my breath.

"The woman's name is Marcia. I sat next to her on the shuttle from the airport." She absently dropped a few mushrooms into a bag. "She was friendly. Said this is the fifth workshop she's taken from Cookie."

"And the man?" That voice, that warning. I tightened my scarf as if it could protect me from his cold words. "He threatened her."

"I'm not sure. He might have been on the shuttle bus. If so, he was in the rear." She turned to me, eyes wide. "Whoever he is, I hope I never see him again."

The morning's fog had lifted, and the sun pierced cold, blue sky as Jean and I made our way to the retreat center from the library, where I'd spent the last hour giving Jean a tour.

"We'll go through the meadow," I said. "Tomorrow I'll show you the path from the library along the river and through the woods—"

"—To grandmother's house we go," she finished.

"I wish. I miss her."

"Me, too," Jean said.

Grandma's house, with its lush, messy garden, lazing ginger cats, and bundles of herbs drying in the kitchen had always been my happy place. Not that home had been unhappy. But once she'd left Grandma's and struck out on her own, Mom had systematically squeezed the magic out of her life and, eventually, ours. I never did know why. Which reminded me—I'd promised to call Mom to report on Jean's arrival.

"If not to Grandma's," she continued, "then on to a fulfilling career as a wellness coach, thousands of followers, and an enviable income." She skipped ahead a few steps and spun with happiness. "I'm so lucky to be here. This is the beginning of something good. I know it."

In my coat pocket, I crossed my fingers. "Take the road left of the café. We'll cut through the trailer park."

In anticipation of the afternoon's grand reopening, the café's windows were papered over, with the celebration's start time noted in magic marker. Lights were off. Darla must have finished prep work for what would be a busy afternoon.

Jean was practically bouncing, her tote bag tucked under her arm, as we threaded through the Magnolia Rolling Estates. It warmed me to see her so happy. I hoped Mom was wrong about the workshop. I pointed out Lalena's pink trailer, where she conducted her business as a psychic. Roz's trailer was dark since she and Lyndon were on their honeymoon. Two figures passed by the kitchen window in Darla's trailer—Darla and her new husband. We emerged into the meadow.

"Hurry up, Josie. I don't want to be late."

"Fine, but watch for potholes." We picked up our pace and crossed the walkway over the new levee where the Kirby flowed into the millpond. From there, it was a few steps to the retreat center's broad stone patio.

The center itself was a log-walled rectangle with a sloping shingled roof and massive stone chimney. A patio with a firepit and a view of the millpond fronted the center. We crossed the patio and pushed open a timber-framed door to enter the large main room with its cathedral ceiling. A fire crackled in the river rock hearth. Three people lounged in club chairs nearby. They turned to us as we entered.

"Hi," Jean said, her voice as welcoming as her wide smile. "I'm Jean Way."

"Rex Markham," the man in the nearest chair said. He rose to take Jean's hand in both of his. "So pleased to meet you."

My pulse leapt. This was him, the man we'd seen at the market. I'd recognize that DJ-style voice anywhere. Coupled with his tan, even white teeth, and preternaturally blue eyes, he made used car salesmen look like Cub Scouts. Jean's smile faltered as she withdrew her hand.

A blonde in her thirties with glossy golden waves raised her palm in greeting. "Sylvia Lewis."

I knew instantly that she and Jean would be retreat buddies. They were both earnest and wide open. A notebook in the canvas tote at Sylvia's side mumbled observations of Wilfred. Apparently, Sylvia kept a journal.

"What kind of coaching do you do?" Jean asked.

"Wellness, with a focus on yoga."

"Me, too!" Jean said. "We'll have to talk."

A graying brunette nodded from the club chair opposite Rex. A thatch of hair tied in a narrow pink ribbon over her forehead brought to mind a senior Lhasa Apso. Cementing the impression, she wore a T-shirt advertising a dog groomer in Boise, Idaho. "Bernie Stanich. Nice to meet you. I haven't settled on my specialty yet. Still feeling it out."

My gaze drifted again to Rex, who, pinkie ring gleaming, steepled his fingers and ignored Bernie. He kept glancing toward to stairs to the guest rooms.

I was about to make my exit, when a petite woman dressed in shearling boots and earth-toned layers rounded the corner. "Good morning, everyone," she said.

That voice, with its hint of Minnesota. Jean and I exchanged glances. It was her. The woman we'd seen at the PO Grocery. Now, with a clear view, it was obvious she wasn't well. She was breathing quickly, and a sheen of sweat covered her brow. She managed a weak smile.

Jean stepped toward her to say hello when a voice interrupted us. "Hello, my crumbs," it said in full, rich tones.

Our collective gaze was pulled to the upstairs landing like stars into a black hole. We were in the presence of greatness. "Crumbs," Jean whispered to me in wonder. "That's what Cookie calls her followers. I'm a crumb now."

Leaning over the second floor's split log banister was a small, wiry woman with short silver hair that matched her curiously gray eyes. Her skin was as smooth as the pages of a fresh-off-the-press novel. Charisma radiated from her, and I knew that anywhere she went, heads would turn in her direction. She didn't have to introduce herself.

This was Cookie Masterson. It didn't take more than three seconds for me to know I couldn't stand her.

Behind her lurked a short man with unkempt, steely hair who looked like he might have been an extra in a gangster movie. Cookie glared at him, and he receded into the hall's shadows before I got a good look.

"Darling crumbs, today we embark on a journey that will change your lives forever. After this morning, nothing will be the same. Nothing." Even without a microphone, her words resounded through the retreat center. I made a mental note to suggest concerts in the lobby for its terrific acoustics.

The crumbs listened with eyes wide. Sylvia's hand strayed toward her tote, then withdrew. Marcia set down her travel mug and felt for a chair. Whatever had sparked her disagreement with Rex Markham seemed to be far from her mind now, but she looked as if she might be coming down with something. Enthralled, Rex stared at Cookie. Only Bernie remained indifferent.

"We will explore my trademarked Ready-Set-Go model in depth. Get ready for an experience you'll never forget," Cookie said. She turned from her impromptu podium and made for the staircase to join the workshop's students.

"See you later, Jean," I said under my breath. I couldn't help but add, "This better be worth it."

Jean, mesmerized, barely paid me attention. "It will. I know it."

# CHAPTER THREE

Instead of the side servants' door, which I normally took, I walked around to the library's front door to experience the grand entrance. I mounted the stairs to the wide porch and inserted the skeleton key before pushing open the carved oak door to the scent of the lemon oil Lyndon used to polish the foyer's woodwork.

Past the tile-floored entry hall, I opened another door, this one fitted with stained glass windows, and emerged into the library's atrium to breathe pure satisfaction. A small oak table adorned the center of the atrium, and, as usual, Lyndon had filled a vase with something seasonal—this week, branches of bittersweet with tiny orange berries. He had planned a bouquet to last his entire vacation. None of us was sure why he and Roz had chosen to tour British gardens in winter, but Mrs. Garlington had pointed out that Roz knew how to pinch a penny, and airfare would be much cheaper now.

"Hello, books," I said. I loved having Jean visit, but it was a relief to be free with my magic.

*Hi, Josie. Hello. Good morning,* came greetings from throughout the library in a crowd of voices, from an Austrian accent in Reference to giggles and sighs from Romance. An elephant trumpeted in Natural History, and a few bars of ragtime drifted from Fine Arts. I was still learning how to harness the magic that flowed so freely from the books. As long as I kept an even mood, things were fine. If not, my emotion, combined with the books' energy, could short out electrical gadgets, hurl books haphazardly, and even start fires. To that end, every once in a while I siphoned off a bit of the books' power by putting them to work. The books loved it.

I stood in the atrium, hands on hips. "Are you ready? Book ballet!" I shouted. Rodney scampered in to watch.

Answering my call, a thick encyclopedia on films wafted from upstairs like a falling leaf and hovered at eye level.

"A film musical, huh? You choose," I instructed.

The book hung, limp, and energy in the library buzzed, quietly at first. Then the energy tightened, and all at once the encyclopedia began to spin. A movie title slipped into my brain: Sonja Henie's *Sun Valley Serenade* from 1941. I laughed. The icicles outside must have inspired the books to choose a movie starring a figure skater.

"Okay," I said. "Ready?" I hummed the movie's theme song. I loved old movies and the books knew it.

The film encyclopedia rose ten feet and raced to circle the atrium as if speeding on skates. I'd intended for it to be a solo show, but a dozen or so books slipped from their shelves to sway at the edges like an enthusiastic audience. Meanwhile, the encyclopedia swirled and bucked, kicking up imaginary legs and waving arms. Tension I hadn't even known was in the air began to dissipate.

I hummed the final flourish and said, "Books! Back to your shelves."

Giggling and trailing imaginary snowflakes, they zipped throughout the library with gentle thunks and swooshes as they slid home between neighboring volumes.

I was so lucky. Having this gift, learning how to use it, had cracked me open in a good way. Before my magic had been unleashed, I'd been like a caterpillar locked in a cocoon clinging to a hidden leaf—or, in my case, locked in my room with my nose in a novel. Now I was a butterfly, free to experience the world fully.

However, it was time for this butterfly to get on with her day. Just as soon as I made myself another cup of coffee, I'd call Mom. I'd barely registered the thought when my phone rang. I didn't need to look to know who it was.

"Mom?"

"Josie. How's your sister? Did she make it there safely?"

I switched the phone to my other hand as I knelt to scratch Rodney between his ears. "I just dropped her off at the retreat center. She's fine."

"Are you sure?" Mothers worry about their children, but having a mother with just enough of the gift of foresight to raise questions, but not enough to answer them, layered on more anxiety.

"Sure I'm sure. She's really excited. I met Cookie." I instantly regretted mentioning the part about Cookie. Mom would sense right away that I hadn't liked her. I launched into another topic. "Is it cold there? It's full-bore winter here."

"Yes, it's cold here," Mom said warily. "What do you expect this time of year?"

I knew that tone of voice. She wasn't buying the weather ploy. I'd have to venture into riskier territory, a subject I hadn't planned to broach until later. "I want to tell Jean I'm a witch. You and Toni know, and it's only fair that Jean know, too." As for Dad, he was clueless. When he wasn't in the classroom, he was in his study with his head in a book about the Girondists or Louis XIV's dining habits.

"I'd prefer you don't, honey."

"Why not?" If it were up to Mom, magic would play no part in our lives at all. I still didn't understand what her objection was, and she refused to talk about it except to say I'd be better off shutting down my magic for good. It was too late for that.

"Jean already doubts herself. She compares herself with you and Toni and feels unworthy. Toni has a solid medical practice and a family—you know Letty is Jean's favorite human being on earth."

Remembering the expression on my baby niece Letty's face when Jean came in the room, the feeling was mutual. "So?"

"And you're doing what makes you happy, running a library. Although it's a little far from home, if you ask me."

"What does this have to do with not telling Jean I'm a witch?"

"Don't give her another reason to feel like a failure," Mom said. "My hunch is this life coaching workshop is her attempt to even the score. The last thing she needs is to think she'll never match up to you and Toni. If she knew you were a witch, it would really get her down. Once she decided you didn't need psychiatric treatment, that is."

"But she *is* worthy." Everyone loved Jean. They couldn't help it. More than that, she loved everyone back. I couldn't get on a bus with Jean without her charming a passenger and passing on advice for rehabbing a sprained shoulder or addressing another passenger's sleep trouble.

"I have a bad feeling about this life coaching business," Mom said. "That child is a natural-born patsy."

"If Jean's getting ripped off, there's nothing we can do about it now. If it helps, there are only a handful of other students, and she'll get lots of attention."

"See if you can encourage her not to waste any more money on that coach, Candy or whatever her name is."

Mom knew Cookie's name as well as I did. "I think it's Snickerdoodle."

"Maybe Mallomar?" She chuckled, then let out a windy sigh. "I can't help but worry. Remember when she was in first grade and that kid stole her milk money for half the year?"

"Sure, but that was a long time ago." Strictly speaking, the kid, a bully with a perpetual runny nose and need of a haircut, hadn't stolen the

money. Jean had noticed his jam-and-bread sand-
wiches and was concerned he hadn't enough to eat.
She'd given him the money. Mom didn't know
about the half a sandwich she'd forced on him, too.

"She hasn't changed, Josie. Look at the place
she rented."

"I thought she liked the apartment. She can
walk to the yoga studio."

"Good thing, too, since she blew out the water
heater. Her landlord was short on cash, so when
the water heater broke, Jean said she'd watch a
couple of videos and try to fix it herself. She
worked a month of double shifts to cover the dam-
age, plus she had to shower at work. Your father
and I paid for her to get chiropractic treatment
after all those extra downward dogs."

I could see this. Jean's soft heart had led her to
trouble more than once. "She means well. It's time
to let go, Mom. Maybe she has to make a few mistakes to learn."

"A broken water heater, a little milk money—
that's okay. Those are learning experiences." Mom's
frustrated tone belied her words. I pictured her,
phone clasped to her ear, circling the kitchen's
butcher block island with her brows drawn. "But
this Cookie person. She's a fraud. It's not just me
who thinks so. There's a whole series in the paper
on the life coach certification racket."

"There is?" The life coach phenomenon hadn't
made it to Wilfred yet.

"Oh, yes. You don't have to have a single qualifi-
cation to call yourself a life coach, you know. You
can promise anything and charge up the wazoo for
bogus certifications. The report I saw, some lady in

Florida was living on a yacht with the money she'd swindled out of people."

I needed to look into this. "Did the report mention Cookie Masterson?"

"Only briefly." Mom's voice dropped. "But that doesn't mean she's not a crook." Another drawn-out sigh. "I'm worried Jean's good intentions will be the death of her. Promise me you'll look after her. I'm counting on you. Okay?"

"I'm not Jean's keeper, Mom."

"Promise me. I won't get off the phone until you promise me you won't let her do anything foolish."

Now wasn't the time to continue the conversation that Jean needed to build confidence by making her own decisions. "I promise. Give my love to Dad."

I glanced at the kitchen clock outside my office door. I had just enough time to find out what Cookie was really about before the café's grand re-opening.


Soon I was seated at Old Man Thurston's wide desk in his former office—now Children's Literature—with my laptop and a mug of coffee. Something about the room's cozy intimacy, oak-lined walls, or maybe the residual energy of the decades of timber business conducted here inspired my best thinking. Today the library was closed and Lyndon was safely overseas. I could carry out research my favorite way.

"Books," I said. "What do you have on Cookie Masterson and on life coaching in general?"

Two magazines flew through the door and landed on my desk. Both riffled open to profiles on Cookie. One was a puff piece from the "Women on the Go" column about how Cookie had been a high school social science teacher who'd downloaded the Ready-Set-Go method in whole cloth from a dream, and now she was changing the lives of tens of thousands of devoted crumbs. Useless. I closed that magazine and pushed it away.

The other story was a feature in the *New York Times* Sunday magazine by big-name investigative reporter Evangeline Philbin. This had to be the series Mom had referred to. In it, Cookie was mentioned as part of a lucrative, unregulated life coaching movement. The reporter wrote that coaching could be helpful in many situations that didn't require a licensed therapist. It wasn't life coaching that the article questioned, it was life coaching academies—like Cookie's—that charged a hefty tuition to issue worthless certifications.

This was interesting, and I wanted to know more.

From the meager offerings that had landed on my desk, I deduced most of my research would have to be online. I started with Cookie's website. Cookie's face gleamed from its welcome page. Below it, testimonials raved at her prowess. *Cookie and Ready-Set-Go changed my life!* and *I can do anything now that I have Ready-Set-Go.* Cookie had apparently trained coaches specializing in everything from wellness, like Jean was learning, to weight loss, closet organizing, pet training, sobriety, and even life coaches for other life coaches.

A whole page was dedicated to her "Find Your Soulmate" coaching program. Photos showed Cookie on the arms of romance-cover-ready men as they gazed at beach sunsets, lounged in hot tubs, and, in one, sipped champagne on what looked like a private jet. Here, Cookie admitted she wasn't ready to settle down for good, but the two-week course outlining her program's three easy steps—that's right, Ready-Set-Go—made sure she had prospects lined up out the door. Maybe I lingered an extra moment or two on this part of the website.

How much did her coach-the-coaches services cost? I scrolled past a dozen testimonials and clicked on a variety of *Ready to change your life?* links before I arrived at an eye-popping number deep in her website. No wonder Mom was concerned.

I closed the laptop. Was Cookie Masterson a cult leader or a legitimate trainer? I pondered the threat we'd overheard this morning at the PO Grocery. Could it be tied to the workshop?

This was the program's first day. Although Mom might not agree, Jean wasn't a complete innocent. Could she resist Cookie's manipulations—that is, if she really was a scammer? Time would tell if Mom's fears were justified.

This was food for thought. Speaking of food, I'd better hurry if I was going to make it to the café's grand reopening before the pancakes ran out.

# CHAPTER FOUR

"Josie, you're just in time," Mrs. Littlewood said. "Darla's about to cut the ribbon."

Unlike last night, when I'd waited for Jean in a desolate parking lot, this afternoon the lot was crammed with people and cars. Practically the whole town gathered around the card table near the café's front door where Darla handed out paper cups of coffee.

Today was a day to celebrate. Darla was Wilfred's de facto mayor, and her café had served as a combination town hall and community square since she'd taken it over several decades earlier. The café was where graduation dinners were held, births were toasted, and home sales signed. Many a breakup had been mourned in the café's tavern side. When Mrs. Garlington was well enough after her hip replacement surgery to leave the house, her first stop was tea and toast at the café, where well-wishers pretended to listen to her epic poem, "Ode to a Rolling Walker."

Darla held a microphone attached to a portable speaker. "Welcome, everyone, to the café's grand reopening. I'm so pleased to see you all."

Clouds of breath rose and gravel crunched beneath boots as the crowd cheered. Darla wore her signature leopard print, this time in a thick woolen scarf, and her voice was clear and firm and as businesslike as usual. Montgomery, her new husband, stood quietly behind her, a knit stocking cap—possibly a product of the town's knitting club—on his bald head, and his hands folded in front of him.

When last spring's flood had left the café a concrete shell, Darla took it as a sign to rethink her business. In the meantime, the café had remained empty. Passing its washed-out walls was like looking at a skeleton and mourning the person who had once given it life. During the summer, it hadn't been so bad. Wilfredians had moved their meetings across the street to the front yard of Darla's sister Patty's This-N-That shop, which at the time had featured vintage appliances. Patty had hooked up stoves and refrigerators to the shop by long orange extension cords, and townspeople had brought tuna melt makings and lawn chairs to pass the hours in each other's company. However, as the weather cooled, Patty sold off her inventory of appliances and switched to candles and birdcages, and the crowds had moved to the library.

At last, the café's restoration was complete, but no one except Duke—the town's handyman deluxe—had seen its interior. Kraft paper covered its windows, and today a wide red ribbon was taped across its doorway. Anyone who'd asked Darla about the new café would get a coy, "You'll just have to wait and see." We did know she'd added a patio off to the side. There was no hiding that. But the interior was a mystery.

My money was on a Southern theme. Darla, despite having only visited the South the summer before, was obsessed with Southern culture. She leafed through the pages of *Southern Living* magazine each month—the library kept a subscription just for her—and loaded the café's menu with Pacific Northwestern takes on Southern food, including a drool-worthy shrimp and grits and a creditable jambalaya with local vegetables. Darla also owned the Magnolia Rolling Estates, named after her favorite Southern flower. Her newest acquisition was a Southern husband. She'd picked him up on her travels in South Carolina.

"Before we cut the ribbon, I want to announce a contest," Darla said. "For years we've simply called this 'the café' or 'Darla's café' or 'the diner.' Now that we're reopening, it's time we had a proper name. I invite you all to submit ideas for consideration. If we select your entry, you win a free breakfast every week for a full year."

"Any breakfast we want?" shouted a portly man from his seat on the hood of his pickup truck.

"That's right. Pancakes, grits, omelets—your choice."

This announcement inspired fresh cheers. I wondered what names would come out of this. Ruth Littlewood would find some kind of bird name. The Crow's Nest, maybe. Dylan, my high school intern, would snag a name from a Cary Grant movie. I imagined him biting his lip and jotting Arsenic and Old Plaice or maybe Bringing Up Barbecue on an entry. Lyndon, if pressed, might propose a botanical name like the Bearded Iris Inn.

"Montgomery, please hand me the scissors." Too bad Patty hadn't been able to source a pair of oversized scissors to add to the moment's drama. Darla lifted pinking shears and, after a few tries, the ribbon's jagged edges fell away. She pushed open the café doors.

"Fellow Wildredians, welcome!" She snapped on the café's lights.

People streamed into the café. What would it look like? For a moment, no one spoke.

"It's . . ." Mrs. Littlewood whispered next to me. "It's exactly the same."

And it was. The same green linoleum-topped tables in the same booths lining the café's walls. The same cash register anchored the back counter, and the same style of stools were bolted to the floor in front of it. Even the same black cat clock with its tail-shaped pendulum tick-tocked from the wall separating the kitchen from the dining room.

Besides being cleaner, everything at the café looked just as it had before it was remodeled.

That is, everything but the dead man slumped over the counter.

We stood, paralyzed by shock. A whimper escaped a woman near me.

A dead man? In the café? Couldn't be. Yet there he was, seated on a barstool, with a knife stuck in his back. A red stain coagulated on his cheerful yellow sweater. There was no point in checking the man's vital signs. He was dead.

Eyes wide, Darla tiptoed around the counter to look at the man's face. From her puzzled expression, I knew he was a stranger.

She straightened and faced the breathless crowd. "Everyone, back off. Don't touch anything. Montgomery, help them outside."

Trembling, I turned to leave, but Darla stopped me. It seemed nothing could rattle take-charge Darla. "Josie, I need you as a witness. You, too, Ruth."

I stepped to the side and Ruth Littlewood joined me. I glanced at Mrs. Littlewood. I knew why Darla had chosen her to stay back. For years, Ruth Littlewood had run a vegetable canning operation in the valley. She was matter-of-fact and completely reliable, and if she hadn't dedicated her retirement to bird-watching, she might have made a suitable secretary of the Joint Chiefs of Staff.

As for me, I was probably chosen because I was a librarian, a profession known for facts. And, until a little over a year ago, an outsider. I'd be a reliable witness.

"Call Sam," I said.

"I'm already dialing the sheriff's office," Darla replied, phone in hand.

The body sagged to the side, and we leapt back. A paper place mat fluttered to the ground.

"Don't touch it," I warned.

"As if," Mrs. Littlewood said.

We edged forward to examine it. The place mat was the type Darla had always used: thin paper with a deckled edge and Greek key design in blue. *READY-SET-GO* was scrawled across it in dried rust red. The color also stained the man's right finger-tips.

"Ready-Set-Go." I swallowed to keep down my breakfast. "That's the workshop at the retreat center."

"More like 'Ready-Set-Gone,'" Mrs. Littlewood observed in a shaky voice.

"Was he part of the workshop?" I scanned the room for text—anything to give me a clue about what had happened. The only writing in the café was on the menus. *Menus, what happened here?* I silently demanded. I relaxed my mind, but all I received were images of scrambled eggs and chicken-fried steak. The menus were too new to have absorbed their users' energy.

Phone against an ear, Darla tapped her foot. "All that waffle batter, wasted. And now this." She perked up as someone evidently picked up her call. "I need the sheriff at the café in Wilfred immediately. Yes, it's an emergency. Didn't I say immediately? Where's Sheriff Wilfred? Get him down here. Now."

While Darla argued with the dispatcher, I slipped my phone from my coat pocket and texted Sam's personal number. Because of his baby, Nicky, he kept his phone on him.

My thumbs flew over the tiny keyboard. *Someone's been murdered at the café.*

"You don't understand," Darla said into the phone. "Let me finish."

"Tell them it's a homicide. That should get them jumping." Mrs. Littlewood continued to stare at the paper menu on the floor.

My phone dinged with a reply at the same time Darla hung up the phone. I blanched at its message.

"Turns out an ambulance is already halfway here," Darla said. "How they found out about it beats me."

"Sam says someone else is dead." Stupefied, I returned my phone to my coat pocket. "At the retreat center." What was going on?

"You're joking," Darla said.

The retreat center. Where Jean was. Someone else murdered. I hurried to the front exit, and before anyone could stop me, I burst out the door in a run.

Never had the path between Wilfred's main drag and retreat center felt so long. I ran through the trailer park, my breath leaving clouds in the cold afternoon. I stumbled briefly on the dirt-packed trail through the meadow—now mostly mud—but regained my footing and powered forward, lungs tight.

*Jean is okay*, I repeated to myself. *She's fine. She has to be.*

Over the levee I ran, the millpond's icy surface placid. A siren wailed in the distance. Ahead, an SUV from the Washington County sheriff's office was already parked at an odd angle to the retreat center's patio.

I crossed the stone patio and burst in the center's front door. And I encountered . . . nothing.

The lobby was still. No body, no commotion. The fireplace crackled cheerfully, the cozy armchairs grouped around it empty. Where was Jean?

Voices from the building's rear caught my attention. At the same time, an ambulance rumbled to a stop outside.

"Jean!" I called and followed the noise to one of the center's meeting rooms.

Sam met me in the hall. "Josie, you have to stay back."

"Why? Where's my sister?" I pressed.

Jean ran down the hall and hugged me, her strawberry blond waves messy. Ever since she was a kid, she'd had the habit of combing her fingers through her hair when she was anxious.

"You're okay." My voice quavered on the edge of tears. "I was so worried."

I felt her nod against my shoulder. Now I was all right. I released my sister. "What happened?"

"She was dead. In the breakout room," Jean said.

"Who?" I asked.

"What's going on at the café?" Sam interrupted.

I never thought I'd be the sort to go for a man in uniform, but Sam wasn't just any man—at least, not to me. I'd been infatuated with him for months. He smiled, a sure sign he was upset, and drew a hand across his prematurely receding hairline. His habit of smiling when he was irked and frowning when happy confused strangers, but I found it endearing. I resisted the urge to hug him in relief as well.

Instead, I kept an arm looped around Jean's shoulders. "A man, never seen him before, is dead at the café. Stabbed in the back. Darla called it in." He'd know the gruesome details soon enough. "What happened here? Not another murder?"

"Can't say for now," Sam said. "We're still figuring it out." His phone trilled and he turned away from us to answer it. "I'm five minutes away. Send a couple of deputies to the Wilfred retreat center, too." A pause. "That's right."

"A workshop participant?" I asked Jean in a low voice.

"One of the crumbs." She looked at me with meaning. "Marcia." The woman threatened that morning at the PO Grocery.

Sam had heard us and raised an eyebrow.

"*Crumb* is a pet name for Cookie's followers," I said.

Sam's gaze lingered on me maybe a second longer than it might have. In his prior work tracking people for the FBI, he'd picked up a way of seeming to read a person's mind with a mere cast of his eyes.

"By the way," I said, "This is my sister Jean. Jean, meet Sam Wilfred. He lives next door at Big House."

Two EMTs with a stretcher pushed their way past us and down the hall.

"I'll be right there," Sam told them. Then, to me: "Josie, you'll have to leave." He turned to Jean. "It's nice to meet you, and I'm sorry it's under these circumstances. If you wouldn't mind, I'd like you to stay here while I ask you and the others a few questions. First I need to get down to the café."

"You do think it's murder."

"We don't know anything yet."

"If you didn't suspect anything, you wouldn't have called in reinforcements."

He smiled. Uh-oh. "Josie, you'll have to—"

"Fine. I'll go." I reluctantly made for the front door. I turned one more time to wave at Jean. As I left, her questioning look was the last thing I saw.

# CHAPTER FIVE

Two people died at the same time, in different locations. One of those people had been murdered. The other? The fact that Sam kept Jean and the others for questioning meant the situation was suspicious. At least one good thing might come of this: The workshop would be cancelled and Jean's money would be refunded. Jean would be devastated, but it was for the best.

These thoughts cycled through my mind as I entered the library and peeled off my coat. At some point, Sam would want to question me, too. Not only had I been present when the body at the café was found, I'd heard Marcia threatened.

For a few minutes, I paced the library's ground floor. Even the thought of rereading one of my favorite vintage crime novels—my usual go-to in times of stress—didn't appeal. I settled at my desk for an hour to work on the trustees' report, but I couldn't focus. I kept checking my phone for the text from Jean that didn't come.

Finally, I shut my laptop. While I waited, why not be useful? I'd take Patty the exercise video she'd asked me to have transferred to our library. VHS tapes were nearly impossible to find now, and the library I'd ordered it from had to dig it out from deaccessions. "I don't even think we'd be able to unload it on the ninety-nine-cent table at the annual book sale," the librarian had told me.

I tucked the tape under my arm and walked down the hill to Patty's This-N-That, directly across the street from the café. Empty birdcages and candles and candles in birdcages filled its front window. The bell chimed as I entered, but the shop was empty.

"Patty?" I called out. Although no one was in Patty's usual perch behind the rear counter, on a nearby TV set, Jane Fonda in leg warmers silently did the grapevine, hands on hips. "I brought your Cher step aerobics tape. The library I got it from said you can have it."

Patty emerged from the stairwell to the basement. Today she wore mint green velour sweatpants and a pink sweatshirt reading *Princess Pumps Iron*. I'd seen Patty watch a lot of hand weights hefted on the screen, but I'd never seen her actually touch one herself.

"Hello, Josie," she said.

Duke popped up behind her. "I tell you, we simply drywall over where I had to punch through the plaster. Not a big deal." He nodded a hello my way.

Behind me, the door chimed again, and I turned to see the short, hollow-eyed man I'd glimpsed earlier behind Cookie at the retreat center. Up close, except for bright eyes the color of sterling silver, he looked even more run-down. Both Patty and Duke stood straighter. Who was he and why hadn't he stayed behind for questioning? He hardly looked like a candidate for Cookie's boyfriend—at least, he was nothing like the buff swains on her website.

"Can I help you?" Patty asked.

"Just looking around," he said.

There was a lot to see. Besides watching other people work out, Patty's major obsession was with things. Random things. One month, she might enthuse over ecclesiastical wear and track down every used priest's collar and nun's habit in the state to stock her shop. A few months later, her interest would shift to scissors, and she'd order mixed lots of Indian scissors and stock up on fine Swiss embroidery snips. There was little chance she was making a living with her shop, and word was her husband had left her enough money to indulge her interests and still get by.

Duke tore his attention from the stranger. "So, like I said, we simply patch it with drywall. It's the simplest solution."

The stranger tapped a wall with his fist. "Plaster wall?"

"Yes." Duke shifted on his feet.

"Why change it?"

Patty slapped the counter. "That's what I said. It's plaster now. Why mess it up? I'd like to keep the integrity of this place."

Duke stepped out from behind the counter and proffered a hand. I had the feeling they'd recognized something in each other: memberships in the brotherhood of the jacks-of-all-trades. "I'm Duke. Patty's handyman. There was a plumbing incident in the basement, and I had to take out part of the wall. We're just discussing it."

The stranger shook Duke's hand. "Desmond. I'm with the workshop up at the retreat center."

"Are you studying to be a life coach?" Patty asked.

"I'm Ms. Masterson's assistant."

I did a double take. I would have pegged Cookie's assistant as someone young and eager, ready to work eighteen-hour days without losing a grin. Desmond had the haunted look of an overworked coal miner who hadn't seen sun or had a good meal in months.

"Plastering's not as complicated as it's made out to be, so long as you have a steady hand," he said. "Sure, you may need to rebuild the lath, be extra-careful with moisture, but the results are worth the trouble."

"It's tiled over. You don't even see the wall," Duke countered.

"But you'd always know."

Patty and I watched the men as if we were watching a tennis match, but instead of rackets, these players wielded practical know-how.

"Maybe you'd like to see the job?" Duke's fascination with construction techniques had apparently superseded any thoughts of dead bodies and life coaches.

"Sure, I'll have a look."

I stepped aside to let Desmond pass and caught sight of a bone-handled knife protruding from a leather sheath clipped to his belt. He and Duke disappeared down the stairs to the basement.

Meanwhile, Patty was examining the back of the aerobics tape. "You think that's her real hair?"

I came closer so I could keep my voice low but still be heard. "Is it okay to let him alone with Duke down there?"

Patty frowned. "You think Duke will hurt him?"

"Not that. The other way around. I saw him, Desmond, at the retreat center this morning, and now two people are dead. Also, did you get a load of his knife? Better safe than sorry."

"You think that's the knife that killed the fellow at the café?"

I shook my head. "That one stayed with the body."

Patty leaned over the counter. "What happened at the retreat center, anyway?"

"One of the workshop participants died. A woman. I don't know any more than that."

We both looked toward the doorway to the basement, and Patty grabbed a large pair of brass scissors from a display case. "Come on."

I followed her downstairs to the former home of the Sing-Along Salon karaoke lounge. Patty had closed the lounge after a murder the spring before. I couldn't help but cast a second glance at the abandoned stage.

We followed the sound of Duke's voice, drifting from the men's room, down the short hall leading to the building's rear. "See here, you've got your studs. It would only take a patch this long. I have a sheet of half-inch greenboard in my shed right now."

"That's easiest, sure, but imagine the satisfaction of a good plaster job." We arrived in time to see Desmond, wrench in hand, tapping the green tiles that traveled halfway up the wall. "Looks like you cracked a few of these. Any replacements?"

Both men were hunched on the linoleum in front of where a urinal had once hung. Once inside, Patty let the door close behind her, cramming four of us into a room that comfortably held only two.

"Has the sheriff finished questioning people at the retreat center?" I asked. I still hadn't heard from Jean.

Desmond stood and faced us. This close, the circles under his eyes really stood out. I had a brief urge to march him to the café for a breakfast platter. "Shouldn't be long now. They started with Cookie, then me, before getting to the crumbs."

"Crumbs," Duke said. "Good grief."

"One of those crumbs is Jean, my sister."

Patty, perhaps realizing she had an exclusive that would make her the toast of Wilfred, stepped in. "Thank you, Desmond, for your expertise on the plaster question. It must be far from your usual work as Cookie's assistant."

His grip on the wrench tightened. "I do a little of this, a little of that."

I exchanged a split-second look with Patty. Like murder? Echoing Desmond, Patty's knuckles whitened on her scissors.

"Why the scissors? You plan to trim something down here?" Duke asked. "The curtains in the Sing-Along are looking ratty."

Ignoring Duke, Desmond had caught our glances.

His voice lowered, and the wrench rose to waist height. "Just because I know Cookie's business doesn't mean I go around killing people, if that's what you're thinking."

"Oh, I would never accuse you," Patty said quickly, gaze darting between the wrench and the knife on his belt.

"Why does everyone think that just because . . ." We hung on his words, but he chose not to finish the thought. "Anyway, the sheriff has my story. All of it." He looked toward the door, now blocked by Patty.

All of what? I involuntarily stepped back. My shoulder hit the stall door.

"Maybe you have an idea of who the killer is," Patty tried again.

"None. Not a one," Desmond replied. "And if I did, I'd tell the sheriff, not you."

"Nothing for us? Nothing at all?" Patty said, still refusing to let anyone leave the cramped men's room.

"I worry about my sister," I added.

"Your sister has nothing to do with this." He dropped his hand at last, resting the wrench on the nearby sink. "I can assure you of that."

So, he did know something. What was it?

Before I could press further, Duke cut in. "Patty, you're treating our guest like a criminal. That's not hospitable, especially when he's giving us such helpful advice. Desmond, would you like to see the plasterwork ceiling in the Grange Hall? I think you'd appreciate it. Pardon us, ladies." Duke pushed behind Patty and held open the men's room door. "After you."

* * *

Back at the library, I resumed pacing the atrium for a few minutes, uncertain of what to do next. My library errands were finished. Jean was still at the retreat center awaiting questioning and hadn't replied to my texts. The café was almost certainly still closed, so I couldn't even relax at the counter with a cup of coffee. Not that I'd ever sit at that counter again. Until Jean was released, I had no choice but to wait.

Just as I had successfully wrangled my focus away from murder, a hollow boom echoed from the basement. Shoot. The furnace had conked out. Lyndon had warned me it might. "Don't let it stay out too long. The old girl can't stand extreme temperatures," he'd said, speaking of the library as it were ailing royalty.

I was on my way to the furnace room, when a rap at the kitchen door drew my attention. The door's window framed Cookie's spiky hair and mascara-laden eyes.

What was she doing here? Warily, I opened the door. "Hello. Can I help you?"

She didn't bother to meet my eyes as she responded. Instead, she looked at the kitchen behind me, taking in its high ceilings, long oak table, and old service bells along the soffit. "Have you seen my assistant, Desmond?"

"He was at the This-N-That a little while ago."

"He has no business going off without me. I need him." Finally, she looked at me. "A library. How quaint. Closed today, are you?" Despite her apparent rush to find her assistant, she stepped past me into the kitchen.

*Disarming Narcissists,* a book whispered a title from Popular Psychology and added, *Surviving and Thriving with the Self-Absorbed.*

I could either kick her out or play along and maybe glean information on how Jean was faring. I forced a smile. "I need to reset the furnace, but I'd be happy to give you a tour, if you're interested."

If Cookie was surprised that the town librarian on her day off would clear her schedule to show her around, she didn't show it. "I wouldn't mind at all."

As I hurried to the basement through the service staircase, I wondered why Cookie hadn't stayed at the retreat center. While she was swanning around upstairs in a public building otherwise closed to the public, my sister anxiously awaited questioning about the death of a fellow workshop attendee. A sensitive leader would have stayed behind to offer comfort.

The basement was clean—thank you, Lyndon—but dungeon-like despite the quavering fluorescent lights in its main corridor. To my right, under the kitchen, was the laundry room and the old root cellar. Next to that was the storage room we used for bookbinding and repairing damaged books. Most of the rest of the basement was a mystery to me, and I liked it that way.

Nonetheless, we needed heat. I took a left beyond the book repair room and made my way to the old house's guts—the furnace room. I drew a long breath before forcing myself to open its paneled door. Inside was surprisingly warm and smelled of damp soil and hot metal. The furnace itself resembled a gargantuan octopus with now-useless arms arching through the room, leaving ink-black shadows frosted in spiderwebs, barely illuminated by a smudged sliver of window near the ceiling. When the Wilfred mill was active, sawdust fed the furnace. Since then, it had been retrofitted with a gas burner.

The instructions for restarting it should be here somewhere. After a glance over my shoulder to make sure no one had followed me, I said, "Furnace manual, how do you restart the furnace?"

A thin voice—could it be Lyndon's?—repeated, "Press the burner's reset button. Press the burner's reset button."

With the help of my phone's flashlight, I found a sheet of paper taped to the side of the furnace. On it in Lyndon's crabbed handwriting was *reset button* with an arrow pointing toward a metal box with a red button. I followed Lyndon's directions. The furnace ticked twice and roared to life. I hurried upstairs, as if I could outrun whatever basement ghouls my imagination had supplied.

I found Cookie in New Releases brushing a hand over the marble fireplace mantel as if it were a normal day in Ready-Set-Go land. I was calculating how best to broach the topic of Marcia's death, when Cookie said, "Do you know anything about the other death—the one the sheriff told us happened at the café?"

Then I realized, *this* was the reason she'd come here. It had nothing to do with finding Desmond or her interest in "quaint" libraries. "I was there when we found the body."

"How did it happen?" Cookie's face was hard to

read, and it wasn't just the makeup or the plastic surgery that had ratcheted her eyes into a permanent expression of mild surprise.

"He'd been stabbed in the back."

She stumbled back a step. "What?"

"He had a knife in his back. He'd written *Ready-Set-Go* on a place mat." Remembering the shaky rust-brown letters, I took a deep breath. "He must have something to do with the workshop. Were any students missing? Did someone who signed up not show?"

"No. I'm as bewildered as anyone." Cookie wouldn't meet my eyes. She dropped her hand from the fireplace and walked to the window to toy with the curtain's bobbled fringe.

When she added nothing further, I said, "This used to be the mansion's dining room. Now it's Popular Fiction and New Releases." I'd always loved this room for its ornate plaster ceiling ornaments and chandelier with crystals missing here and there.

Days off were hard on the books, who relished the attention of the library's patrons. As I'd feared, they decided to get chatty. "Read me! *New York Times* bestseller," a thriller to my right announced, gunfire and screeching tires in the background. I struggled to keep a neutral expression. Not to be outdone, a novel farther down the shelf bragged, "*Publishers Weekly* starred review." Sounds of the ocean and a creaking ship's masts escaped from its pages.

I pretended to straighten a book and mouthed, "Don't distract me." Turning to Cookie, I said aloud, "Would you like to see the rest of the ground floor?" She followed me across the atrium to Children's Literature in Old Man Thurston's office. Here, too, the books were talkative, some singing nursery rhymes and others telling stories of kittens and bicycles.

I firmly resisted their chatter. "Could you tell me what happened at the retreat center? My sister is one of your students." I refused to call her a crumb. "I can't help but worry."

Cookie might have expressed concern for Jean, but she didn't. Her attention funneled from the ether to me. "It was most unfortunate. One of my best students, Marcia, died."

"I'm so sorry. Had you known her a long time?"

She nodded. "Five years. She took all my online courses and four in-person workshops. This would have been her fifth. She was making great strides in developing her client base." Cookie's face stretched into a smile that reminded me of the emotionless grins of Halloween skeletons. "Truth is, she wanted to be me."

"I imagine your success attracts lots of people," I said, refusing to include Jean among them. "Since Jean is in the workshop, I can't help but wonder how the student died."

Cookie shook her head. The spikes in her hair didn't move. "We don't know. At first we thought it was a heart attack. She was sweating and couldn't catch her breath. Could barely keep her head up. My assistant settled her into the workshop room next door. Then . . . she died."

"I'm so sorry. What a nightmare. I suppose you'll have to cancel the workshop now."

"Oh no." Cookie led the way into the atrium,

then to the former drawing room, now Circulation, to gaze out the French doors, past the rose garden, now a bed of thorny stems. "My crumbs count on me. I need to wake them to possibility, to what they can achieve. You don't get what you want by wishing upon a star. It's Ready-Set-Go that makes dreams come true."

"Jean will be happy to hear that," I said reluctantly. Now I was certain. Even the unexpected death of a longtime student wouldn't keep her from turning a buck. The woman was a money-grubbing crook.

"Inspiring others is my mission in life." She turned away from the window. "I don't mind telling you, I've accomplished more than most people. I'm wealthy, respected, and have a busy romantic life. I want for nothing. Everything I desire, I get. It's no secret how it happens, either."

"Ready-Set-Go," I replied, resisting the urge to mimic vomiting. Ready-Set-Go seemed to be the answer to everything, from the common cold to sending a man to Mars.

"Ready," she murmured, then fixed me with a stare. Her focused gaze sent an icy shiv of adrenaline through me. "Don't believe what you read."

"What do you mean?"

"Some people say my coaching institute is a sham." She shook her head with vigor. "If they could see the good we do, the lives we've saved."

"Oh." I inhaled to calm my racing pulse.

"My teachings have patched up marriages, shown people their life's calling, brought them health and love. Even my assistant. Without me, he'd be rotting in some prison somewhere."

Rotting in prison? I remembered how disdain-
fully she'd treated him. "I've seen the newspaper
series on the coaching industry." I chose my words
carefully. "It advises people to be careful before
committing to life coaching training. The courses
are expensive."

"If students didn't invest substantially in my
work, they wouldn't take it as seriously." All at once,
she smiled, and her almost militant charisma softened to a warm friendliness. "Let's forget all this
drama, shall we? I'd love to see more of this amazing library."

# CHAPTER SIX

I was still processing the hour I'd spent with Cookie when my phone dinged with a text from Jean saying she was on her way home. Cookie's sheer force of personality had convinced me she taught a solid workshop, and she had come off as genuinely shocked when I'd given her the details of the death of the man in the café. Yet, I was certain she'd come to the library with an agenda. I wasn't buying that it had been to find her assistant. Why didn't I trust her?

Minutes later, an SUV from the sheriff's department pulled up with Sam at the wheel. He followed Jean into the kitchen.

"How was it? How are you?" I asked Jean.

"I'm all right. It's your turn now." She glanced at Sam. "I'll wait upstairs."

"You don't have to rush off," I said.

"I need to call Mom and check in, anyway."

"Good luck with that," I told her as she left the kitchen. A moment later her steps sounded on the service staircase.

I turned to Sam. "Let's sit in the conservatory where it's warm." Not that being near him wouldn't heat me through. We crossed the atrium, and Sam's presence pulled at me as if he carried a magnetic charge. "You're usually home by now. Where's Nicky?"

"Mrs. Garlington picked him up from the sitter. He's probably listening to 'the Itsy Bitsy Spider' on the piano while Derwin regales him with stories about the daily mail rounds."

We took chairs near the tile stove. Sitting and talking with Sam was the most natural thing in the world. He looked at me and frowned. Happiness. Heart now a puddle, I smiled in return. "It's been a long day, huh?"

"It's not over yet. Two deaths, one a murder? Not something we see every day."

"Marcia. Could she have been killed, too? Even the plotlines of your operas don't get this macabre." I considered this. "I take that back—*Lucrezia Borgia* was pretty intense. Anyway, it's suspicious that two strangers died the same morning, both having to do with the workshop."

"Why do you say 'the workshop'?"

"I'm thinking of *Ready-Set-Go* written in blood on the counter." I leaned forward to deliver my coup de grâce. "Naturally, you understand that the killer had to have written it. Not the victim."

"You mean because the victim was stabbed in the back?"

So, he'd thought of it, too. "A dying man wouldn't

have been able to reach the middle of his back to ink his finger with blood. Had to be the killer."

"Solid deduction." Sam's frown deepened. "But the message was written in ketchup."

"Ketchup?" I practically heard the *wah-wah-wah* of a tuba as my pride deflated. "And there was ketchup on his fingers, I suppose?"

He nodded. "Nice try, Detective Way."

As usual, Rodney appeared from nowhere and prepared to leap into Sam's lap. "No, Rodney. Don't torture him." Sam was allergic to cats, proving no man was perfect.

Rodney shot me a disdainful look and settled into the kindling basket. He'd already pawed the kindling to the floor and dug out a cat-sized hole.

"Who is the dead man, then?" I asked. "Cookie told me all the workshop participants showed up."

"Josie, I'm here to ask you questions, not the other way around. What happened this morning at the PO?"

I leaned back and crossed my arms over my chest. "If that's how it will be, fine. But I doubt I can tell you anything Jean didn't."

"Try."

I recounted the morning's conversation, from first hearing voices to stooping at the shelf to seeing Marcia's, then Rex's backs as they left. "Anything new there?"

Sam looked at his notes. "She missed the detail with the cans of cat food, but otherwise everything matches. You say Rex Markham bought roses?"

"Red ones. You know the type the PO stocks— dark red buds wrapped in cellophane. Why do you ask?"

"We found the stems and a few roses in the garbage outside the retreat center. Plus bits of rose petals in the victim's room. It makes me wonder—"

"Wonder what?"

Sam closed his notebook and stood. "Thank you."

"What, Sam? Don't leave me hanging. You've told me a hundred times how useful I am in your investigations." I stood, too. Outside the conservatory's glass walls, day had collapsed into an early evening dark enough to be night. The library's windows would be frosted in the morning.

"This is murder, Josie. It's not stolen chickens or a lost dog. It's better for you to stay out of it."

"But, my sister." Surely he understood that.

He stepped forward, close enough that I could have run my hand over the stubble on his jaw, if I chose. "If I learn anything that will affect your sister, I'll let you know, okay? In the meantime, lock the door after me."

I guess it would have to do. "All right."

I walked Sam to the kitchen door and, as he'd instructed me, bolted it. Instead of crossing the lawn to Big House, he got into his SUV and backed out the driveway. When I returned to the atrium to take the stairs to my apartment, Jean was leaning over the banister, watching me.

"Why didn't you tell me you were in love with Sam Wilfred?"

"I don't know what you're talking about," I said to Jean, two stories above me. I made for the stairwell. When I emerged at my apartment, I walked straight to the kitchen, avoiding the living room, where Jean stacked firewood in the grate. One of my apartment's perks was a real wood burning fireplace left over from the days when my living room was a gathering place for the mansion's live-in staff. "There's butternut squash soup in the refrigerator."

Jean followed me. "Why are you so cagey about Sam?"

I busied myself with ladling soup into a saucepan. "Hmm?"

"You're avoiding my question."

"Go keep an eye on the fire," I told her. "I'll be there in a minute."

"Fine. Be like that. This conversation isn't over."

A quarter of an hour later, ensconced on the couch with a warm bowl of soup on the coffee table in front of her, she looked more like the Jean I knew: calm and almost cheerful. Rodney curled up next to her, soaking in her warmth and that of the fire. I took the armchair and pulled up my knees, covering them with a quilt.

"You haven't told me yet about this afternoon," I said.

"What about you? Finding Marcia was bad enough, but stumbling over a man with a knife in his back?" At my surprised look, she added, "Sam told us. He probably wanted to see if anyone had a suspicious reaction."

"Did they?"

"No. As far as I could tell, we were all shocked. We'll get to that in a minute, but first, stop changing the subject. What's the story between you and Sam?"

"What story?" It didn't matter if I'd never mentioned Sam, Jean would guess how I felt.

"Stop playing dumb. Why aren't you two together? You obviously have a thing for him, and he likes you, too." At my doubtful glance, she added, "I can tell."

"His wife died last spring. It's too soon." This was the excuse I'd told myself over and over.

"But you spend lots of time together, and you're close. Maybe best friends? I'm right, aren't I?"

She was right. We were close, and the label of "best friend" made my heart leap. I'd never thought about it that way, but we'd spent so many evenings together talking—Sam about his cases and experiences of fatherhood, and me about library patrons and arguments with Roz. He was leading me through Verdi's operas, and I was choosing some of the library's best golden age detective fiction for him. We'd had lots of dinners in town full of laughing and good-natured arguments. We'd paddled a canoe around the millpond with Nicky bundled between us and picnicked on the mountain. But I couldn't call them dates.

"Maybe," I said.

"Your face is all red," Jean said.

"It's the fire."

"Uh-huh."

"It's just an infatuation, that's all. Nothing serious."

Jean folded her arms. "Tell me about him."

At first, I resisted. What was the point? But I knew Jean wouldn't let the subject drop. "Sam is a descendant of Thurston Wilfred, Wilfred's founder, a timber baron we call Old Man Thurston. Sam

is"—I wrinkled my brow and counted generations—
"Thurston Wilfred the fifth. Nicky's the sixth. They
all have nicknames, of course. No one calls them
Thurston."

"Interesting, but let's move on to the good stuff.
When did you meet him?"

She didn't waste time getting to the point. If
Jean used this kind of approach with her wellness
clients, they'd certainly get their money's worth.

"A few nights after I arrived in Wilfred. He has a
key to the library. I found him downstairs, sleeping, with a Hardy Boys mystery in his lap. As for
when I knew I had feelings . . ."

"It was right away, wasn't it? I can tell."

I nodded and felt my face and chest burn once
again. "A crush, that's all. He was here on a job for
the FBI. Just before he left town, I found out he
was married—nothing had happened between us,
of course," I rushed to add. "He was getting a divorce, and I think he got the hint I was interested
in him and was alarmed to think he might have ac-
cidentally encouraged it." Remembering, I was
mortified. "Anyway, he left, then returned with a
wife and baby. Then his wife died. That was less
than a year ago."

Jean clasped her hands in her lap, and Rodney
crawled up to nose under her palm. "Nice over-
view, but I'll need details, please."

Over the next half hour, I filled her in, slowly
at first, then with more detail, about our non-
relationship relationship. It was a relief to give air
to my feelings. I told her about Sam's quiet focus,
and how while he could seem to be oblivious, he
gave a person laser attention. I told her how, when

he was on call, he seemed to be able to fall asleep but snap awake when something needed his attention. He cooked when he needed to think, I told Jean, and he loved opera.

"He hasn't been seeing anyone?" Jean asked.

I shook my head. "Remember, his wife just died. A few women have been interested in him, primarily an actress who passed through town last summer." I cringed, remembering how "hands-y" she'd been. "He's friendly, but seems tuned out to romance."

Jean absently stroked Rodney's back. "Remember how you used to hate charades?"

"Sure."

What did this have to do with anything? Mom had read in some English novel that gentlemen and ladies played charades at country manors and insisted we launch our own tradition after holiday dinners. I detested them. I didn't like the spotlight on me, and I've never been one for unnecessary competition. For years, when the dishes were in the dishwasher and Mom clapped her hands for post-meal games, I'd tried to slink away.

"Bear with me," Jean said. "Then you knocked out *Mill on the Floss* in less than a minute. Remember? You had this uncanny ability to impersonate book titles. Now you help Mom with cleanup so we can get to the game faster."

"True." *Mill on the Floss* had been a cinch. All I'd had to do was pretend to floss my teeth and then roll my hands. "So what? You want me to ring his doorbell and act out *Romeo and Juliet*?"

"No. You're misunderstanding me on purpose. Once you saw yourself as a charades player, everything changed. Get it?" Jean's voice rose. "That's how it is with Sam. He's new in his job, a new father, and just lost his wife, and no matter how bad their relationship was, her death couldn't have been easy. He simply doesn't see love. On some subconscious level, romantic relationships don't play into his life. He doesn't see himself as a charades player."

I sank deeper into my armchair. "What does that mean for me?"

"He needs a reality check. Something to yank him out of his rut. Something big."

I raised my eyes to Jean's.

She read the question in them. "I have no idea what that might be. But he is just as caught up with you as you are with him." At my skeptical glance, she added, "I guarantee it."

"Maybe I could say something to him," I ventured.

"Definitely." She nodded vigorously. "Change how he thinks about you. It's up to you to do something about it. Ready-Set-Go, Josie. You've been stuck at Ready for too long."

# CHAPTER SEVEN

After dinner, Jean followed me to my tiny kitchen, Rodney at her heels. "Mom said she made you promise to look after me."

Someone else might have found Mom's request to be sweet and protective. Jean, I knew, was peeved. "What was I supposed to say to her?"

"I need you to stick up for me."

"You know how Mom is. She only said it because she loves you. I—"

A banging at the kitchen door downstairs drew our attention. Jean set down the dishcloth. "What's that?"

"I'll check."

In stocking feet, I hurried down the steps, took a hard right in the atrium and arrived at the kitchen door. Filling its window were the faces of the knitting club's members. One of them hoisted a basket of cherry red yarn to show what they wanted.

I cracked open the door to the winter evening's cold. "Library's closed today. Besides, it's after hours."

Maureen, a comfortably built brunette obsessed with granny squares, stepped forward. "Can't you let us meet in the conservatory, anyway? We won't make trouble. You'll hardly know we're there."

"I have you marked on the calendar for Thursday afternoon."

"We need to meet now, and there's nowhere else to gather. Besides, you aren't doing anything, anyway."

"How do you know?"

She gave me the once-over, noting my stockinged feet and jeans. "You aren't, are you? It's an emergency."

What, someone had to have a homemade pot holder, stat? Not only that, the knitting club rarely did any actual knitting. One member had been working on the same teapot cozy since spring. "What kind of emergency?"

Neil, a pimpled boy with a prominent Adam's apple, stepped into the porchlight. Ever since he'd asked for my help finding nineteenth-century knitting patterns, he'd become one of my favorite library patrons. "It's the murders. We need to blow off steam, and we can't meet at the café. It's still a crime scene."

"I don't know—" I began.

"You always tell us that a library is a town's beating heart," Mona said, her arms full of a pit bull–

mix puppy, her latest foster charge. "Can't you let us in? It's cold out here."

The knitting club members watched me, seeming to hold their breath. In the background, knitting patterns methodically chanted overlapping strings of knits and purls and binding off.

"All right. Just this once." I let the members in—Neil, four women, and a wriggling puppy. Occasionally Duke attended, but apparently not this evening. From my office doorway, Rodney stared daggers at the puppy. "I'll put coffee on. The stove's lit in the conservatory."

When I checked in a few minutes later, the knitting club had turned on lamps and settled in a circle of chairs around the tile stove. The light cast soft reflections against the conservatory's glass walls. Mona sat nearest the fire to keep the puppy warm. They pulled out their knitting, but only one woman, partway through the sleeve of a mammoth Aran sweater, actually held her needles. Rodney ambled in and climbed into the kindling basket. The puppy whimpered at him and lunged, his tail wagging wildly, but Mona clutched him by the collar. Meanwhile, Rodney played it cool.

"Two bodies," Maureen said to me, reaching into her basket for a hook. She was the club's sole crocheter. "You saw the man in the café. I heard you hightailed it to the retreat center. Did you get a look at the other stiff, too?"

"No," I said. "I just wanted to check on my sister." I should have known. This was their emergency. Wilfredians had a grapevine efficient enough to make Jack's beanstalk look like an alfalfa sprout.

The knitting club had wasted no time gathering fertilizer to feed it.

"I hear they found words written in blood at the café," Gloria said. Gloria's knitting output consisted largely of pot holders and Southern belle dolls with knitted skirts intended to cover rolls of toilet paper. We had a pink one in the bathroom upstairs. "Had something to do with her program. Suspicious, I'd say. I caught a glance of the workshop leader at the PO on my way over, and she looks like someone Hollywood invented, with the help of plastic surgeons."

"Like she walked off a TV set," Maureen offered.

"For an infomercial," Gloria added. "I don't trust her."

I felt like a traitor, but I had to agree. "Have you noticed how she never looks you in the eye?"

While the knitting members talked, Rodney turned his back to the puppy and flicked his tail. He looked over a shoulder to check the dog's reaction. The puppy whined.

"Hush, Boris," Mona said, placing a hand on the dog's back. "And she's named Cookie. Like the snack food. Suspicious."

Pleased with the puppy's reaction, Rodney pretended to swat something back and forth in the kindling box, just out of sight. Once again, I caught him glancing back at the puppy, who now struggled to stand on Mona's lap and was whining more loudly.

"Hush," she repeated, hand gentle on the dog's head. "If you keep this up, I'm going to have to put you in the car with your hot water bottle."

I silently admonished Rodney. He shot me a "so what?" look.

"She wouldn't be stupid enough to leave a clue that obvious with a murder victim," Neil said. Knitting needles were tattooed on his forearm, and he was the one knitter with real skill.

I'd better step in before speculation got out of hand. "Cookie was running the workshop when the man in the café was killed. I'm not wild about her either, but it couldn't have been her. No one saw her anywhere near the café. Unless one of you did?"

The room's silence provided the answer to that question. Finally, Gloria said, "I don't care. I don't like her looks."

"Doesn't make her guilty," Mona said. "Aren't you afraid for your sister?"

"Definitely. Sam brought her home tonight, but what about the rest of the week?"

Rodney, sensing victory was near, stared at the puppy, then burst into zoomies, racing the conservatory's perimeter. All at once, he halted near the banana tree and licked a paw. His show had the anticipated effect. The puppy barked and struggled to escape Mona's lap.

"Boris, I warned you. Come on. I'm taking you home."

If cats could smile, Rodney was grinning ear to ear. With a languid swagger, he returned to the kindling box and settled in for a nap.

Maureen ignored the drama and shook her head. "How about the new café? We should team up for Darla's contest to name it. Takes more than one person to finish a café breakfast platter, anyway."

Mona, puppy in her arms, halted at the conservatory's door. "That's a great idea."

Gloria said, "I could go for that."

"Why not take it further?" Annie said. She rarely spoke, but when she did, it mattered. This evening she hadn't even pretended to knit. Her basket of moss green wool sat untouched. "Now that we have the retreat center and visitors, Wilfred needs a branding campaign. Slogans, colors, the works."

Setting out the coffee cups, I asked, "I like the idea, but why would the knitting club do Wilfred's PR?"

"Do you see a chamber of commerce? No? I didn't think so." Point made, Annie settled back and crossed her legs. "Once the retreat really gets going, people will be pouring into town. We need to distinguish ourselves. We can work Darla's café into the overall campaign."

"And get breakfast for a year," Maureen said. Her crochet needle hadn't yet touched yarn, but it made a good tool for gesturing.

"For a slogan, how about, 'People are dying to come to Wilfred'?" Neil asked. "We have folks kicking the bucket left and right. Let's take our greatest asset and run with it."

"I love it," Gloria said.

"You don't think it's too gruesome?" Mona asked.

"Nah. People really go for stuff like that. Check out the TV listings. Look at true crime podcasts. I bet Josie would tell us that murder mysteries are popular."

"Super-popular," I admitted.

"Then why not make the most of it?" Neil said.

"It'll get Wilfred a lot further than bragging about scenery and fresh air."

"I've got another one," Maureen said. "'Have killer fun in Wilfred.'"

"'Wilfred will knock you dead,'" Annie offered.

The kitchen's coffeepot beeped. "I'll get this," I said. When I returned with the coffeepot and a pitcher of cream, Jean had taken Mona's chair near the stove. She refused to look at me, but I could tell from the way her lower lip jutted out that she was angry. My heart sank. She'd been listening.

"Aren't you afraid?" Mona asked her. She still lingered at the door, finally letting the puppy down on a leash.

"Why?" Jean replied. "Cookie isn't a killer. The murder has nothing to do with us."

"I hear the dead man wrote *Ready-Set-Go* on a place mat. In blood," Gloria said.

I didn't want to burst their bubble with the fact that it had been ketchup. I was worried, though. Jean didn't know that the knitting club wasn't a cheerful group of crafters discussing recipes and homemaking tips. They could be a tough crowd. Not long ago, I'd seen them walk past the Hinkles' house, and Stan Hinkle's dog, known for terrorizing passersby, had actually run to the back door and scratched to be let in.

"In blood? He did?" she whispered. Her expression hardened, and she swatted away Gloria's statement. "A coincidence. He'd probably heard of it, that's all."

"He might have read about it in the paper. Seems I read something, too, about life coaches," Maureen said. "A bunch of crooks."

I groaned. I set the coffee urn on a side table and turned to watch Jean.

"I guess I'd know." Jean's voice was unnecessarily prim. "After all, I researched Cookie and her workshops and have been following her work for months."

Maureen wasn't going to let it go. "I'd watch out for her. I know that type. Ruthless."

"What makes you say that? Have you taken a course from her?" Jean asked, her voice rising.

"Testy, are you?" Gloria said.

"Jean, let's go upstairs," I said. "Come on, Rodney."

He looked at me with citrine eyes and blinked. Unless I could offer up something warmer than his basket by the stove, he'd stay put.

"No, Josie. I want to stay here and talk about Cookie. These people have it wrong."

The room quieted. All five of the knitting club's members stared at her. "What do we have wrong?" Annie said.

"Jean, we'd better be going." I pasted my gaze on her. *It's best this way. You're not going to get anywhere. Take my word for it.*

Jean hesitated before rising. "Fine." At the doorway, she spun to face the room. "But I'm right. You'll see."


Jean stared out my living room window into the darkness. "Why didn't you stick up for me?" She stood with her back to me and arms folded over her chest.

"There was nothing I could say," I pled. "You

don't know those guys. They feed off drama. Give them another minute, and they would have had you weeping."

She dropped her arms and turned to me. "I was in the atrium. I heard you agree with them. You think they're right and I'm stupid for taking the workshop, that I'm getting ripped off. You're entitled to your opinion, but couldn't you have at least kept your mouth shut?"

I wouldn't tell Jean to calm down. It would only anger her further. Neither would I lie to her. "No matter how I feel about Cookie, I believe in you."

From Jean's raised eyebrow, it was clear she doubted me. I held my breath as she stacked another log in the fire and poked at it, drawing sparks. "All right," she said finally. "I'm sorry. I'm just touchy."

Despite her words, by the clench of her jaw I knew she hadn't forgiven me entirely. Better change the subject. "After this afternoon, we're all touchy. Do you want to talk about what happened at the retreat center? We never got to finish our conversation."

Rodney had apparently decided to help my cause, and he popped up from downstairs and trotted to the couch to jump into Jean's lap.

She let him headbutt her chin. "I've already told my story a dozen times. Not that I saw very much."

"Tell me. Everything looked perfectly normal when I dropped you off. Marcia seemed tired, maybe, but that's all."

Jean pulled up her feet. Rodney settled in her lap. "For the first hour or so, everything was normal." Jean slipped a hand between Rodney's ears, and his purring amped a few decibels. "Cookie met with us in the lobby and gave us a rundown of the workshop schedule. Nothing unusual. We went around the room and each of us talked about our life coaching goals." Her face lit up. "Cookie says wellness coaching has a bright future. Health is wealth, right?"

Bogus life coaching is Cookie's wealth was more like it, I thought. "You have a gift for knowing what people need, health-wise. What next?"

"Marcia said she didn't feel well and . . . and Cookie encouraged her to go to the kitchen for a glass of water. She left, and Cookie kept up her talk. I think Rex was telling us about his chain of Tub 'N Tans."

Maybe he was training to be a tanning coach. "How long was she gone?"

Jean shrugged. "I couldn't tell you. Maybe half an hour? When she didn't come back, Cookie sent Desmond to check on her."

Remembering Desmond's matter-of-fact demeanor earlier at Patty's, I never would have guessed he'd discovered a dead woman only hours before.

Jean pulled up her quilt, jiggling Rodney. "We were getting ready to go into one of the workshop rooms to dig into the Ready step when Desmond came out and whispered something to Cookie. Cookie's face turned totally white. She called 911 right away."

"Do you think Marcia died of natural causes? Could you tell?"

She shook her head. "She'd seemed healthy that morning at the grocery store. Remember?"

I did. She'd been energetic—feisty, even. I ran through the workshop's participants in my mind. Sylvia, the slender blonde with the wavy hair whose gaze was glued in fascination on Cookie; Rex, the tanned man with the mien of a used car dealer; Bernie, who mumbled and couldn't seem to focus; Marcia, the victim; and, of course, my sister.

"What do you know about Desmond? I met him this afternoon at the This-N-That."

"He's Cookie's assistant. Other than that, nothing." She narrowed her eyes and raised them to mine as if daring me to say something against Cookie's staff.

I tried a different angle. "How did Marcia die? Could you tell? Maybe she had a heart attack."

Jean's features relaxed. "I don't know. I really don't. We—Sylvia, Rex, Bernie, and I—were kept separate from Cookie and Desmond." She lifted Rodney and set him at her feet. He dug a nest in the pool of quilt and settled in, face to the fire. "There was one strange thing, though."

"What?"

"Cookie told us Marcia's room was torn up, like someone was looking for something." Answering my unspoken question, she added, "She'd gone to her room to find Marcia's purse, for information on her next of kin."

"This sounds more and more like murder."

"What about the dead person at the café?" Jean asked.

I told her what I knew, which wasn't much. Two strangers, two dead bodies, and at least one a murder. Both found within an hour of each other. "One thing, though." I didn't want to freak out

Jean, but she needed to know. "As you heard downstairs, he'd written *Ready-Set-Go* on a place mat. The workshop must be involved somehow."

"Oh no. The killer couldn't have been Cookie, no matter what you think of her. Don't even go there." I opened my mouth to respond, but Jean wasn't finished. "Why would she call out her own workshop? That would be plain stupid. Next, unless the stranger was stabbed days ago, she couldn't have done it. She'd been at the retreat center since she arrived last night."

The fire popped as a log fell. I rose to nudge it into place. "How can you be so sure? She might have written it to throw suspicion away from herself, not because she's stupid, but because she's smart." I added quickly, "Just playing the devil's advocate."

Jean's voice rose. "She's dedicated her life to helping people help others. People like that aren't murderers." She smoothed the quilt over her lap. "Besides, I told you. She was with us the whole time. Impossible."

I couldn't refute that. There was no way Cookie could have nipped out across the meadow, stabbed a man, and returned to the workshop in the time it took to use the ladies' room.

"Cookie came by this afternoon," I said. "After her questioning."

Jean sat up. "She talked to you? Alone?"

"I showed her around the library."

"What did you think of her? Did she say anything about me?"

I measured my words. "She says you have promise. I thought maybe she'd cancel the workshop, but she insisted she'll continue."

Jean smiled. "That's what she told us, too. She's so dedicated." Her smile faded as she looked into the fire. "I know you doubt her." I opened my mouth to reply, and Jean held up a palm. "Don't say it. I know you think I'm making a mistake. Mom does, too. You'll see. This workshop will be a turning point in my life. And Cookie is not a murderer."

"Oh, Jean, you can't go back." I felt Jean's anger rising, but I couldn't help myself.

"Why not? What's done is done. It's over now. The sheriff is on it."

"Until the murderer is found, it's not safe."

"I thought I'd explained, but you still don't understand." She was furious enough that Rodney moved from the quilt and stretched on the hearth, belly toward the fire. "Do you know what an honor it is to be here? Cookie rarely offers workshops this small. You don't get how lucky I am. I'm not going to back out now." She tucked her chin.

She had more to say. I could tell. "What?"

"You're just mad."

"Mad?"

"You don't like having your ideas about me blown apart. I'm finally finding my way in life. You and Mom have me stereotyped as baby Jean who wears cute clothes and charms people and is always broke and getting into trouble." Her voice climbed in pitch. "I can do so much more than that."

"Of course you can. I never doubted it." I

worked to keep my words calm. "Why are you so touchy? All I did was suggest for your own safety that you stay away from the workshop."

Jean wouldn't look at me. "Toni has her medical practice and her family. You have your job here, which you clearly love. This is my chance to make something of myself, something big. I don't plan on teaching yoga at the community center for the rest of my life just so you can feel superior."

I'd had no idea Jean felt this passionately about it. None. She'd always been so easygoing. The most worked up I'd ever heard her before now was talking about Vipassana breathing techniques and the evils of white sugar.

Her voice shifted from angry to pleading. "You understand, don't you? I have to do this. Can't you, for once, just mind your own business?"

Did I like it that she was spending thousands of dollars on a life coach that smelled as phony as a three-dollar bill? No, but I would come to terms with that. It wasn't my money to spend.

I pulled Jean into my arms for a hug. She smelled of warmth and orange blossom shampoo. "I get it. I'm behind you all the way. I'm worried, that's all. Can you give me that? I haven't seen you in so long, and I can't bear the idea of something happening to you." I released her. "Come on, I have a great lavender-chamomile tea."

# CHAPTER EIGHT

The knitting club had finally gathered their projects—and in Mona's case, puppy—and left the conservatory. I'd collected their coffee mugs and locked up the library for the night. Jean and I had managed to pass the rest of the evening without arguing, by looking through my scrapbook and laughing about old memories. Jean gave me the update on Letty, our niece, who was turning out to be a real talker. I banked the fire and bolted my apartment door. What a day.

Throughout the evening, I'd been feeling the tug of my grandma's magic lessons. When I'd learned I was a witch, I was alone in Wilfred, and my only possible mentor—my grandmother—was dead. However, she'd left me a chest full of sealed envelopes. In each envelope was a lesson she'd written over the years, somehow knowing I'd eventually need them. And I had. When it was time for me to move on to the next lesson, the chest almost sang to me.

With Jean settled for the night on the couch, I closed the door connecting the bedroom and living room and quietly slid the chest from under my bed. The chest seemed to sigh as I moved my hands among the envelopes, trusting magic to guide me to the lesson I needed. Energy vibrated through my hand, and my bedside light flickered. The star-shaped birthmark on my shoulder—the one that marked me as a witch—burned.

After the day's events, this lesson could be about anything. Evil, maybe. Or spells of protection. Heat shot through my fingers when they brushed one envelope in particular. I drew it from the pile, relocked the chest, and slipped between my cool sheets, eager to see what Grandma had for me tonight.

I unfolded the letter and her scent rose, a mixture of rosemary, sage, and molasses cookies. As always, my heart caught as her voice filled my head.

> *Dear Josie,*
> *Today's lesson—or is it tonight's lesson?—is fundamental for those gifted with magic, and I hope it comes early in your apprenticeship. It's about knowing what's your business and what belongs to someone else.*

Really? A murderer was on the loose, and my lesson was about knowing when to mind my own business?

> *This might be especially difficult for you, because you're a truth teller and compelled to seek*

*justice. It already shows. Even in kindergarten you
mediated fights over who would play with the
blocks. Just yesterday you saw a stellar jay picking
on a chickadee, and you ran to the garden to scare
it off. Your instinct is to get involved wherever you
feel you can do good. But not all business is your
business.*

*Your mother had trouble with this, too.*

I set the letter on my lap. This was interesting.
Mom had never even mentioned magic in my presence until last year, when I forced the conversation
after my own powers had appeared. As I pondered
this, Rodney, purring, planted himself on the letter. "Move, baby," I told him.

*Your mother has the second sight, and although
it's only a shadow of your gift, she can sense the
drama of people around her. In line at the grocery
store, she knows if the person ahead of her is waiting on the results of a medical test and if the
cashier is worried about paying bills. She may even
suspect the results of the test or the amount of the
cashier's checking account. None of that is her
business, and she must let it go, as if it's information on billboards she drives by. Catherine solved
her problem by squelching her magic altogether.
But that's another story.*

*This lesson might seem too ordinary or obvious.
As you read, you might be thinking, "Why do I
need to know this?" However, knowing what's
yours to take on and what to leave behind is at
magic's foundation. You'll need to be careful as
you decide what is constructive and what is inter-*

*ference in the plans fate already has for an individual. If you are careless, you could inadvertently throw a wrench into the wheel of fortune and ruin generations of lives to come. Your knowledge is a great responsibility.*

*When receiving information, a smart witch asks herself two questions: Is it my business? And, if it is, Can I truly help? Although it may be difficult, sometimes you must walk away and trust destiny to know better than you. I don't know yet exactly how it will reveal itself. Perhaps you already know.*

Oh, I know, I thought. Walk into the library, and books fall all over themselves to tell me what patrons need, from marriage counseling to a brake job.

*First, whatever issue the individual faces might be a lesson they must solve alone to become a stronger, more resilient person. That father-daughter conflict you sense might need to be uncovered and confronted bit by bit by the daughter to strengthen her for later relationships. The novel you see someone pick up—the novel you're sure they won't enjoy—might contain an anecdote its reader will recall at an important moment later in life. Each person has their own path to walk, and unless they reach out for your help, you must let them move ahead their own way. Let that person embrace their challenges at their own pace. Let fate play its role.*

*Next, you may see the problem, but as ardently as you want to address it, you may not have the expertise. It's far too tempting to get involved in situations that you might unknowingly worsen.*

*Yes, you have the magic to see a difficulty others don't recognize. That doesn't mean you know how to address it.*

*Although I sense your magic will come from the books you love so much, I can't see every corner of your power. If the flow of information around you begins to wear you down, remember to ground your energy. My grimoire can help you with that.*

*As always, you are in my heart, and a piece of me remains with you.*

I admitted it now: I'd been feeling the urge to wade into solving Wilfred's murder—potentially two murders. Almost without trying, I'd been gathering information on motives and suspects. It was the truth teller in me. Surely, though, finding a killer couldn't be thwarting destiny? If I was meant to stay on the sidelines, why had I been given magic—plus such a strong drive to see justice done?

I tossed the lesson and its envelope to my dresser. I'd return it to the chest in the morning.

Just because I was a truth teller didn't mean I was the only person who could find a murderer and bring him to justice. A whole system of police and courts existed to do that. Besides, my interference was hurting my relationship with my sister.

I needed to draw back. The sheriff's office could take care of this, and I could trust Sam's judgment. As long as Jean was safe—and she was—I had to let it go. The deaths were none of my business.

# CHAPTER NINE

"We'll lay out our mats here," Jean said.

The morning's crisp winter sun through the cupola cast pools of jewel-toned light on the atrium's wood floor. The furnace had kicked in this morning without incident. Despite yesterday's drama, Jean was bright and rested and didn't seem to bear me a grudge for not sticking up for Cookie yesterday. She wore fuchsia leggings and a lime green sports top. She unrolled a yoga mat with one bare foot.

My "mat" was a beach towel, and my exercise ensemble was a pair of sagging long underwear topped with a stained T-shirt that read *Librarians Do It by the Book*. I'd tied my unruly hair into a ponytail.

"Yoga will help us decompress," Jean said. "I don't know about you, but I had terrible dreams last night."

I remembered my magic lesson. "The sheriff's office will get to the bottom of it. I'm sure. Our job is to stay out of the way."

Jean kneeled on the mat and looked at me. "Who are you and what did you do with Josie? I thought you were hot on learning more about the murderer."

"Nope. It's not my business." Then, looking at the mat: "Are you sure this is a good idea? I won't sprain anything?"

"You spend too much time hunched over the computer or with your nose in a book. You need to open your chest." She thrust her shoulders back and raised her arms behind her. "It will feel great. Now, watch me. We'll start with a simple cat-cow."

Jean dropped on all fours to her mat, and I followed suit on my beach towel. Rodney slinked in from breakfast in the kitchen, and, licking his chops, stood directly under my chest.

"Kitty," I said.

"Never mind him. He'll move when he has to."

Under my torso, he sat and looked at Jean. His ears tickled my stomach.

"Lift your head and let your belly sink toward the floor. Exhale. Feel your shoulders open up. Hold that pose a moment."

Fascinated, Rodney left my beach towel and sniffed at Jean's face. She looked blissful, oblivious to his whiskers on her cheek. A few books from Health offered suggestions: *Focus on your breath. Find your center.* A manual on boot camp calisthenics barked orders while a book of yoga poses whispered encouragement, accompanied by an airy Pan flute.

"Good," Jean said. "Inhale deep into your stomach and tuck your head. Let your back rise into an arch." She adopted a pose that mimicked Rodney when he wanted to strike fear into an assertive squirrel.

I copied Jean's movements, and she was right—it felt great. I understood why her classes were so popular. I glanced up to see Marilyn Wilfred's portrait smirking at us. I never could tell if the portrait was truly animated or if it was my admittedly vivid imagination.

Jean dropped to sitting cross-legged and twisted to one side, her arms stretched behind her. "I didn't know you had a pen pal in Norway."

"What are you talking about?" I sat, too, and twisted, although not with Jean's suppleness.

"The letter on your dresser. To someone called Gerta. I saw it when I was looking for a mirror."

Breath stuck in my throat. That was no letter. It was my magic lesson. I'd dropped off to sleep before returning it to the trunk. "Gerta" was the only word I could manage.

"Did you meet her in library school?"

Grandma must have put a spell on the lessons so that only I could read them. Clever. I wondered if I could cast that sort of spell, too. "If I told you about Gerta, you wouldn't believe it. Now, what do I do with my breath again?"

"Roll to your stomach for cobra pose."

I lowered to my belly and Rodney leapt onto my back. Before I could tell him to scram, he launched and ran toward the door, his nails skittering on the floor.

"Josie?"

I pushed back to sitting. It was Sam, in his uniform and watching us with a slight frown. In other words, he thought we were funny.

"Don't you ever knock?" I said. The library had been a gift to the town from Sam's aunt, and a key hung from the rack near Big House's kitchen door.

"I was headed upstairs to knock on your apartment door. I didn't know you'd be flopping around the atrium." He turned to my sister. "Hi, Jean. How are you after yesterday? I promise that Wilfred's usually a lot calmer."

Jean watched the two of us with bald curiosity. "Slept great, thanks. We made a fire and stayed up and talked. I love this place. I feel like I'm in one of Josie's gothic novels." She rose to her feet with a grace Rodney might have envied. "We were just doing some yoga. You might try it, too. You look like a few sun salutations wouldn't hurt. If you'd like, we can roll out another beach towel."

For a moment, I indulged myself in imagining Sam at my parents' dinner table. He was already comfortable with Jean, and he'd get along great with Toni, I knew it. Nicky might have fun playing with my baby niece, who was a year or so older than he. Thrilled I'd brought a man home, Mom would fuss over him, watching his every bite to offer more of whatever he seemed to like best. Dad would undoubtedly launch into an involved discussion of Talleyrand's tactical errors during the French Revolution. Meanwhile, Sam would watch and listen to it all with his unreadable expression that hid his sharp, observant mind.

"Thank you. Another day," Sam said. "I promised I'd give you updates on the case, and I wanted you to know we've identified the victim at the café."

"Who was he?" I asked, yanking myself from my reverie.

I'd known Sam long enough to see he had something more to impart than the victim's name. He was looking for a reaction.

"Anders McGhie. Cookie's husband."

"No," Jean said right away. "That's impossible. Cookie isn't married."

"I talked with her yesterday afternoon. She didn't mention a husband," I added.

This was what Sam had been waiting for. "We have their marriage certificate."

Jean shook her head. "Cookie's single. Everyone knows that. She has a whole module on Ready-Set-Go about meeting the partner of your dreams. It's one of her biggest sellers."

"I can't speak to the nature of her relationship with her husband, but we didn't find a divorce decree."

"Was there any evidence of something between Anders and Marcia?" I asked.

"They were wearing identical Irish claddagh rings engraved with each other's names," Sam said.

I remembered the flash of silver on Marcia's hand from yesterday morning. "Cookie might have found out and been jealous. Or, her husband or Marcia threatened to reveal their relationship. That would sink Cookie's dating program and cost her money and credibility."

Jean shook her head again, this time more vigorously. "You think Cookie killed them? Impossible. She was with us the whole time. Why won't anyone believe me when I say she's innocent?"

"She has a solid alibi," he admitted. "There's still a lot we don't know." He pointed toward my back.

To my horror, my T-shirt was stuck in the back of my bra. I pulled it loose with as much nonchalance as I could muster. As I met Sam's eyes, I wondered if what Jean had told me was true, that Sam had feelings for me he didn't recognize.

"Thanks. Any idea yet on how Marcia died?"

"We're running tests, but it looks like she was poisoned."

Two murders now. My chest tightened.

"Likely something in her morning coffee. Her travel mug, the one witnesses say she drank from, is at the lab."

"Cookie couldn't have done it. We all saw her," Jean repeated.

"Do you know when Marcia might have been given the poison? At the PO that morning, she seemed fine. She looked less well when I dropped Jean off at the retreat center at noon."

Jean nodded. "Like she was coming down with something. No energy. Then she excused herself. Cookie was concerned. She suggested Marcia take a time-out."

"We told you about what we saw between her and Rex. What does he have to say about it now?"

Sam raised an eyebrow. "Don't worry, Josie. This is my job."

I tried again. "How about fingerprints on the knife in Anders's back?"

"We didn't find any, but that's not surprising, especially given how cold it is. Whoever killed him must have been wearing gloves. Seriously, Josie. We're on it."

*Mind your own business,* last night's magic lesson seemed to whisper from where I'd left it on my dresser. "Right." I took a deep breath. "You're absolutely right. You know your job."

Sam's eyebrows raised, as if he didn't believe me. "In other, better news, the café's open for breakfast."

I picked up my beach towel and slung it over my arm. "Now we're talking. Come on, Jean. How do you feel about Southern food?"

# CHAPTER TEN

I could hear the chatter of breakfasting Wilfredians even before my hand touched the café's
door. The diner was packed, and it wasn't just because of the two deaths, but because the café had
been closed too long. People were hungry not just
for Darla's stellar cooking, but for community.
This time there was no ribbon-cutting and no paper
over the steamed-up windows. It was the café, just
like it used to be, as if the past nine months of clo-
sure had never happened.

"Welcome, Josie," Darla called from the back
counter. She wore black, presumably in mourning
for Anders McGhie. However, a cheetah-print blouse
peeked from under her cardigan. We met her near
the cash register and she hugged me briefly. "This
must be your sister."

"Jean," I said, "this is Darla. If we had a mayor, it
would be her."

"Pleased to meet you." Darla raised her voice to be heard above the din. "Both redheads. Amazing. And to think the hair just comes out of your scalp that way, no dye necessary. I envy you."

"Thank you," Jean said. I've always admired her poise. It was nice to have reached a détente after last night's spat about Cookie.

"We're full up this morning, but if you don't mind Montgomery's company, you can sit with him." Darla gestured toward a booth near the patio door.

"We'd love it," I said.

I glanced at the counter where we'd found Anders McGhie facedown with a knife between his shoulder blades. Black crepe paper draped the stool, and a handwritten sign with a simple *RIP* was taped to its back. A bundle of gold chrysanthemums lay on the seat—the only empty seat in the house. A further scan of the room showed Bernie, Rex, and Sylvia huddled at one table with Duke and Desmond chatting at the next. Remembering my magic lesson, I squelched to urge to pull up a chair and question them.

"Welcome, ladies," Montgomery said as we slipped into his booth. "What'll you have?"

Montgomery was a small, bald man who at a passing glance might've been mistaken for a nerdish middle-schooler with alopecia. In fact, he was a retired tourism manager with a sonorous voice, interest in philosophy, and Southern accent as rich as pecan pie with bourbon syrup. After a library trustees meeting one night, Darla confessed that her interest in him was piqued by that intoxicating voice. "He was a tour guide in Charleston," she'd told me. "Two words out of his mouth, and I was hooked like a famished trout." He read to her each night. From the rustle of wind through Spanish moss and cries of "Scarlett!" coming from their double-wide at the Magnolia Rolling Estates, my guess was they were deep into *Gone with the Wind*.

"Two shrimp and grits platters," I told the waitress, a high schooler Darla had pulled in for help. "Jean, you'll love them. And coffee, please."

"Make mine a green tea," Jean said.

"Montgomery, this is my little sister, Jean."

"A good, old-fashioned name," Montgomery said. "Had an aunt named Jean. Her father worked the railroads during the Depression. She was named for one of the cooks. Jean Eleanor."

"It's short for Eugénie," Jean said.

Montgomery set his fork on his platter and looked from Jean to me. "And your full name is Joséphine, I wager?"

"We have an older sister called Toni."

"Marie Antoinette," Jean said. "Dad teaches French history at the community college."

Satisfied at his deductions, Montgomery untucked the paper napkin from his collar and folded it over his plate. "Darla warned me the café would be busy, but I never expected anything like this."

"It sure is good to be back." I hadn't realized how much I'd missed the friendly check-ins with Wilfredians and the quiet "hellos" from paperbacks in their purses here and there.

"Darla and I weren't sure if opening the café was appropriate. A sad occasion, to be sure," Montgomery said. "We decided to open the doors anyway, let our neighbors process the deaths." He pushed his empty platter to the table's edge to be bussed. "Besides, we had all this food."

"You did the right thing," I said. "I wonder"—Grandma's words about minding my own business rose to mind, but I wasn't asking anything any other Wilfredian wouldn't—"Did anyone see the victim around town before we found him here?"

"Exactly what the sheriff wanted to know," Montgomery said. "They interviewed everyone at the Magnolia. Apparently, Duke caught a glimpse of a stranger coming through the trailer park. You know how he keeps an eye on the meadow."

Duke was a member of a World War II vehicle club, and his cherished M26 Weasel was parked in the meadow. He wasn't going to let anyone take off with it, although it labored to achieve speeds even I could outrun.

"A man?" I asked.

"He's not sure. Whether it was the victim or the murderer, we don't know."

Our food arrived, and I dug in. The grits, earthy with thyme and bits of chanterelle mushroom, were as delicious I remembered. At some meal soon, I was looking forward to Darla's Northwest-adapted jambalaya with salmon, and a slice of her huckleberry pie. If the rapidly dwindling supply of shrimp on her platter was any evidence, Jean was enjoying breakfast, too.

"If the murderer came from the retreat center, he probably would have come through the Magnolia Estates," I said. "He'd risk being seen on the access road."

"I wish I could say I spotted the killer, but I

didn't." Montgomery shook his head. "Darla and I were prepping the café until ten or so. We were too busy to keep an eye on the path to the trailer park. Besides, the windows were papered over. After that, we took a nap. We'd been up since five."

Marcia, with Rex shortly behind her, would have made her way back to the retreat center from the grocery store while Darla and Montgomery were at the café. It made sense that Montgomery had seen nothing.

"I'll stay alert," Montgomery said. "I'm a bit of a Miss Marple, myself. A student of human nature. For instance, I see that you, Josie, have focused on the grits, while your sister is eating her shrimp first."

I glanced at my platter. He was right. "I suppose I'm saving the best for last."

"You enjoy the anticipation," Montgomery noted.

I hadn't thought about it, but he was right. I nodded.

"As a whole," Montgomery said, slipping into professorial mode, "we tend to be a people who either save the best for last or dive in for the good stuff right away. Me"—he tapped his plaid-shirted chest—"I proudly eat the best first. When I see quality, I don't hesitate. That's why when I lit eyes on Darla, I made sure we'd have dinner together that very night."

We all turned to watch Darla ring up a customer with one hand, her other hand slapping an order on the kitchen pass-through. Busy as she was, she cast a smile our way.

"Life is short," he added.

Now we turned to the black-draped stool.

"In matters of romance, Josie definitely prefers to wait," Jean said.

I kicked her under the table. "If only a study of human nature could reveal murderers."

"They say the most powerful motives for murder are money and jealousy," Montgomery said. "I'd add ego. Self-aggrandizement has driven half the world's wars, I'm sure. Never underestimate how toxic injured pride can be." He shook his head as if remembering some long-ago instance. "On a more practical note, we found bits of red rose petals on the patio. Torn up, like someone was angry. Didn't I hear that the tan fellow purchased a dozen?"

I twisted in my seat to follow Montgomery's gaze to the table across the room where the workshop participants sat. Sylvia's eyes strayed toward the black-bedecked stool, and her hand rested on the spine of her notebook poking from her bag. Next to her, Rex, with the air of a down-market TV game show host, waved a fork and expostulated about something. What was it he'd wanted with Marcia at the PO? Bernie seemed lost in her thoughts. Today her hair puffed slightly on top like a standard poodle's. I couldn't miss the glances of the rest of the café's customers, either, as they undoubtedly pondered thoughts similar to ours.

"Hardly a motive for murder," Jean said.

Behind the table, Duke and Cookie's assistant, Desmond, seemed to be arguing—a good-natured argument. Duke shaped something imaginary in his hands and made a sawing motion. Desmond laughed in response, the smile giving light to the hollows beneath his eyes. He laid his bone-handled knife on the table. Duke turned the blade, admiring it.

"They say the second victim, the lady, was poisoned. And"—Montgomery twirled a finger in the air to emphasize his point—"the dead man, the one we found here? Cookie's husband."

How had this news leaked already? Sam had told us barely an hour ago. Honestly, the speed of Wilfred's grapevine rivaled a fiber optics network. "Everyone's here," I said. "All the possible suspects. Except Cookie."

# CHAPTER ELEVEN

After walking Jean to the retreat center, I was happy to give myself over to work. Grandma's lesson had warned me to stick to my own business. There was no reason to doubt Sam's ability to get to the bottom of the murders. Besides, if our assumptions held, the deaths involved two people in a closed relationship, Cookie's husband and his lover. As long as Jean was safe, I planned to back off.

That went for letting Jean learn her own lessons, too. She was enthusiastic about Cookie's workshop. If it was a rip-off, then it was a lesson for Jean. If Grandma was right and my interference could tip destiny, by keeping Jean from the workshop I might prevent her from meeting someone or learning something—even something incidental—that could change the course of her life for the better. Here, too, I would back off.

It seemed my lesson would continue to be put to the test. Standing on the library's porch, earnestly avoiding eye contact with me, was a woman to whom the weekend before I'd recommended a pamphlet on prenatal health. The problem was that she'd been looking for a good mystery novel. The state of her womb was none of my business, no matter how loudly the pamphlets had lectured from their rack.

"Good morning, Emmy," I said. "Can I help you find anything?"

Unbidden, the title of a manual on breastfeeding slid into my head. Keeping a professional smile plastered on my face, I imagined my brain as a chalkboard and erased the thought.

She walked ahead two steps without replying, then spun to look at me. "How did you know I'm trying to get pregnant?"

"What?" I said, playing for time.

"Last week, you gave me something about prenatal vitamins."

"I did? I'm sorry. I must have been distracted when I grabbed that brochure." I widened my smile. "Psychic librarian! Or maybe you had a Madonna-like glow."

For a moment, she looked at me uncertainly, then, to my relief, broke into a grin. "Weird, huh? Anyway, the pamphlet was helpful. This time, though, I really do want a mystery."

My whole body relaxed. Grandma was right. I had to mind my own business. Just because I knew what someone needed to read, even if I'd never heard of the book, didn't mean I had to dole out the suggestions.

"Come this way to Popular Fiction."

"Hello," Lalena called from kitchen. Sailor, her terrier mix, trotted behind her, led on a fat pink ribbon. Today Lalena wore woolen knickers and striped socks with a long, ribbed sweater pulled over it. In case she looked too much like Oliver Twist, she'd topped it off with star-shaped earrings and a matching brooch from the 1970s. "Reporting for work."

From there, the day began peacefully, with Lalena suggesting her favorite books to patrons, regardless of what they'd requested, and me practicing minding my own business. One patron asked where to find cookbooks, and I resisted pointing out a book on bathroom remodels. When another patron asked about what to feed her budgie, the books nearly screamed a title on holistic arthritis treatment, but I handily ignored that, too. Not only was I able to block book suggestions that were too personal, I found I had more energy. Acting as a human card catalog for the patrons' subconscious needs had been more wearing than I'd realized.

Midafternoon, the vibe began to shift. It started when I reached into a drawer for a pad of paper and found the 1940s Delano Ames novel *She Shall Have Murder* on top of a stack of yellow pads. As I shelved a new release, I'd gasped as the spines of murder mysteries popped from their shelves, accompanied by faraway shrieking and sirens. The final straw came that afternoon in the kitchen, when I opened the refrigerator for milk to doctor my coffee and found a dog-eared copy of Agatha Christie's *The Body in the Library* staring at me from on top of Lalena's lunch in the crisper drawer. This was too much.

"What do you want?" I whispered, retrieving the chilled book. "Is this because murder is on my brain, or is it a warning?"

"A what?" came a voice behind me. I spun to find Orson at the doorway to the atrium.

"Someone left a book in the refrigerator. Imagine that." I held up the paperback, then dropped it to the table. The book was too frigid to touch for more than a few seconds, much colder than a mere refrigerator could make it. We both stared at its vintage cover, featuring a young woman in a strapless gown lifeless on the floor of a dark room. It took me a moment to catch my breath.

"*The Body in the Library*. Funny. We're taking bets at the tavern on who the next victim will be." Orson was a bartender on the tavern side of the café, which was why I rarely saw him before noon.

"My sister's in that workshop."

"Oh, I know. We placed long odds on her. No, my money's on the tanned gent." Orson shook his head. "Drinks cosmopolitans."

The books weren't normally practical jokers. They had something to tell me—or something to warn me about. My uneasiness about Jean's workshop deepened. Every instinct I had told me to get her away from the retreat center, no matter what I had to do to make it happen. But my grandmother had instructed me to mind my own business, and her magic lessons were nearly always spot-on.

I returned to Circulation so Lalena could take a late lunch. She was painting her thumbnail peony pink while Sailor snoozed in a basket under the desk. Rodney, ever the heat seeker, was curled up next to him. Mona had brought in the basket when she'd seen Rodney squeezed in the conservatory's kindling box. He still preferred the box.

"Look at those two," I said. How I loved that cat, troublemaker he was.

"I know. They're adorable." She set the nail polish next to a book, one of the vintage mysteries that had been in the library since Marilyn Wilfred's days. She tapped its cover. "I found this in their bed. Isn't that strange?"

It was *Unfinished Crime* by Helen McCloy. I flipped it over to read *WEB OF TERROR* in capital letters. That was it. I didn't know how I was going to pull it off, but there was no way I was letting Jean return to the workshop tomorrow.


Library closed for the day, I waited in my office for Jean to return. Stuck in my mind was the vision of *The Body in the Library* with a spinach leaf frozen to it from Lalena's salad.

Dark fell early this time of the year, and the thick cloud cover cut visibility even more. I'd instructed Jean to make her way home through the meadow, then up the road, rather than taking the shorter, but more secluded, trail through the woods. Every two minutes I texted to make sure she was okay. Her responses became more and more terse.

Finally, Jean's face appeared at the kitchen door. I leapt to unbolt it for her. "You're home!"

Instead of being happy to see me, Jean looked irked. "It's not like there are a lot of other places to go. Not in this town. Although after all your mother-henning, I was tempted."

"You can't blame me for being worried." When she didn't respond, I added, "Come upstairs. We'll make a fire."

Jean wasn't going to like my warnings. I knew I could enlist Mom to help convince her to return, but Jean would be seriously peeved I'd even try—maybe even angry enough to leave the library and move into the retreat center until the workshop was over. I couldn't let that happen. If only I could tell her about my magic and the books' warnings.

Upstairs, I was formulating my battle plans, when I heard Sam calling my name from the atrium. I looked over the banister. Sam frowned up at me, and red and blue light splashed his uniform from the moon through the cupola's stained glass. My heart beat double-time at that happy frown. Could Jean be right, and he really did care about me but was too clueless to know? Hands spread over the oak railing, I leaned forward.

A British-accented baritone rose from fiction. "But, soft! what light through yonder window breaks? It is the east, and Juliet is the sun!"

Sam couldn't hear this, of course, which saved me years of mortification. "Did I startle you?" he said. "You look kind of . . . strange."

"No, I was just"—I glanced down the hall, willing my expression to lose the Shakespeare-inspired mooning—"I was just thinking about literature."

"Okay." He shifted, and the jewel-toned light dropped away. "Would you and your sister like to come to my house for dinner? I made a Bolognese sauce yesterday, and there's plenty for all of us."

"We have plans, but thank you so much for the offer." As much as I loved my evenings in Sam's kitchen, I didn't need Jean monkeying with my non-love affair.

"What offer?" Jean emerged from the living room, her face still pink from the winter chill. Rodney appeared from nowhere and wound through her ankles.

"I stopped by to see if you'd like to come to Big House for dinner. I can toss pasta with cheese and butter for you, Jean, if you don't eat meat. Plus, we'll have a salad."

"We accept," Jean said.

I glanced at her. *Don't make a fool of me*, I thought, knowing she'd get it.

She read my expression clearly and smiled. "We'll be right down. Josie, get your coat."

A moment later, we joined Sam in the atrium. She looked first at me, then at Sam. Her mental wheels were turning, and I didn't trust their direction. She smiled sweetly. "I'm sure looking forward to this dinner."

"We'll lock up," I said. Theft wasn't a problem in Wilfred. Murder, yes. Robbery, not so much. But after the recent goings-on, I wasn't taking chances. "Hold my coat, please." I handed it to Jean while I dug for my keys in my purse. As Jean pulled her hands from her pockets, something fluttered to the floor.

"What's this?" She knelt to retrieve a sheet of paper torn from a small spiral-bound tablet. "This isn't mine."

I was all too aware of Sam leaning over my shoulder to look at the note. "Don't touch that," he said with enough authority that Jean yanked back her hand.

"No," I whispered. "Please." I didn't need to read the note to know what it said.

*READY*, it read in block letters. Next to the word was a taped list of workshop participants cut from a program, with a jagged black line through Jean's name.

Jean swallowed. "That's our agenda from yesterday."

Maybe the murders weren't my business before, but they definitely were now.

# CHAPTER TWELVE

We sat at Big House's kitchen table, a near double to the table in the library's kitchen, except that here the room smelled of garlic and tomatoes, and Mozart played in the background. Normally, I would admire the old house's expertly turned moldings and coved ceilings and wonder about the generations of Wilfreds who grew up in it. I would take in Nicky's stuffed animals and Sam's odd bachelor touches—the high-end sound system, the tool kit occupying the space where someone else might have set a vase of flowers— and think about Sam and Nicky rattling around the spacious rooms on their own. I would wonder if I had a place here.

But tonight wasn't a normal night. Tonight, someone had threatened to kill my sister.

Jean and I were on one side of the kitchen table, and Nicky sat in Jean's lap, grabbing at her cutlery.

He could walk now, albeit like the town drunk in diapers, so it was safest to contain him in someone's lap when we couldn't watch him.

Sam glanced toward a side table, where the paper reading *READY* was now sealed in an evidence bag. He pulled a notepad from his briefcase. "I'll need a statement from you, Jean."

"I don't have much to say. I went to the retreat center, studied with Cookie. I didn't do anything special." Considering her life was at risk, Jean acted remarkably cool.

My plans for subtly persuading Jean to leave the workshop went out the window. "You have to fly home right away. I'll work on getting your ticket changed. You're not going back to the workshop."

"It's a piece of paper. That's all," she replied. "You're not the boss of me."

I leaned forward. "It's a murder threat. Someone has to show some common sense here."

"Why would anyone want to kill me? I haven't done anything."

Sam looked from me to Jean. "If we can pause the sisterly bickering, I'd like to ask a few questions."

I leaned back and folded my arms. "Fine."

"Jean, where was your coat during the workshop?"

Jean gently removed Nicky's hand from her fork. "Hanging on the coatrack near the retreat center's front door."

I pictured the vintage wool coat, dangling from its hook, open to the world. Anyone could have slipped anything from a note to a live cobra into one of its deep pockets. "Hmpf."

"Was it always in the same room with you? For instance, when you had lunch or took bathroom breaks?"

"No. Why would I take my coat with me to the restroom? I didn't have any reason not to trust the crumbs." She straightened. "I bet it's all a joke."

"We'll get in touch with the other workshop participants to see if anyone else received the threat. No one has called it in, or I would have heard."

Jean inhaled deeply, held it, and let out a gusty sigh. Clearly some sort of yoga breath. "I suppose a stranger could have dropped something into my coat. Not just workshop participants. Some crazy person might have snuck to the retreat center and slipped the note into my pocket." She shook her head, and Nicky copied her. "I just can't see any of the other crumbs leaving a threat like that. Although . . ."

"Although, what?" I said.

Sam simply watched, his expression deceptively placid.

"It's nothing, really. During the break I made a comment to Sylvia about how I had to do some lion breaths to calm myself after all the information we were taking in. She had no idea what I was talking about."

Neither did I. Lion breaths? "Why is that a big deal?"

"She calls herself a wellness expert, but she doesn't know squat about yoga."

"Tell me about Ready-Set-Go," Sam said. "What does it mean?"

"Why aren't you asking about Sylvia?" I interjected. "You know something, or you would have followed up on Jean's comment." Nicky grunted and lifted his arms to me. Jean handed him over, and I parked the baby's compact warmth on my lap.

"Josie, you have to trust me. Now, Jean, please continue."

"Ready-Set-Go is basic, yet profound." Now that Jean's hands were free of the baby, she waved them in the air for emphasis. "To accomplish any goal, any dream, you need a plan. As Cookie says, simply wishing on a star isn't going to cut it. The Ready-Set-Go methodology lays out a path for making dreams a reality. It's so important that Cookie trademarked it."

I grimaced. Jean sounded like a fully indoctrinated cult member.

"And Ready?" Sam asked. "What happens in that step?"

Happy to talk about the workshop, Jean's wariness vanished. "Ready is the foundational step. In Ready, you flesh out your goal and really examine how you want to feel, what you want to accomplish. You visualize your end state. You make it as real as you can in your mind."

"Give me an example," Sam said.

Jean only pretended to examine the air for a topic. Something in her expression put me on warning. "Let's take Josie. Say, Josie decided she wanted a boyfriend."

"Jean, that's—"

She lifted a hand in a "stop" motion. "Calm down. This is all theoretical. You clearly wish to remain a spinster for eternity."

"Gah," Nicky said.

"In the Ready step, Josie would admit to herself, concretely, that she wants a relationship. With that goal in mind, she would focus on how the end result would make her feel—not on her preconceived ideas of what her boyfriend looks like." She turned to me. "Josie, how would you say that end result would feel?"

"Shut up." Jean would pay for this.

Sam glanced at me with a frown. He found this amusing. Big-time. "What do you mean?"

"She might think she wants a particular person or a particular type of person—you know, tall, dark, and handsome. Or whatever. Really, though, she wants a feeling. The feeling of being with a good friend and being appreciated for who she is. As well as being attracted to that person." Jean was really going at it now. I willed the floor to open and swallow me whole. "By not anticipating the physical representation of the end state, she'll be flexible and consider a variety of options and, so, be more likely to achieve her goal." She beamed at us.

"All right, example over," I said firmly. "What about the shredded rose petals Montgomery mentioned were found on the café's patio?"

Sam ignored me. "So, in leaving that card in your pocket . . ."

He didn't need to finish his sentence. Jean's hands dropped to her lap. I didn't want to think about what the killer was visualizing—not if it had to do with my baby sister, no matter how irritated I was with her at the moment.

"Like I said, maybe it was a joke," Jean replied in a small voice.

"We can't discount this. Joke or not, we have two people dead already. The note is a threat, and we need to treat it that way."

"The murderer may not be finished," I said. My pasta, so appetizing a few minutes ago, didn't tempt any longer. I pushed the plate away from Nicky's roving fingers and kissed the scalp under his curly black hair. He smelled fresh and milky, of pure baby.

"Until we get to the bottom of this, I don't want you going anywhere alone," Sam told Jean.

"Maybe the workshop should be called off," I said. "Can the sheriff's department insist on it?"

"No!" Jean said. "Stop it, Josie. The note was a joke. I know it. I bet Rex put it there. He seems like a joker."

"What makes you say that?" Sam asked.

"He writes encouraging messages to Cookie on the whiteboard. Things like that. Today, he wrote, *What's sweeter to eat than a Cookie? Nothing.*"

"Those aren't threats," I pointed out. "They're love notes in questionable taste. She needs to call off the workshop."

"It's up to Cookie," Sam said. "We don't have the authority to shut anything down." He leaned in, forearms on the table. "Also, we might have more of a chance of finding the culprit if the retreat continues. Monitored, of course."

Next to me, Jean relaxed.

"There's no way you're using my sister as bait," I said, my voice low.

Nicky sensed my sudden anger and let out a whimper. I kissed his cheek and slipped him into the bouncy seat Sam had clipped over the pantry doorway. He shrieked a laugh and kicked his chubby legs.

"She's not bait," Sam said once I'd settled back into my seat. "I would never do that."

"Don't I have a say?" Jean placed both palms facedown on the table. "You forget that I'm an adult. This workshop is my time and my money. The risk is mine, too. I'm here for a reason—to be certified as a wellness coach. Nothing is going to stand in the way of that, certainly not a stupid piece of paper with a word on it."

"What if Cookie feels differently? What if she cancels the workshop?" I asked, hoping she would indeed do that. Jean would be richer and safer. I could keep her in the library with me until the sheriff's office had collected its evidence, then escort her to the airport.

"She won't," Jean said.

"How can you be so sure?" Sam asked.

"The workshop is part of her Ready-Set-Go vision. Once a plan is in place, she says, it barrels forward like a mighty train, and nothing will stand in its way."

Jean was repeating motivational pap. Expensive motivational pap. I made a disgusted sound. She glared at me. Sam took it all in.

"Can you tell us what you know so far about the murders?" I asked Sam.

"A little bit. There's a lot we don't know yet and some I can't disclose."

Sam and I had discussed many of his cases as we sat in the dusk on his kitchen porch looking over Wilfred. He hadn't kept much from me then. Of course, those cases had to do with things like pilfered eggs and graffiti at the high school in Gaston, the town next door.

"You told us who the victims were," Jean said. "Are you positive the guy in the café was Cookie's husband?"

Sam nodded. "They'd just celebrated their twentieth anniversary."

"And the other victim was one of Cookie's prior students," I confirmed.

"Marcia Borne. A longtime student and a successful coach in her own right. A coach for coaches, according to her website."

"Which made her one of Cookie's competitors," I pointed out.

"Cookie's husband wasn't on the shuttle from the airport," Jean said.

"No, he'd flown out separately and rented a car in Portland. It was parked in Gaston at the Parker House. He'd told the manager to prepare for two guests."

It didn't take a genius to figure this one out. "Clearly they were together. Romantically, I mean. An affair. It points to Cookie as the prime suspect."

"That's logical," Sam said, "But according to Cookie, she and her husband had an understanding and jealousy wouldn't be a strong motive. Not only that, it's impossible that Cookie killed her husband. Cookie was teaching when he died. As for putting something in Marcia's coffee, the timing is off there, too. The medical examiner says Marcia was likely poisoned in the morning before the workshop began, when Cookie was in her room. Everyone else at the workshop had the same opportunity to poison Marcia."

"Except Jean," I said.

"Correct. Because she was staying with you, and you were with her all morning."

"You're confident about the times of death?" I asked.

"We'll know for sure after the autopsies, but according to the medical examiner's initial estimate, yes."

"What about the argument we saw between Rex and Marcia? Anything there?"

"I questioned Rex. He didn't deny talking to Marcia. He said he knew about her affair with Anders, and he wanted her to back off."

"Why would he do that?" I asked. "Especially since he appears to be after Cookie himself?"

"He said he didn't want Cookie to be publicly humiliated. Apparently, Anders didn't make a habit of tagging along on her workshops." Sam leaned back. "But that's enough. I've already told you more than I should have, and I only revealed this much because of the threat against Jean. I know you're worried." He shifted his gaze to Jean. I recognized the look on his face, that inscrutable, quiet focus. I also knew never to underestimate it. "Had you met Cookie or either of the victims before you came to Wilfred?"

"I knew Cookie, yes, of course."

"When did you meet?"

"We never met in person. I knew her through social media and podcasts. I guess I felt like I knew her." Jean's expression became more earnest. "You don't understand. Cookie is an open book. She has nothing to hide."

Sam's face softened. "Everyone has secrets, Jean."

# CHAPTER THIRTEEN

Sam escorted us across the lawn separating Big House from the library. I was uneasy. There was so much we didn't know, and so much Sam knew but wouldn't reveal. As I unbolted the side door, I could feel the books' humming, feeding off my anxiety.

"Be sure you lock up. Windows, doors, everything. Did Lyndon fix that basement window?"

"The one by the furnace? Yes." The old furnace's sawdust chute was converted into a window at some point in the eighties. The latch had never quite worked right.

"Keep your phones near you. If you hear anything unusual—anything at all—call me. Okay?"

"Okay," Jean said. "I'm exhausted. I'll just run upstairs and leave you two." She cast me a meaningful glance and hurried inside.

Once her steps had faded, Sam pulled my elbow

so I faced him. "Josie, I know you want to protect your sister."

"And?" He stood so close. Our breath clouded the frigid night.

"You trust me, don't you? You believe I'm capable?"

I knew what he was getting at. I nodded. I did trust him, and I did believe in his ability to suss out a murderer. He wasn't showy about his intelligence, but it was there, ticking through evidence, making deductions, steadily working toward a conclusion.

However, Sam didn't have my motivation. It wasn't his sister in the killer's crosshairs. Besides, he wasn't a witch.

He cupped my other elbow so that now I stood within his arms, only a few feet from his chest. "Then you will back off and let me do my job, right?"

He seemed to radiate some sort of force field that plunged me into a drowsy trance. "What?"

"You asked a lot of questions tonight. I admire your sense of justice. But this is murder. You need to step away and trust I'll get to the bottom of it."

I jerked back and snapped out of the spell. "I've helped you with your cases more than once. Why can't I help now?"

"This isn't petty theft." He stepped closer, and I retreated. If he sucked me into that vortex again, I might never come out. "You saw Anders at the café. Remember the knife in his back? The blood? I don't want that to be Jean. Or you. If you start asking questions, you'll move right onto the murderer's to-do list. Got it?"

Mute, I nodded. And I crossed gloved fingers behind my back.

He smiled—never a good sign—and yanked my hand forward so quickly that my fingers were still crossed. "Just as I thought."

"That was nothing. I always cross my fingers when I'm nervous, I—"

"Uh-huh. Now I'm going to sweeten the pot. If I get wind at all—and I mean at all—that you're nosing around about the murders, I'm going to take your sister into custody."

"Jean? You can't do that."

"Oh, yes I can. She could have easily poisoned Marcia, and I have only your word she didn't stab Anders. After all, she's the only workshop participant who wasn't at the retreat center when he was killed."

My head whirled. He couldn't possibly be serious. "What about the threat she found tonight?" I said, then realized what Sam was thinking. I dropped my head. "Right. Throwing suspicion elsewhere." I lowered my voice. "You don't really think she's guilty, do you?"

"It doesn't matter what I think. What matters is that you step aside and let me do my job." He grasped my hands in his. "Got it?"

There was no chance to cross my fingers now. "Got it."

Jean settled on the couch with several blankets over her for warmth, plus a backup quilt. However, she didn't look sleepy at all.

Since we'd arrived home from Sam's, she hadn't said anything to me about the workshop, but I could tell she hadn't forgiven me for wanting her to drop out of it. As she walked, toothbrush in hand, to the bathroom, she shot me a "how dare you tell me what to do" glance. When she arranged the quilts over her, she pointedly looked away from me. Even Rodney, snuggling close for pets, got only cursory attention.

"Sam told me to lay off the case. Just so you know," I said.

She raised an eyebrow, but refused to turn her head in my direction.

"He said if he gets any hint I'm butting in, he'll throw you in jail."

"What?" She sat up so fast that Rodney jumped from her lap to the floor. He recovered quickly, ambling into the bedroom as if that were his objective all along.

"He pointed out that you're the only crumb who wasn't at the retreat center when Anders was killed. He said maybe you did it, and I'm covering for you."

"That's ridiculous! I would never hurt Cookie that way."

"I suspect it was an empty threat, but with Sam you never know." I sat on the edge of the couch facing her. "Anyway, I'm backing off. I'm going to mind my own business. For real."

"Thanks, Josie." Jean grabbed my hand and squeezed it. "I hate being mad at you." She returned her hand to her lap and fidgeted with the ties on the quilt.

"You're not tired at all, are you?"

She shook her head.

"One of the perks of living in a library is that you never lack for books. I bet a few chapters of something relaxing will put you right to sleep."

"You can try." She lay back with an arm behind her head. "I bet I'm up all night."

I relaxed my brain and a title slid neatly into it. Perfect. I skipped down the stairs and, once I was sure Jean couldn't see me, I lifted a hand and whispered, "Come." The volume I sought whirled from Children's Literature and alit on my outstretched palm. I held it against my chest. *Do your work*, I willed it.

Upstairs, I handed the book to Jean.

"*The Golden Treasury of Bedtime Stories*? A kids' book?" she said.

I had to shake out my hand. It had fallen asleep just holding the stories. "Remember? We had that one when we were kids. You always loved it. I thought it might be comforting tonight."

She was already opening the book. I went to my bedroom and closed the adjoining door. As I changed into pajamas and a chenille bathrobe, I heard the lambs baaing, princesses singing, and the chugging of the little engine that could, all twisting into a soporific haze. I gave the book twenty minutes to work its magic and peeked out the door. Jean was fast asleep. Poor girl. She'd had a rough day. We both had.

I crept out of my bedroom, lifted the book from her chest where it had fallen, and clicked off the light. Then I tiptoed downstairs to Old Man Thurston's office and lit a candle. Jean was in danger. It was time to put my magic to work.

I wasn't much at casting the types of spells the general public associated with witches. Verses in Old English? They didn't do a thing for me. As a dedicated reader and poetry lover, I found most rhyming spells goofy. My grandmother had provided a few spells for me in her grimoire, but they mostly centered around potions, her specialty.

Instead, to bend energy to my intentions, I usually worked directly with my source: books. Sometimes I lifted a passage from a childhood favorite, *Grimms' Fairy Tales*, and applied it to my situation. For instance, the part of *Sleeping Beauty* where the kingdom awakens from a century-long sleep was key to reinvigorating my magic. Other times, I simply encouraged the books to do what they did best, depending on their storylines.

Tonight, I wanted to cast a spell of protection over the library. Jean needed at least one safe place. I placed my palms flat on Old Man Thurston's desk. Its oak surface had been worn to a satin sheen over the generations, and it had absorbed the energy of thousands of business contracts and bills of lading for timber, dusted with the singsong stories of the children's books living here in more recent decades.

"Books," I said. "Tonight we're going to cast a spell to protect the library."

Cheers peppered with cannon fire arose from History, and sighs heaved from Popular Fiction, probably the romance novels. The prickling of my skin reflected the library's rising energy. I heard the gentle bump of the cat flap as Rodney emerged from upstairs, where he'd undoubtedly curled up on Jean's couch. Seconds later, he was on the desk, purring with the intensity he invokes when I'm using magic. He head-butted my hand.

I closed my eyes. "Send me four strong books, books full of courage and strategy. Send me four books to protect this home."

My whole body thrummed as I became a conduit for the energy unleashed from the library's thousands of volumes. From Music, books blasted competing military marches. I steadied my breath, as my grandmother had taught me, so that instead of amplifying this energy aimlessly—a mistake that could result in burning down the building—I became its prism.

My eyes snapped open as the first volume thunked in front of me. *War and Peace*. Okay. Maybe a bit on the nose, but it would do. Plus, the energy of all its readers since its publication more than a century and a half earlier would charge it with an extra boost of power.

In quick succession, two more books joined this one: *The Personal Memoirs of Ulysses S. Grant* and the *Iliad*. Oh, this could be interesting. Spell casting was like making prints. The artist can carve the block of wood or etch the plate, then apply ink or paint, but she never knows exactly how the finished product will come out. Here, it was the same, if not more so. I could assemble the spell's magical ingredients and hone my intention, but the final product was anybody's guess.

"One more book?" I said.

In response, *For Whom the Bell Tolls* rolled into the room with a drunken swagger. I'd have some Hemingway to deal with, it seemed. For most books, it was the story, the author's intentions, and the readers' visualizations that fueled energy. Hemingway was such a legend that readers would see him in all of his work. There was no avoiding his personality infusing my magic.

"Attention!" I said.

The books snapped spine-up and tilted to face me like a row of soldiers. Faraway bugles sounded and horses whinnied, with the winds of a Siberian winter howling in the background. Gunshot and—could it be?—a barroom piano sounded. Here was my army, and I was its general.

"Company, halt!" I commanded. "Our mission is to protect this library. You will admit only those people who mean no harm. Others—the enemy—will be turned away at the perimeter. Understood?" As I spoke, the birthmark on my shoulder tingled and energy coursed through my cells. My months of practice allowed me to funnel this magic cleanly into the four sentries.

The books barked their assent in English, Russian, and what I had to assume was ancient Greek. Instead of standing at attention, Rodney scratched an ear and set to cleaning a hind leg.

I loaded the books into my arms and walked across the room to the library's farthest northwest corner, here in Old Man Thurston's office. Under the brocade curtain I tucked *War and Peace*. "On guard, sentry," I told it. Rodney patted the novel once and twitched his tail.

Now for the southwest corner. That would be in the conservatory. Through the darkened library I walked. Cold seeped through the conservatory's glass walls, but thanks to the stove, it was still warm enough that the scent of one of Lyndon's blooming orchids perfumed the air. I rested the *Iliad* on the floor behind a table. Most patrons would be distracted by the banana tree and not see it.

Next for the library's southeast corner. The kitchen. I pulled out a stepstool and slid *For Whom the Bell Tolls* into the cupboard above the refrigerator. It would stay hidden here, but still able to work magic. As I closed the cupboard door, the moans of Spanish guerillas wounded by shrapnel escaped. "You'll be all right," I whispered.

The fourth book, *The Personal Memoirs of Ulysses S. Grant*, would carry out its guard duty in the library's farthest northeast corner, Circulation. I hoped the general wasn't too chatty, since I'd be spending my days within earshot.

Now for the final step. I retrieved the lit candle from Old Man Thurston's office and carried it to the table in the atrium, the library's heart. A dull glow from steely moonlight through the cupola spilled a jewel box of color on the wooden floorboards. Beyond the reach of the candle's glow, the library was so dark that I could barely make out the gilt edge of the frame surrounding Marilyn Wilfred's portrait. My birthmark felt hot and I pressed a finger into it.

The magic of generations of women in my family—all the way back to Scotland and beyond—funneled into this very moment. I felt as if I could be a harried mother two centuries ago, escaping her cottage at midnight, standing on a cliff to siphon the moon's power. Or, a priestess in a heavy woolen cape in a room that smelled of wet stone. In reality, I was a librarian in a bathrobe, intent on protecting my baby sister, but also a link in an unbroken chain of centuries of magic. Rodney's tail flicked against my bare calf.

I raised my arms, and the pitch of the library's energy rose with them. I held it between my fingers like a steel cable, vibrating and hot enough to scorch my bones. I stood firm. "Books. Protect this library. Make it a sanctuary for all that is good, and banish that which will harm us."

I dropped my hands and, at once, bolts of golden energy arched from the books I'd placed in the library's four corners. Above me, they connected in a jolt that flashed through the atrium like lightning, sealing a web of protection. In the sudden illumination, I saw Marilyn Wilfred's lips curl up. Then, as suddenly as it had struck, the atrium was dark again.

I put a hand on the table to steady myself. Being a conduit for all that magic was exhilarating—and draining. I knew I'd sleep well tonight, both from exhaustion and from the knowledge we were safe.

We now existed in a cage whose bars steeled against anything that could hurt us. Patrons seeking their usual action-adventure DVDs, diet books, and biographies could pass through easily, feeling nothing but a sense of safety. Other people with less pure motives would find reasons to avoid stopping by, or, if they planned to come over, their cars would stall or phones distract them. If they made it this far, they would find themselves confused and curiously unable to open the door.

"Come on, Rodney," I told him. "Time for bed." With satisfaction, I blew out the candle.

# CHAPTER FOURTEEN

After reluctantly seeing Jean off for the workshop, I opened the library for the day. I only wished I could have put a spell of protection over my sister, too, but my magic didn't work that way.

At least Sam had promised he'd post a deputy at the retreat center. A quick text this morning revealed that his queries as to whether any of Jean's classmates had found a paper with *READY* among their things had come up dry. I wasn't sure whether to be relieved or even more concerned for Jean. But I did know I wasn't going to leave the matter entirely in the sheriff department's hands, despite Sam's warning. Jean was my sister, she'd had a direct threat, and I was going to do everything I could to protect her. Sam simply wasn't going to know about it.

"Hey," Lalena called from the kitchen door. Sailor trailed behind her. She crossed the atrium and seated herself at the Circulation desk. Once comfortable, she slipped off her boots to rest her heels on the credenza, and withdrew a silk-wrapped deck of tarot cards from her bag. "Good morning, Josie."

I watched from the doorway. "Thanks again for filling in."

"You're welcome. I don't mind the library so much, but I'm not a fan of desk work."

No joke. Picturing Lalena in her vintage kimonos and old dresses with tattered hems parking herself in a cubicle instantly elicited a large red circle with a slash over it.

She looked around, as if she'd never been in the library before. "It feels different here."

"How?"

"I don't know. Different. Calmer, maybe." She shrugged. "Anyway, if you don't mind, I have Mrs. Garlington in for a reading at ten." Before I could respond, she added, "I can do it right here." She patted the desk. "Everyone knows her business, anyway. She probably wants to check in with Martin."

Martin Garlington had vanished nearly fifty years ago, right after Derwin was born. Since then, Mrs. Garlington had composed several poems throbbing with heartache, purchased a cemetery plot and headstone for him, and announced herself a widow. At least once a month she met with Lalena to contact his spirit. Apparently, Martin was doing well in the afterlife, spending time enjoying woodworking and eating nutritious meals. Occasionally, perhaps prompted by terrestrial Wilfredians, Martin advised Mrs. Garlington to remind their son Derwin, Wilfred's postman, to shelter magazines from the rain and please not to tramp the floral bed in front of the Tohlers' bungalow.

"Do you mind keeping an eye on the library while I work in my office? It will only be for a few hours."

"That's fine."

My office was a cozy nook under the library's main stairwell, just off the kitchen. It had been the mansion's pantry, but now, instead of shelves of preserves, it held a desk with a casement window above it, an armchair, a filing cabinet that just fit under the sloping ceiling, and a low row of bookshelves with library records. It was true I had library work to do—the trustees would expect their quarterly report, and cataloguing was always backed up—but this morning I planned to research the retreat's participants. Starting with an in-depth look at Cookie, this time focusing on her personal life, not her business. Once I had background information, I'd sketch out where everyone was at the time of the murders.

As I opened my laptop, I had to wonder why anyone would want to kill Jean. I ruled out a serial killer, striking at random. So far, the victims were related to the workshop. As I saw it, Jean was chosen for one of two reasons: Either she knew something that could point a finger at the killer; or the murderer was trying to muddy motive or direct attention to someone else.

Looking at motive, Cookie had the strongest reason to kill Anders and Marcia. What Sam had told us yesterday pointed toward her husband and star student having an affair. They'd arrived in town at the same time and were planning to spend the night together. If Anders's existence had come to light, Cookie's lucrative soulmate program would tank. Plus, there was Cookie's ego. And, who knew? Maybe Cookie had actually loved him. Jealousy was a strong motive.

I tore a sheet of graph paper from its pad and wrote *motive, means,* and *opportunity* across the top and underlined them. Down the left-hand side, I wrote the names of the retreat's participants—I refused to call them crumbs—starting with Cookie.

Sam was sure that despite motive, Cookie hadn't had the opportunity to kill either of them. I knew from my vast diet of golden age mystery novels that murder could be planned in ways crafty enough to mislead almost anyone. Was there a way—any way—Cookie might have pulled this off?

According to Sam, Marcia had likely been poisoned. The medical examiner estimated she took the poison before the workshop, but the full report wasn't in yet, so it was possible that Cookie caught onto the affair and slipped something into Marcia's coffee later on.

So, Cookie may have had the opportunity to kill Marcia. As for "means," once the toxicology report was finished, the sheriff's department could take care of tracking that.

But what about Anders? Could he have been killed elsewhere and dragged to the café? Unlikely, since no trail of blood led to the building or was on the café's floor, and no one had seen it happen. He must have died where he sat. Besides, Anders was a big man. I couldn't picture whippet-thin Cookie dragging him into the café. Furthermore, Anders's death had to have taken place between when Darla and Montgomery were prepping the café and the opening ceremony, when the body was discovered. That whole time, Cookie was leading her workshop. Five witnesses put her there.

No. Sam was right. Cookie couldn't have pulled off Anders's murder. At least, not on her own. Which brought me to the next suspect.

Rex Markham. Slick, needy, and handsome in a George Hamilton-ish sort of way. He'd threatened Marcia at the PO Grocery and didn't hide his infatuation with Cookie. He might want Anders dead to open the field. What could I find out about him? I pulled my laptop closer.

Browsing *images* brought me a few hits. Rex was from Billings, Montana—interesting, he had more of the Palm Springs look about him—and owned a chain of Tub 'N Tans, which would explain his nut-brown hue. He'd been married at least three, no, four, times. Pictures of him and his various wives were set in country clubs and homes with acres of white furniture.

His most recent wife had died a little more than a year ago, and the cause of death wasn't listed. Searching his name with *coaching* yielded nothing. From photos, it looked like he had money and wouldn't be pursuing Cookie for her cash, but fancy cars and expensive vacations could camouflage staggering debt.

*Wife-murdering gigolo,* I jotted on my chart. Might as well go big.

Next, I typed in *Sylvia Lewis*. Dozens of entries came up. Sylvia was an old-fashioned name, and many of the hits were obituaries. One Sylvia still living was a real estate broker in Nebraska. Social media was a dead end, too. I switched to images and found a few photos from club meetings and an obituary of a woman prominent in her church in a farming community in California. One of the young women grouped around her casket resembled Sylvia, but the photo was blurry, and I couldn't positively ID her.

*Impersonator,* I wrote next to her name. Motive might be tricky, but I'd get to that later.

Next up, Bernie Stanich. I tried *Bernie, Bernadette,* and *Bernice* into the search field. At last, here was a suspect who checked out. Bernadette Stanich was a divorced mom of two kids in college. Real estate listings pegged her as the owner of a suburban split-level house in Boise, and a street-view photo showed the sign for a dog grooming parlor in her garage. According to social media, she'd had a death in her family, and her feed was full of "sorry for your loss" posts. Other posts mostly had to do with dogs and her kids. Nothing about coaching.

*Clean, therefore probably a murderer,* I wrote.

That left Cookie's creepy assistant. The assistant's first name was Desmond, that much I knew. I tried searching a combination of *Cookie Masterson Desmond* and *Cookie Masterson assistant* and finally got a hit on a photo identifying Cookie's assistant as Desmond Finn. Putting his name into the search bar came up with a big zero. It was as if Desmond Finn didn't exist. *No web footprint. Potentially in cahoots with Sylvia.*

*Open questions,* I jotted. *What was the poison and who had access to it? Where were suspects at the time of Anders's murder?* The biggest question was the hardest to write. *Who wants Jean dead?*

# CHAPTER FIFTEEN

Noodling on the internet would only get me so far. I needed to dig into primary evidence—in other words, talk to real people. I took the service staircase to my apartment and grabbed my purse and coat, then stopped by Circulation, where, to a handful of curious Wilfredians, Lalena lectured on spirit visitations.

"No, Mr. Isaac. They will generally appear to you as you remember them in their happiest state."

"But can you come back and haunt?" Mr. Isaac asked. He'd worked in the mill before it closed thirty years earlier, and although his career had transitioned to selling aluminum awnings in Forest Grove, he still the meaty, though now grizzled, build of a mill hand. "I mean, say you leave someone your farmhouse, and they tear out the roses to put in a carport. Can you haunt them until they change it back?"

"Errands. I'll be back before lunch," I mouthed from the doorway. Lalena gave me a thumbs-up.

My ancient Corolla took a few minutes to warm up in the icy morning. Despite its lack of power—honestly, sometimes I thought a lawn mower could outrun me—the heater worked great, and before long I had warm feet and was driving into farm country and away from the forest that backed into Wilfred. Smoke trailed from the chimneys of the odd house I passed here and there, and steam rose from the noses of horses and cattle dotting the fields. Ten minutes later, I was slowing into Gaston, home of the Parker House bed-and-breakfast, where Sam had let slip that Anders had spent the night.

Unlike its grand namesake in Boston, Gaston's Parker House was a wood-framed house that had started as a Victorian cottage and had been added onto over the years so that it resembled a caterpillar constructed of different architectural styles. A sign reading OFFICE dangled from the front porch's gingerbread trim. I opened the door to an overheated parlor fitted with a desk and faux Chippendale armchair. A large television on mute displayed the national news. I rang the bell on the desk.

A hassled-looking woman with short gray hair pulled in different directions popped her head in from the adjoining kitchen. She dried her hands on her apron. "Looking for a room?"

The Parker House must have a small library for guests, because into my head materialized book recommendations: *Decorative Napkin Folding* and *Time Management When You Have No Time.* In other words, the Parker House had standards, and its proprietress was overworked.

"I know you're busy, so I'll only trouble you a moment. I'd like to ask about a recent guest."

"You've come about the murdered man, haven't you?" Her tone of voice made it clear she didn't intend to chat about it. "He wasn't killed here. Unless you're from the sheriff's office"—she gave me a quick head-to-toe assessment—"and from the look of it, you're not, I have nothing to tell you. I have a business to run."

*Ten Five-Minute Breakfasts,* a nearby magazine whispered.

"You do all this yourself?" I advanced a few steps. Beyond the innkeeper, the narrow kitchen was a mess of dirty pots and mixing bowls. The oven timer dinged.

"I've got to get this."

"Let me help." I followed her. I set my purse on a chair and pulled a bowl to the sink to rinse. "I'm Josie Way. I'm the librarian in Wilfred."

The woman hesitated, but seeing me at work on her dishes, she relented. "Mrs. Parker. Careful with those water glasses. They're real crystal." She pulled two tins of muffins from the oven, filling the room with the scent of warm butter and cinnamon.

"Maybe it seems strange that a librarian is interested in Anders McGhie, but my sister is in a workshop that his wife—rather, widow—is running. You might have heard that one of the workshop's students also died. I can't help but be worried about my sister."

The innkeeper's features didn't change. I'd try a different approach.

"You know how slowly bureaucracy runs. It's all red tape and procedures. The sheriff's office cares more about doughnuts than finding murderers." *Sorry, Sam,* I thought. "I want to be sure everything possible is done to find the murderer."

"What can you do that the sheriff's office can't? They tore the place apart, collecting carpet samples and heaven knows what else."

I dried the bowl and rested it in the drainer. "Sure, they looked for hair and DNA, but I want to look for something else. Just get the feel for the room, or a sense of something out of place." Something a book might know, for instance. "Sometimes intuition gives better results than science. Did Anders McGhie have breakfast that morning?"

Noting my progress with the dishes, Mrs. Parker took a seat at the small kitchen table and let me work. "Ate like a horse, he did. I'll tell you what I told the sheriff: He came in for breakfast around nine o'clock and plowed his way through two scones, an apple muffin, a bowl of cereal, and a banana. He was alone."

"When did he leave?"

"Don't know." She pointed to a cupboard over my head. "Glasses go there. I didn't make up the bed. The guest had hung his DO NOT DISTURB sign on the knob."

I pulled over a step stool and carefully lined up the glasses in the upper cupboard. I bet Sam hadn't had to do housework to get his info. "How long did he book the room for?"

"All week." She slipped off a shoe and rubbed one foot with the other. "Before you ask, folks from the sheriff's office turned up early that same evening. I showed them to the room, and they were there for a few hours. They took away the guest's suitcases. After they left, I put the room right myself. Nothing's out of place. Although later . . ."

"Later, what?" Sink now empty of dishes, to keep conversation flowing I wiped down the counter. Mrs. Parker slid the empty muffin tins to me. I grabbed the dishrag. Whatever it took.

"Never mind."

"It would make me feel so much better to see the room. Just for a few minutes." I reached for the muffin pan and ran the sponge around each of its pockets.

Watching me, Mrs. Parker stood and rested her hands on her hips in satisfaction. "You missed a spot there, on the side." When I'd scrubbed it clean, she said, "I suppose you could have a quick look, as long as you don't touch anything. The new guests don't arrive until this afternoon."

I set the muffin tin in the now-full drainer and dried my hands. "I promise."

"Follow me."

As Mrs. Parker led me out the Victorian house's original back door to a hall, I pondered why Anders had come to Oregon at all. Was he so in love with Marcia that he couldn't leave her alone for even a week?

"This," Mrs. Parker said, "is our Roaring Twenties annex."

*Annex* seemed like a generous word for what was essentially a lean-to with a wide porch and two rooms, labeled the Scott and Zelda suites. In a few strides, we'd passed through the chilly porch. Mrs.

Parker opened the door to a continuation of the building—this bit indoors.

"Here we have our three Sputnik rooms."

"I see the theme."

What might have been a generic mid-century rectangular addition boasted a satellite-shaped hall light and wallpaper with rockets on it. I could only imagine what the rooms themselves looked like.

Mrs. Parker slowed. "Your sister is in the workshop, is she?"

"I'm worried about her. I have the feeling more is going on than the sheriff's office knows. Do you have sisters?"

Mrs. Parker paused at the door at the end of the hall. "Five of them."

I considered my words. "I didn't say anything earlier, because it isn't public knowledge, but last night my sister got a death threat."

Mrs. Parker faced me. "No kidding? That explains your detective act."

"I can't help it. I can't just stand by."

She stood between me and the door. "Then there's something you should know. After the sheriff and the evidence folks left, I cleaned the room and put it back into shipshape. Later, when I went to restock the paper for the commode, I could tell someone had been there."

"When was that?"

"First thing this morning. The drawers had been opened and closed, but not completely, as if someone didn't want to make noise. It was subtle, but definite." Remembering, she shook her head. "I think someone even looked under the mattress.

When you've made as many beds as I have, you notice things like that."

Whatever they'd been looking for, then, was flat enough to slide under a mattress and small enough for a drawer. "How did they get in?"

"The sliding glass door was unlocked. I'm sure I locked it after resetting the room."

I was sure she had, too. Mrs. Parker didn't miss a trick. "Did you report it to the sheriff's office?"

She fixed me with a cold stare. "I didn't and you won't, either. I have a business to run, and this room is booked for the week. Do we understand each other?"

Therefore, the room was double-booked for the week. I had the hunch she wasn't returning Anders's money anytime soon. "My lips are sealed."

At last Mrs. Parker inserted a key in the bolt. "This is the modern wing, where the gentleman who died had stayed. Only one room, but it's a suite with its own hot tub." She flung open the door and turned on the light.

*Whoa.* My gaze swept left to right, then took it all in again. Here, *modern* meant 1970s with all its trappings: green shag carpeting, mirrored wall tiles veined in gold, and a hanging lamp depicting the Venus de Milo surrounded by strings of fishing line dripping oil meant to mimic rain.

I pointed toward the bed. "Is that—a waterbed?"

"King-sized," Mrs. Parker said proudly. "See those bear skins?"

Still gaping, I nodded.

"Genuine artificial fur." She handed me the room key. "Five minutes, hon. I've got to get back to the tea cakes. Lock up when you're finished, and look but don't touch, okay? I'll know if you touch anything."

"Okay. Thanks."

Before the door even closed, I was scanning the room for books. I'd settle for a dog-eared copy of *Valley of the Dolls* or even Greg Brady's autobiography, but the faux-wood veneered dresser held only a brass lamp and an amber glass ashtray with a NO SMOKING placard on it. I parted the beaded curtain to the bathroom. No books there, either.

Across the room, a curtain covered the sliding glass door. I drew it, careful not to touch the glass, and saw a deck and hot tub. The lock here would be easy to pick, and the room's position at the end of the lot meant someone careful could break into the room without being seen.

Between the police, Mrs. Parker, and lack of books, not much was left to provide clues about Anders. Wait—what about the nightstand? Maybe the Gideons had left a Bible. I perched on the waterbed's edge and slid open the drawer. No Bible, but I did find a telephone directory from the 1990s. I'd have to tell Mrs. Parker she'd missed a historic detail.

I pulled out the telephone book and—I couldn't resist—lay back on the waterbed and let myself bob on its waves. I set the book on my belly, folded my hands over it, and closed my eyes. "Telephone book," I said, "what can you tell me about the room's last occupant?"

As I floated on the mattress, the directory began to speak. *Sheriff's Department, 9-1-1. In Case of Emergency*—

"No, not them. I know the sheriff's department was here. I mean the guest. Anders McGhie. What can you tell me?" My five minutes would expire any second, and Mrs. Parker would be the type to march in and drag me out by my hair. I didn't know what exactly I was looking for, but I'd take any clue to Anders's state of mind.

The telephone book murmured telephone numbers, probably those that guests had used most often over the years. Restaurants, the airport, rental cars. Names and addresses chattered a quiet audio stew. Then, one number stood out. *Divorce attorney*, the telephone book enunciated and recited a number for someone who had probably retired years ago. *Specializing in equitable property disbursement. No case too difficult.*

# CHAPTER SIXTEEN

If the telephone directory at the Parker House had correctly communicated Anders's concerns, then Cookie and Anders were divorcing. Or, at least, that had been Anders's intention. Given the relationship between Marcia and him, this wasn't surprising. Since Cookie already advertised herself as a single woman, it seems she would have been on board with a divorce. In some highrise, attorneys would be battling out a separation of assets. However, even if Cookie had calculated murder as cheaper than divorce, she couldn't have killed her husband. It simply wasn't possible.

With this on my mind, I drove back to the library. The taut spell of protection still shimmered its dome over the building. I came in the kitchen door to a salute and "Enter!" from *For Whom the Bell Tolls*. The sooner Jean was within its care, the better.

I'd expected to find Lalena tapping her toes with an eye on the clock and mind on her lunch. Instead, she was huddled over the circulation desk with Bernie Stanich, palm up, in the chair across from her. Bernie had ditched last night's poodle stylings for her pageboy with a bow, this time red, holding back her bangs. She showed the intense, slightly fearful look Lalena's clients did when they consulted her—even people who normally laughed at fortune-telling.

"I believe you already know what your palm reveals," Lalena said.

This was part of her patter. Once, when I'd questioned her about it, she'd said, "I help people get in touch with what they know, but can't or don't want to recognize." She'd argued this service was more valuable than a bogus read of the future. "Why should I tell them to pack their bags for a cruise to Panama or that they'll soon come into money when, deep inside, they know their real trouble is a boring job or a daughter who won't listen to them?"

Bernie leaned in. "I'm afraid it could get ugly."

My instinct was to edge closer, but I didn't want to break Lalena's spell by drawing attention to myself. Too late. Sailor caught a whiff of me and trotted over, tail wagging, from his basket.

Lalena waved. "I hope you don't mind that I'm reading Bernie's palm on work time. It's an impromptu professional swap. She trimmed Sailor for me."

Sailor panted up to my feet. For the first time in weeks, I could see his eyes. My desk scissors and tufts of fur on the desk showed why.

"If I had my clippers, I could give him a proper trim."

I extended a hand to Bernie. "We've met. I'm Jean's sister Josie."

"Jean's sister," she repeated, then, unexpectedly, smiled. "I see the resemblance. Not just the red hair, either."

"I love having Jean here. It's been months since I've seen her."

Bernie nodded with enthusiasm. "Cherish her. Sisters are wonderful."

"I do. You must have sisters, too."

"One." Her smile melted into melancholy. "She died not long ago."

I remembered the "sorry for your loss" comments and sad face emojis I'd seen on her social media stream. "I'm so sorry to hear that."

Lalena rose. "Since you're back, Josie, I'll take lunch now. Bernie, remember, in your heart you know what's best. Be true to the best you." With that banal, yet timeless pronouncement, she left the room, Sailor behind her.

I took her place behind the circulation desk. Bernie stayed put, seemingly lost in thought. The title *On Grief and Grieving* played in my mind like an urgent television commercial. "You must really miss your sister," I said. Grandma had warned me to mind my own business, but this was compassion, not nosiness.

"I looked up to her. She married well—until the last one, that is—so she didn't have to work, but she always encouraged me to be my best self. When she saw how great I was with animals, she helped me get my dog grooming certification and gave me the down payment to set up shop." Bernie's eyes reddened. I pushed a box of tissues across the desk. "She died of pancreatic cancer. It was fast. And awful." She pulled a few tissues and clutched them to her chest. "I was with her to the very end. Me and Junior, my labradoodle."

"A privilege."

She nodded. "I took her to our childhood home in the country. The hospice nurse was only a short drive away, and I knew the river and the woods would do her good. She always loved it there. I did, too. But now . . ."

"Now, what?"

"I'll never be able to go back. She left the house to her husband, and he lets it sit empty. Won't even respond to my calls asking him to let me visit."

"I'm sorry. It sounds like you might not have the best relationship with him."

"We go way back. I was the one who introduced them." She opened her mouth as if to explain further, then seemed to think better of it and pushed back her chair. "I'd better be going. I don't know why I'm going on like this. I guess it was my palm reading, or maybe it's because I feel so safe here somehow."

"Oh, no," I said. "You don't have to hurry. Tell me about the workshop. Is it really so dull that you skipped out this afternoon?" Getting to know Bernie in person would be a lot easier than following her trail through in cyberspace.

Bernie hesitated before replying. "The workshop's all right."

Just all right? "Jean raves about it."

"It's just . . . I don't know."

"It took a lot of effort to come here." And money.

"My life is at a crossroads. I thought maybe . . ."

"Coaching sounded good to you?" If it had, she must have changed her mind. I wouldn't have been able to pry Jean from the workshop with the Jaws of Life, but Bernie was wandering the countryside instead of taking advantage of her privilege as a crumb and sitting at Cookie's feet.

She leaned forward. "Lalena said I have the answers inside me. Listen. If you knew something that could save lives, but it meant taking certain liberties . . ."

This inability of Bernie's to finish a sentence was starting to get to me. "Do you know something about the deaths that you haven't told anyone?"

She stared toward the empty dog bed beneath the desk as she considered my question. "I know something about the murderer."

"You need to tell the sheriff."

She picked up a pen and examined it as if she'd never seen one before. "It's not that easy."

"There's something you want to tell me," I said gently.

One of the Tohler brothers wandered into Circulation and looked curiously at Bernie and me. I flinched as his books clunked into the return box, but the noise didn't seem to register on Bernie.

"It's like this," Bernie said.

I nodded with encouragement.

"One of the workshop participants is a murderer."

"It does look like that might be the case." I fought to keep my frustration below the surface. "You suspect someone in particular?"

"Do you think Lalena is right? I mean, about already knowing what your life decisions should be?"

This was a tricky question to negotiate. "In general, yes. Unless fear or anger are giving you false answers. Or desire, I suppose. Why do you ask?"

She pushed the pen away and seemed to come to a decision. "I do suspect someone." Her chest rose with a deep breath, but she said nothing more.

"Why do you suspect someone?"

She glanced at me before turning her gaze to the window. "I saw someone—the morning of the murders—while I was out."

From what I'd gathered, no one had left the retreat center that morning aside from Rex and Marcia. This was a new wrinkle. "You were out?"

She averted her gaze. "I saw someone."

"Was it Sylvia?" Jean was sure Sylvia was a fraud, and I hoped that giving names would inspire Bernie to choke out her own suspicions.

"Sylvia?" Bernie seemed genuinely perplexed that I'd bring her up. "The one with the hair like a golden retriever's? No."

"Desmond?" I had to keep trying.

"No." She looked at me as if I'd lost my mind.

"Rex, then," I said.

From the change in Bernie's expression, I knew I'd hit home, but I wasn't sure if it was adoration or horror I'd invoked. She opened and closed her mouth like a guppy surfacing for air, then shut down.

"Did you see Rex?" I asked.

She rose so quickly that she nearly toppled the chair. "I'd better be getting back."

"Did you tell Sam—the sheriff?"

Her face reddened, and I wondered if she was going to cry. "Not yet. I don't know if I should."

"Why wouldn't you?" I asked. "It sounds like you have evidence."

"It's not what you think." She clutched her purse to her chest. "I don't know why I'm telling you all this. Somehow, I feel so safe here. Like nothing could hurt me, and I guess . . ." She turned abruptly. "I'd better be getting back."

"Goodbye," I said to her back. A second later, the front door closed.

She knew something about Rex, but she wasn't prepared to reveal it. Had she truly seen something? And why was she at the workshop at all, when she barely spent time at the retreat center? I tapped a pencil on the desk as I turned our curious conversation over in my mind. Bernie might know who the killer is. That is, if Bernie herself wasn't it.

# CHAPTER SEVENTEEN

Opening and closing the library were my favorite times of day, but this evening I hurried to get through my closing duties. There was no way I was letting Jean walk alone from the retreat center to the café, where we planned to have dinner.

Now my sights were on Rex. I had the feeling that getting information from him would be like conducting lengthy negotiations with a commission-hungry used car salesman, and I didn't look forward to it. However, I knew I could engage him by asking about Cookie and take it from there.

I walked the library's perimeter, drawing the curtains, shelving wayward novels, and catching bits of book chatter here and there: a New Release thriller on heavy rotation emanated car chases and gunfire; a local history left on a table by an amateur genealogist dryly recited birth dates and census data; mariachi music and Spanish conversation flowed from a guidebook to Mexico.

A couple of high school students—a boy and girl starting a romance, it seemed—chatted in a corner of Natural History. I shooed them out for the evening. Other patrons had left, now likely peeling potatoes in Wilfred's kitchens, reminding grammar schoolers to do their math homework, or putting on coats and hats for dinner at the café.

In the conservatory, I banked the fire for the night in the tile stove so Lyndon's banana tree and orchids would continue to flourish despite the biting cold outside. Finally, I grabbed my coat and locked the doors.

When I arrived at the retreat center, Jean lounged in an armchair in the main room, chatting with Sylvia, who listened intently from a cushion on the rug. The fire gave a comforting glow from its river rock hearth. The picture might have been lifted from the après-ski scene of a novel set in the Alps—if that novel were a murder mystery.

Jean was deep in conversation. "It took everything I'd saved. But I had to come to this workshop. I'm sure you of all people understand."

"Definitely," Sylvia said. "Cashing out your grandmother's inheritance? That shows real commitment."

"Dreams require real commitment," Jean said. "Step two of Ready."

"What convinced you it would be worth it?"

Jean looked at Sylvia in surprise. "What do you mean? You're here, aren't you?"

Sylvia quickly laughed. "Of course."

Except for Jean and Sylvia, the lobby was empty. The evening's darkness muffled the room's edges. Through the floor-to-ceiling windows, the millpond lay black, and Wilfred's lights felt faraway beyond the meadow.

"Where is everyone?" I said. "I didn't think I was that late."

"Cookie ended the session early so we could relax and digest the past couple of days. Desmond and Bernie went down to the café. Cookie's upstairs. Rex said he'd stay behind, too," Jean said. "Oh, and guess what? I'm going to lead a yoga session tonight! Restorative yoga to release tension. Right here. Cookie said it was a great idea. You'll come, too, right?"

I smiled. "I'll sit in the back."

"Sylvia, Josie and I are going to the café for dinner. Would you like to join us? That's okay with you, right, Josie?"

Absolutely good for me. It would give me the chance to feel out Sylvia's background, which was nearly nonexistent online. After Bernie's confessions this afternoon, I also wanted to get more of a handle on Rex.

"The deputy sheriff is still here?" I said.

"Out there." Jean pointed to an SUV parked to the side of the retreat. A dim light inside showed the deputy was reading. "She said she'd drive us into town."

Then it would be safe. "Why don't you and Sylvia go ahead? I want to have a quick look at the books upstairs. You know, librarian stuff. I'll be right behind you."

The second-floor landing was home to a tiny

outpost of the library: three waist-high bookshelves surrounding an armchair with a side table and reading light. The library's trustees had donated it to the retreat center, and it was up to me to keep it stocked. Two of the shelves held books to relax and entertain workshop participants and included local histories and photocopied walking maps, as well as mysteries, women's fiction, and thrillers. The third shelf held a rotating display of books I selected to accompany the retreat. For the coaching workshop, I'd chosen books on self-improvement and motivation.

But, my goal here was more than to check in on the books. I pretended to examine the shelves until I heard the front doors close and the sheriff's SUV drive away.

"Books," I whispered on the landing. "Everything cool here?"

A chorus of sleepy yeses reached me. The books hadn't been getting much action, it seemed. One of Roz's romances glowed. I touched its spine, and images filled my head of Bernie reading from bed. Instead of vicarious love, however, I sensed grief.

"Other readers?" I whispered to the books. Pictures of the workshop's participants flitted through my head, but it seemed that other than Bernie, none had borrowed books. The only person the books hadn't shown me was Desmond. He must not even have scanned the shelves in curiosity.

I stepped back and looked up and down the corridor. Light shined from under the door of the corner guest suite at the far right—the largest suite and undoubtedly Cookie's. To my left, light seeped to the hall from a room halfway down.

Its door opened, and Rex stepped out. "Oh, it's you."

"Just checking on the books," I said cheerfully. "Is there—"

Before I could engage him further, he shut his door.

I wasn't going to be defeated this easily. I walked down the hall and rapped on his door. "Rex?" The chatter of a television set played in the background, and he didn't respond. "I wanted to ask you about Cookie," I said in a voice I hoped was loud enough to reach him, but quiet enough not to disturb Cookie.

The door opened a crack, and one eye and half a tanned face appeared. "Yes?"

"I'm concerned about her."

The door opened wider, but not enough to admit me. "What about?"

"My sister's life was threatened last night. You heard about that?"

"Sure. The sheriff asked if any of the rest of us got a note. I hadn't, and as far as I know, no one else did, either. What does this have to do with Cookie?"

His teeth were so white and skin so tan I felt I was talking to a ginger snap with buttercream icing. I took a stab. "Someone saw you in town the morning of the murders."

This was too sudden. I'd miscalculated. Rex frowned. "I bought flowers for Cookie."

"After that," I said.

"Are you accusing me of something?" The doorway narrowed again. "This has nothing to do with Cookie, does it?" His mouth flashed all his teeth in a wide, fake grin. "I'm on to you. If you bother me again, I'll report you to the sheriff for harassment. Good night." The door closed, and the thunk of a bolt punctuated the conversation's end.

Shocked, I stood back. Maybe I hadn't anticipated he'd happily confess to being a murderer, but I certainly hadn't expected this.

To my right, Cookie's door opened. "Josie," she whispered and crossed her lips with an index finger. I had to look twice to be sure it was actually Cookie who spoke and not her timeworn mother. Instead of the made-up, gel-coiffed dynamo I'd seen before, here was a tired, bare-faced woman. I glanced toward Rex's door and hurried to Cookie's end of the corridor.

"I don't want to alert Rex. He's been . . . attentive lately." Cookie craned her neck to make sure the hall was quiet. "Come in."

Jean had told me the Ready step included being open to adapting to opportunities as they arose. Rex might have been a bust, but Cookie was willing to talk.

She shut the door quietly behind me.


"Have a seat," Cookie said. "I see you looking at me. Surprised, aren't you?"

She was right. I was surprised. As I took an armchair, I couldn't help but notice the bruise of circles under her nearly nonexistent eyes and her tired, sagging cheeks emphasized even more by the room's unforgiving light.

Cookie's room was the most deluxe of the retreat center's bedrooms. She merited her own fireplace—cold and empty tonight—and a work area with a desk and credenza. One suitcase was in the open closet with tunics and blouses hanging above it. Another suitcase lay open on the floor beneath the credenza. Its contents—a mass of men's clothing—were heaped in it. An open toiletry bag sat on the desk, showing shaving items, prescription pill bottles, and a tortoiseshell comb. Anders's items, returned to Cookie.

Hoping I hadn't been too obviously nosy, I shifted my attention to Cookie. "It's been a hard few days for you."

She sighed and took the chair opposite mine. "The hardest in my life, and my life hasn't been an easy one."

Yes, she'd lost people dear to her, if you defined as "dear" a husband she'd denied having and his lover. Then there were the private jets, constant media coverage, and honking gigantic rock on her right ring finger. None of those would wear on her. Or would they? What did I know about her life, anyway?

"You doubt me," she said. "You're thinking of Cookie Masterson, famous life coach and social media sensation." She shook her head. Without gel, her hair was sparse and roots showed white. "Cookie is a construct. She's a persona I put on every day and shed just as soon as I can. Few people see me like this."

At her honesty, my wariness melted a bit. Still, she was no innocent. She was choosing to let me see her without her armor, and she undoubtedly had a reason. "Why do you do it? Why not simply be you?"

"It just grew. I started with a few coaching clients. I wanted to inspire, to show my students what they could achieve, so I put on a good face. Literally." Her eyes might have nearly disappeared without their armor of mascara, but they managed to pierce all the same. "My work snowballed. I discovered I spoke to something fundamental in people. Everyone dreams of a better path of life than the one they find themselves on. They want more, and they thirst for a way to get there. To get that great job, five-bedroom house, soulmate. I lay out a simple process." She closed her eyes. When she reopened them, I saw something different there: vulnerability. "Now, tens of thousands of crumbs count on me. They depend on my words to help them decide whether to leave their spouses or have another child. It's a huge responsibility, and it weighs on me. All because of three little words."

"Ready-Set-Go," I whispered. Although Cookie's full-bore charisma of the past few days hadn't pulled me in, this new vulnerability did. And it made me think. Was I settling for less than I could get? Was a tiny library and clueless love interest all I deserved?

"Exactly. Ready-Set-Go. You can achieve anything with Ready-Set-Go." She leaned back and her former reserve set in. She reached into an open bag of potato chips and stuffed a few into her mouth. "Maybe you even wonder if I'm taking advantage of your sister? This workshop probably cost her more than she's paid for anything in her life."

Cookie might have been reading my mind. "She's so happy to be here, but, yes, it was expensive."

She snorted a laugh. "In fact, I'm the one who's

taken advantage of. You have no idea how many charlatans sign up for my workshops with the sole objective of stealing my Ready-Set-Go program. I'm in the middle of three lawsuits right now. As if no one could see that One-Two-Three or Rootin'-Tootin'-Scootin' aren't direct rip-offs." The anger in her voice softened. "As for Jean, it's a pleasure to have her in my workshop. She truly wants to help others. If only all my students were like her."

"Thank you," I said. "I think she's pretty wonderful, too."

"Bright, trusting, and motivated."

These were not the words of someone who wanted to kill Jean. Maybe I'd been wrong about Cookie all along. "I'm sorry about—about your husband. And Marcia."

"I never should have hidden Anders. He was my support through all of this." She rolled down the top of the bag of chips and shoved it away. "He was the one who insisted on remaining out of sight. He said it would encourage the crumbs more if they thought they could find true love along with me." She dabbed at her reddened eyes with a sleeve.

"I thought you'd filed for divorce?" My bluff with Rex had failed, but maybe it would work here.

Seeing the flash of shock on her face, I'd caught Cookie off guard. "Oh, that." She shook her head. "How did you find out?"

Bull's-eye. "I don't remember. Maybe you mentioned it?"

Cookie shrugged. "When I developed my relationship coaching course, we drew up divorce papers to throw people off the trail, but that was ages

ago. No, we had no intention of ever divorcing."
Cookie must have known I was thinking of Marcia,
because she quickly added, "Perhaps I'd been ne-
glecting Anders. I should have paid closer attention, and I'll never forgive myself for that. I swear
to you, though, he and I were soulmates."

"Were you together long?"

"Over twenty years," she said. "We met when we
both taught at the same high school, if you can believe that." She shook her head as if hardly believ-
ing it herself. "We hit it off right away. He wanted
more for his life, just like I did. We'd sit for hours
in the teachers' lounge, dreaming about what we
could do. With his creativity and my business
sense, we had no limits." She shrugged. "His marriage was in bad shape, and I was single. As soon as
his divorce was final, we were married."

So, Marcia wasn't Anders's first affair. "I see."

"The show must go on. That's what Anders
would have wanted." She drew a fortifying breath
and seemed to emerge from the past. "Thank you
for talking with me. I knew you'd want some reas-
surance that your sister will be all right. I want to
thank you for something else, too."

"What?"

"Talking with you, I realize how far I've let myself drift from the real me, from what's important.
That's going to change."

As in the *Wizard of Oz*, I'd seen behind the curtain. The wizard was human. At last, I understood
her pull to Jean. "I admit I'm worried about Jean.
Knowing you're keeping an eye on her means a
lot."

Cookie waved her fingers dismissively. "A joke.

That's all it was. You have my word I'll watch out for her safety. If anyone's at risk here," she added, "it's me. It's my workshop that's threatened. It's the Ready-Set-Go brand. If word gets out about the deaths, my livelihood is on the line."

"Do you have any ideas of who the killer might be?"

She lowered her eyes and reached for the bag of chips, then withdrew her hand. "I don't know. A few things are suspicious, though."

"Like what?" I couldn't count on this new, unmasked Cookie to reveal everything to me, but it was worth a try.

"My assistant Desmond has a past. I've done my best to rehabilitate him, but sometimes his actions give me pause. I've told the sheriff."

"Have you known Desmond a long time?"

"All my life," she replied.

"You mentioned him the other day," I said, hoping she'd expand. She didn't.

"Then, yesterday." Cookie's curiously gray eyes, nearly lost without their uniform of eyeliner and mascara, met mine. "After the sheriff left. Everyone had gone down to the café, except me, and Sylvia was the last to leave. I saw her coming out of Marcia's room. I can't figure out why."

"What was she doing?"

"That's just it. I'd heard drawers open and close. She'd kept the lights off."

"Did you say anything?" Jean had questions about Sylvia, too, although apparently they weren't enough to prevent her from being Jean's workshop bestie.

"She closed the door quietly, as if she didn't

want to be heard. I saw her glance down the hall, but I was at the other end, in the shadows. After Marcia's death, I simply didn't have the energy to confront her. I'd been trying to get in touch with Anders, but he wasn't answering. Of course, now I know why." Cookie raised her gaze to mine. "You understand why I didn't say anything."

"I do." It had been a brutal day for Cookie. "Jean is with Sylvia right now."

"I can't say Sylvia is a murderer, but something is going on." She furrowed her brows, then broke it with a calm smile clearly meant to dismiss me. "I wouldn't worry about your sister. Why would anyone want to kill her? The note was a nasty joke. If I ever find out who wrote it, there'll be hell to pay, I promise."

She'd mentioned Desmond and Sylvia. "Did you know Rex or Bernie before the workshop?"

The overhead light brought out the lines on Cookie's upper lip, set firmly in conviction. "Rex tells me we've met before, but I don't remember it. Bernie I don't know at all. She skips out on enough of our sessions that I'm not even sure I'd recognize her if she walked in right now."

"I see." I pulled on my gloves. "Thank you for looking out for Jean, and I hope you get some rest tonight."

Cookie rose to see me out. Her voice was almost cheerful. "It was so nice to talk with someone who understands me. Good night, and be safe out there."

# CHAPTER EIGHTEEN

Now I was eager to get to the café to confront Sylvia. Why would she have been going through Marcia's things? Didn't Jean tell me someone had searched Marcia's room the day of her murder, too? Then there was Anders's room at the Parker House. I took off in the dark toward the café.

As I crossed the levee, I glanced back at the retreat center. It stood dark and quiet, as if deserted and my conversation with Cookie had been a dream. A cawing crow drew my attention. With a clatter, he alit on the retreat center's sloped roof. One by one, more crows swirled in the gloaming and settled next to him until they covered the roof in moving blue-black bodies and sharp beaks, crying out as if in warning—a warning for me. I caught my breath and turned toward town.

I passed through the Magnolia Rolling Estates

and rounded left toward the café. Inside, Wilfredians chatted and dug into food-laden platters, and the air was warm with the comforting aroma of Darla's cooking. The coaching workshop participants, including Jean, had pushed tables together to take over the dining room's center.

"Too-da-loo," Rex said. He stood at the head of the table holding a to-go box. Even in a puffy down jacket he looked like he was retiring to the pool house. Last I'd seen, he'd been at the retreat center. He nodded an expressionless hello as he passed me.

I took the seat he'd just vacated facing Jean and Sylvia. "Rex didn't stick around for long."

"He stopped by for something to-go," Sylvia said.

"A slice of huckleberry pie for Cookie," Jean added.

Rex was ready to step into the dead husband's place without missing a beat. "How's dinner?"

"Great, but huge. Want to finish my fish stew? What took you so long to get here, anyway?"

I pulled Jean's bowl to my place. "After I checked the books, I dropped in on Cookie."

Jean cocked her head, and Sylvia came to full attention. "Why did you do that?"

"She heard me on the landing. She wanted to reassure me that you'll be fine, and that she's keeping an eye on you." In response to Jean's warm smile, I added, "I underestimated her. And you. I'm sorry about that."

One of the things I loved best about Jean was her willingness to forgive, but she wasn't quite ready to let this go yet. "I was sure you'd understand Cookie if only you go to know her. Now I hope you'll stop preaching to me about my decision to come here."

I glanced at Sylvia, who was watching us like we were the final set at Wimbledon. "We can talk about this later."

"No," Jean said. "The sheriff is investigating the murders, and I'm safe. The rest is"—she fixed me with her gaze—"none of your business. If you really care about me, you'll drop the subject." She pulled her bowl back to her place. "It turns out I'm hungrier than I thought." Her tone sweetened. "Sylvia, did you enjoy the discussion today?"

Oh boy. Jean was peeved. I'd have some making up to do on our walk home.

Beyond Jean, Patty—Darla's sister and owner of Patty's This-N-That—was lost in conversation with Bernie. "I can't help it. I lose interest in something after a while and have to change what I sell."

Bernie rested her chin on her palm. This evening, two hanks of straightened hair were clipped over her ears. Each hank bore a tiny pink bow. I'd seen a similar hairdo on a spaniel at the Westminster dog show.

"What is it you're really seeking?" she asked. "What do you hope the change will bring you?"

Patty dabbed at an eye. "I don't know. It's been like this ever since my husband died."

"You're fascinated by life's variety. Something in it comforts you."

"Maybe. It's just so tiring clearing out the store and bringing in new inventory. I keep thinking this time it'll be for good. Then something else interesting comes along. For instance, I have a line on some old fishing equipment—"

"Have you thought about opening an antiques mall? That way the spaces would be full of all sorts of things to interest you, but it would be up to other people to stock it."

Dumbfounded, Patty stared at her. "I do have the space."

"It seems to me you've used your shop to express your grief from losing your husband. Maybe it's time to feel those emotions instead."

Patty looked as if all the candles she'd stocked in the This-N-That had burst into flame in her mind. "By gosh, I think you're right." She leaned forward, and her words were lost in Jean and Sylvia's conversation.

"It's a lot of information," Jean was saying. "I had to do a few rounds of pranayama breathing to calm myself."

"Great idea," Sylvia said.

"You know, three shorts, hold, and one long exhale."

"I do it all the time."

"And then tap your throat and stamp your foot twice."

"The most effective way," Sylvia said.

Jean leaned back. She hadn't touched her stew since she'd reclaimed it. I slid it back to my place and dug in before she could stop me.

In the booth next to Bernie and Patty's, Duke and Cookie's assistant Desmond were in deep conversation. Duke, while generally friendly if occasionally crude, had always seemed to me to be a loner, but he and Desmond had really hit it off. What was Desmond's secret that Cookie had alluded to? I hoped Duke wasn't going to be disappointed.

Darla appeared at our table, drying her hands on the bar towel dangling from her apron. "Josie, county health regulations. No cats allowed." She nodded toward a booth where Rodney sat in Mona's lap eating a morsel of salmon from her fork.

"How did he get in here?" I said. "I'd better take him home."

Jean rose, too. "I'll come with you. I'll see you later tonight at restorative yoga, Sylvia, Bernie. We need it after the past few days."

"Come on, Rodney. Shoo." I held open the door and he slipped out, licking his lips.

We were barely in the parking lot, the cat scampering ahead of us, when Jean said, "I don't know what's going on, but now I'm certain. Sylvia's a fraud."

I waited until we were well out of earshot of the café before I questioned Jean further. "A fraud?"

"I don't know what she's here for, but it's not to be a wellness coach."

"What makes you say that? She seems really into the workshop." I remembered the notebook chattering in her tote bag. "She takes lots of notes."

I picked up Rodney and he squirmed against me. I stooped to drop him to the ground again, but he tunneled inside my coat. I buttoned him in and cradled him, purring, against my chest.

"Into the workshop, yes. Knowledgeable about wellness, no."

"What do you mean?"

Jean turned to me as we walked up the hill. "Did you hear when I asked her about her pranayama breathing? She had no idea what I was talking about."

"Neither did I," I pointed out.

"It's a basic yoga breathing technique. Anyone who'd taken a few yoga classes would know it, and it would be second nature to an instructor."

"That bit about stamping your feet did sound over the top," I said. "Maybe she does other kinds of wellness. You know, vitamins and things."

"I asked her when we first met, remember? She specifically mentioned yoga." Our steps moved in unison over the bridge.

"She's fit," I said. "She could be into wellness."

"Gym-based stuff. Machines and weightlifting, I bet. Maybe the odd Pilates class."

"Cookie told me Sylvia was poking around Marcia's room the evening she died. She saw her sneaking out. Also, while you were in the workshop this morning, I stopped by Anders's motel. The owner said someone had searched his room, too, after the deputies left. Didn't you tell me Marcia's room was a mess earlier in the day, too, like someone had been through it?"

Jean nodded. "Someone is looking for something. I wonder what it could be. You drove to the hotel? You don't mess around."

"I can't help it." How I wished I could tell her about my magic, about my DNA as a truth teller. "I was careful. Sam won't find out." Unless he happened by the Parker House again.

"I was with you that night, so I have no idea if Sylvia left the retreat center," Jean said. "She could have."

Jean hadn't reacted well the last time I questioned Desmond's background, so I didn't bring up Cookie's comments about him. Instead, I said, "Cookie really thinks highly of you." Even in the dark, Jean glowed.

"What did she say?"

"That you really care, you're motivated, and you're a good student. She thinks you'll go far. She's right, you know. You're good."

"How can you tell?"

"You have the ability to look at someone and understand right away how they feel. It's a gift." Just as I could sense someone's state of mind and know what they needed to read next, Jean could read a person's physical condition. More than that, she wanted to help improve it.

"It's nothing extraordinary. You look at them, you see them. That's all."

"You make it sound so easy. I'm telling you, not everyone can do it."

I wished I could tell her about our lineage as witches. She had magic she took for granted. Lots of people did, really. Darla's hospitality, Roz's imagination, Lalena's insight, Duke's native understanding of machinery—all of these were glimmerings of magic.

"Maybe Sylvia is lying about her coaching abilities, but I can't see her murdering anyone," Jean said. "Especially me. She's so friendly. She asks so many questions and seems truly fascinated by what we say."

"Killers don't always wear black and cackle like fiends, you know."

We rounded the corner to the road leading to the library and home. Sensing it, Rodney popped his head out of my coat. I kneeled to let him jump to the ground to scamper toward the library and his food bowl.

"I did a little bit of checking up on the computer this morning about the workshop's participants," I said. "Nothing came up for Sylvia Lewis and wellness—at least, nothing matching her description. It's as if she doesn't exist."

In the dim illumination of Big House's porch light, Jean's face tightened. I braced myself for a scolding for getting involved in her business. Instead, she said, "Lights are still on at Sam's. Want to see if he's in? I want to tell him about Sylvia. What you said about her searching Marcia's room— he should know. We have time before tonight's yoga session."

"Jean." I lowered my voice. "Sam needs the information about Sylvia being a fake, but don't tell him we've been doing any digging around, okay? Promise? I told you what he said about detaining you."

She looked into my eyes, her breath clouding the night air. "Okay."

"Plus, remember how he refused to say anything about Sylvia's identity? He already knows something about her."

Big House's front porch was tidy and welcoming with its pots of winter cabbage someone—more likely Mrs. Garlington than Sam—had planted.

But the front porch was where official visitors rang. We were family.

"Let's go around back to the kitchen door."

Sam was doing dinner dishes. When he let us into the kitchen's warmth, Nicky stood in his playpen and pointed a wet finger at us with an emphatic "bah-bah."

"Hi, baby," I said and scooped him up. He grabbed a hank of my hair and pulled, laughing.

"Hi, you two," Sam said, drying his hands on the dish towel slung over the oven's handle. "Did you come on business, or is this a friendly visit?"

"Both," Jean said before I could reply. She pulled out a dining room chair, leaving the one closest to Sam for me. "Have you found out anything new about my killer?"

My gaze shot to Sam. I was used to Jean's blunt ways, but he might not find them as charming.

"Why? You haven't had another threat, have you?" he said.

"No threat, but something odd," Jean said. "Something that might interest you."

"Maybe Josie discovered something at the retreat center tonight?" His glance held a warning.

"How did you know I went to the retreat center?"

"We have a deputy stationed there, remember?"

"I swear I wasn't nosing around. I was checking the books." Partially true, at least. "It's my job. Plus, I didn't want Jean walking to the café alone."

He looked at me a moment too long before apparently accepting my explanation. "All right." He took a seat and turned to Jean. "Tell me about it."

Something in Sam's briefcase whispered to me. The briefcase—soft-sided, black leather—leaned on the back of a chair. I edged closer and rested a palm on the chair's seat.

"I wonder," Jean said, "before I get started, is there anything we need to know?"

Crafty, that Jean.

"This is an ongoing investigation, Jean. I can't tell you much, but you can be sure I'd let you know if we had anything that affected your safety." Sam frowned slightly, meaning he was amused. He'd read Jean's ploy. His expression then morphed to what I'd learned was his ghosting face. When he was with the FBI, his job was to track people, or "ghost" them. When he was absorbing the most information, he appeared blank, almost checked out. "Now, what did you want to tell me?"

Words from Sam's briefcase started to crystallize. Chemical names and numbers with decimal points leaked into my mind. A toxicology report.

"What do you know about Sylvia Lewis?" Jean asked.

Sam moved the briefcase and sat next to me. *Shoot.* The report faded. I doubled down on my focus, although Sam's presence made it more difficult. "The same we do about each of the workshop's participants. Why?"

"Whoever she is, she isn't a wellness expert. She doesn't know a thing about yoga."

*Initial results,* the toxicology report said. *Comprehensive results after full panel analyses.*

"I don't think she's here for coaching instruction at all," Jean said.

*High levels of Dilantin detected in victim's blood.* I struggled to keep my expression neutral. Marcia had definitely been poisoned. Sam had been right, and it was murder after all. Then, an addition: *Concentrations approximately four times larger than found in Anders McGhie's blood.*

"I can't comment on that," Sam said, "But rest assured we've looked into each participant's background."

I let my mind relax, urging the contents of Sam's report to reveal themselves more fully. Beyond the toxicology report, only a few words drifted in: *blood spatter* and *roses.* Sam's laptop was also in his bag, but my magic was no good at reading digital text.

"You should look at her more closely," Jean said. "Maybe her ID's a fake. She's a nice person, but she's no wellness expert."

He seemed entirely unsurprised. "Point taken. Anything else?"

I was just about to turn my mind away from Sam's briefcase when a few words arose in black and white, so clearly I could both see and hear them. *Desmond Finn,* they said. *Felon.*

# CHAPTER NINETEEN

I returned my full attention to Sam and Jean. "What do you know about Desmond? When I talked with Cookie tonight, she mentioned he had a past."

"Did she say more than that?" Sam asked.

I shook my head. "She was vague."

"Then I'll be vague, too. Desmond does have a past—as do most of us. I'll point out that Cookie wouldn't keep him on as staff if it were anything to worry about."

My voice rose. "What's privacy compared to my sister's life?"

"Take it easy, Josie," Jean said. I knew what she was thinking: *Shut up and don't get us into trouble.*

"Gah," Nicky opined.

Sam leaned back and folded his arms. "And why is Cookie telling you this, Josie? You didn't happen to be asking her about him?"

"No," I quickly replied, glad to be telling the truth. "Cookie heard me when I checked in on the retreat center's library. She and I talked for a few minutes, and she wanted to reassure me that she'll watch out for Jean. I mean, her husband was stabbed in the back and a longtime student overdosed on some weird drug. What do you expect?"

A moment passed as both Jean and Sam stared at me. I'd blown it.

"Some 'weird' drug," Sam said.

"I mean, that's what I'd assume."

When Sam replied, his voice was cold. "But she mentioned her assistant."

"She did." I remembered Desmond at the café that evening and the silver glint of his knife on the table. "It came up. Somehow."

"I see."

He wasn't coming completely clean and it irritated me. I irked him, too—I knew by his slight smile.

"Come on, Jean," I said. "Let's go home."

"You're not telling me something," Jean said.

"What makes you say that?" I bolted the library's kitchen door behind us, even though the spell of protection continued in full force. I felt as safe as if armed Marines patrolled the perimeter.

"I'm not sure how, but you know something about the murders. I felt it when you looked at Sam just now. Plus, you mentioned a 'weird drug.' What were you talking about?"

I took my time untying my scarf and unbuttoning my coat. I couldn't casually toss off, "Oh, I had a little chat with Sam's notes, and they told me one of the suspects is a felon and one of the victims took a fatal dose of Dilantin."

"You're not going to tell me, are you?" When I didn't respond, she narrowed her eyes. "You're chicken. Scared to do something Sam won't like."

She knew how to push my buttons. "No. I told you I've asked around."

"But you won't tell me about what poisoned Marcia."

Again, I remained silent.

"Fine. Get your laptop. I'm tired of this BS. Let's start our own investigation."

Mom had been clear: *Keep an eye on Jean* and *Under no circumstances tell her you're a witch.* She hadn't said anything about teaming up on murder investigations. Sam had also been clear: *Keep your nose out of the investigation, or Jean is going to jail.*

I suppressed a flicker of excitement. "Are you sure? It's risky. What if Sam finds out and takes you into custody?"

"He knows I didn't kill anyone. Besides, everything's risky right now." Jean flicked off the kitchen lights while I was hanging my coat in my office. I followed her through the atrium to the conservatory. "We'll set up here. We have half an hour to pencil out a strategy before I'm due at the retreat center for yoga."

Jean and I were teaming up to investigate. I couldn't help but smile as I turned on a few side lamps. Rodney blinked sleepily from the kindling box next to the tile stove, which still radiated a low heat. He stretched his front legs. The winter night pressed in on the conservatory's glass walls and ceiling, but here it was warm.

"Okay." Jean plopped a lined pad and two pens on a small table. "Come here, kitty." Rodney leapt to the desk, then dropped to her lap. "Lay it out, Josie."

"What?"

"Don't tell me it was a complete accident you stopped by to see Cookie tonight."

I lowered my eyes. "Actually, it was. My plan was to talk with Rex, but Cookie cracked open her door. She was practically begging me to come in."

"I'm not angry. I just want to know what you know. So we're on the same page."

Judging from the set of her lips, she was serious. "Hang on a second." I went to my office and returned with my notes. "Maybe you're right, and I have done some thinking on it."

Jean pulled the notes toward her and flipped through them. "This is good. Looking at opportunity, motive, and means is good. But I have a better idea. Let's use the Ready-Set-Go methodology."

"What?"

"To plan our investigation."

This was a new Jean. The Jean I knew let someone else take the lead and tried her best to make them happy. She could be stubborn, true, but I'd never seen her take charge outside of a yoga class.

I sat back and a book series shuffled in front of my mind's eye. The covers featured two girls in 1950s dresses, socks, and saddle shoes in a variety of situations: sneaking through a forest, shining a flashlight in a creepy mansion, staring down a rocky canyon at an old shack. "We're the Dana Girls," I said.

"The what?"

"The Dana Girls. It was a mystery series featuring teenaged sisters as sleuths. We have most of them in Children's Literature. In fact"—could it be? Yes—"the little sister was named Jean."

"No kidding? She was the smart one, I bet."

"She was the playful one with the 'humorous tilt' to her nose."

Jean pressed a finger to her nose. "I always liked Mom's Trixie Beldens, anyway. Enough of that. Let's get started."

"Okay. I'm game." Rodney, catching sight of my open lap nearer the stove, leapt over. I rested a hand on his silky back.

"We start with Ready. This is where we examine if it's the right time to undertake the project. We take stock of our resources and our liabilities," she recited. "We ask ourselves if this is truly the right time and place. Too many people ignore this step and find themselves in trouble. Even a few minutes spent in the Ready phase pays off."

Jean had not wasted time during the workshop. She'd practically memorized the curriculum. "Go on."

"Resources," she continued. "I'm in the workshop, so I can observe the suspects."

"Good," I said.

"You're a librarian and accomplished at research."

I nodded.

"Plus, you have an in with the investigating sheriff, and you know Wilfred well. If we need to question people in town, they'll talk to you. Already I'd say we're in nice shape. True, we don't have a team of crime scene analysts, but what's there to know, anyway? One victim was stabbed and another one poisoned."

If only she knew about my magic. "We're in better shape than most."

"Liabilities," she said.

"Someone's out to kill you," I promptly replied.

Her shoulders sagged. "Yeah, that's a big one. I don't buy the 'mean joke' idea."

"We can't afford to." The winter wind rattled the conservatory's glass ceiling, but the chill I felt came from somewhere else. "As for timing, this is the best timing possible. We can't wait. It's now or never."

"Another aspect of Ready is to gather the information we need to begin." As Jean spoke, she looked into the darkness and swaying fir trees behind us. "We must be open to anything, expect anything."

I felt a surge of pride in Jean. She was afraid. I didn't need our connection to know it. But she was brave, too, and she wasn't going to sit back and whimper.

"I told you about my trip to the Parker House. Nothing there, except that the owner is sure someone was in the room after she cleaned it." Remembering the telephone directory's recommendation of a divorce attorney, I added, "We need to consider Cookie's relationship with Anders."

"Why? Did Cookie tell you they were getting a divorce?"

"No. In fact, she said the opposite, that their marriage was solid."

"Then why do we have to look at their relationship?"

Time to move the discussion along. "I also did an initial run on the workshop's participants, and I didn't find anything surprising, except that both Sylvia and Desmond came up dry. I couldn't find a word on them—no social media, no mentions in newspapers."

"Sylvia strikes me as someone who would have an online presence."

I pictured her immaculate haircut and California sunny looks—and the keen look in her eyes. "Me, too. But search *Sylvia Lewis* and all you get are retirees in Florida. Mah-jongg clubs at senior living homes specialize in Sylvia Lewises."

"She seems so social, though. I can't believe she spends her days holed up at home," Jean said. "Could she have an alias?"

"Why would she?"

"She gave me her business card. Just a sec." Jean fished through her purse and laid a business card next to my laptop. "*Sylvia Lewis, Yoga Instructor, Lazy Buddha Studio.* Looks legit."

As I typed *Lazy Buddha* into the computer's search engine, a solid *boom* sounded from below us.

"What was that?" Jean asked.

I pushed away from the table. "The furnace. Every once in a while, it dies. Don't worry—Lyndon told me what to do. Hang tight." On second thought, I added, "Don't answer the door to anyone except Sam."

I hustled to the basement, keeping my gaze fastened on the furnace room, away from the hallways that smelled of damp and rats. How such a welcoming place as the library could have such a horror show of a basement, I didn't know. I pushed the reset button and made for the conservatory like there was a demon on my back. As I hurried back upstairs, a thought crossed my mind. I'd first guessed Cookie might have killed her husband and Marcia out of jealousy. Cookie's motive was strong, but her alibi was unimpeachable. Could she have enlisted someone to kill them for her?

Upstairs, I found Jean at my laptop. "The Lazy Buddha checks out," she said. "Sylvia Lewis is even on their roster as an instructor. I'm telling you, though, there's no way she teaches yoga." She raised an eyebrow and turned the laptop toward me. "Plus, there's this."

The computer showed a staff photo of Sylvia Lewis—an elderly brunette. "She might have had a dye job," I said with doubt in my voice. "Maybe some good night creams. The eyes sort of look like hers."

"This photo didn't come from the future, Josie. If it's her, she spent a fortune on plastic surgery."

"What if Cookie hired her to kill Anders and Marcia?"

Jean swiveled in the chair to face me. A smile broke over her face. "Smart." The smile disappeared and she shook her head. "But gruesome. Strangely, I can almost imagine Sylvia stabbing someone. She looks so friendly and carefree, but sometimes I'd swear something else is going on in that head. It's the way she looks at you, you know what I mean? Like every word you say is gold, but she's thinking about something else the whole time."

I nodded. I'd seen that look, too.

"I'll try to get a look at her credit card the next time we're at the café," Jean said. "See if it's in her name."

"And I'll call the yoga studio tomorrow."

Jean slowly came to her feet. "That will have to be enough for now. The retreat center awaits."

# CHAPTER TWENTY

Until tonight, I'd never seen Jean in her own world. Now here she was, a yoga mat laid out in front of her on the retreat center's wood plank floor, preparing to lead the crumbs in a session of something she called "restorative" yoga. A fire crackled in the lobby's stone fireplace, and tiny flakes of snow, lighter than dandelion tufts, drifted by the windows.

"Would you like to help lead the class, Sylvia?" Jean asked.

"If you don't mind, I'd prefer to follow along with everyone else." She laid a blanket at the rear of the room. "It's been a long day."

Besides Jean and Sylvia, "everyone" was me, Bernie, Desmond, and Rex. According to Desmond, Cookie had stayed in her room to "regroup." Rex seemed the least committed—he kept glancing up toward the guest rooms where Cookie was probably soaking a few dozen cotton balls with makeup remover.

The center's front door opened to Duke, stomping his feet on the mat to shake loose the ice particles clinging to his work boots. "Am I late?"

Desmond smiled a greeting and tossed his hand in a salute.

"Welcome, Duke," Jean said. "You're right on time."

He shed his coat to reveal sweatpants and a Gaston High School T-shirt before taking a spot next to Desmond.

I settled toward the edge of the group, where I could watch Sylvia. Bernie laid her blanket across the room from Rex, but seemed drawn to him, her face filled with an unreadable emotion. What was going on there?

"We've had a hard few days," Jean said. "Cookie's instruction has been inspiring—"

"Definitely," Rex said, glancing once again toward Cookie's room.

"—And we've had . . . tragedies to process. Your body might be responding to the emotion in ways you don't understand right now. Your sleep might be disrupted; you find you can't eat—or you eat more than you'd intended; you worry about things that never used to concern you." Jean's voice was calm and manner motherly, yet firm. Her witchy DNA as a healer showed strong and sure. "Now. Sit in a way that feels comfortable to you." She gracefully slipped into a lotus position. "First we'll focus on breathing."

I sat cross-legged and watched. Upstairs, a door shut. Rex's gaze shot toward it.

As Jean led us through a series of relaxing poses, I kept an eye on the rest of the group. Jean was right about Sylvia. She was lean and strong, but built like a runner, not a yogini, and her lack of familiarity with the poses showed in the split-second pause between Jean's demonstration and her own stiff replica.

"Now, come to your feet. We'll relax into mountain pose," Jean said. I didn't miss her glance toward Sylvia to see if she'd understood. Surprisingly, Duke rose into position before the rest of us. Sylvia followed his lead. "Feel the earth anchor you, ground you."

An hour later, the fire dying, we were scattered limply over the floor with blankets covering us. I felt as if each of my muscles, inside and out, had been stretched and left to settle, lulling me near to sleep. A thought intruded—*One of us is a murderer*—bringing me back to the moment. Sylvia also seemed to snap to. She sat abruptly. "Thank you, Jean. I'd better get up to my room."

"Sylvia. Wait," I said. "There's something I want to ask you."

Everyone looked at me. They understandably wondered what was on my mind. It couldn't be about yoga, and I wasn't a crumb. "How do you get such lovely highlights in your hair?"

Her frozen look melted. The rest of the crowd sat up and folded their blankets, chatting.

I scooted toward Sylvia, safely at the room's edge and, as long as I kept my voice low, out of earshot. Jean kept the other crumbs out of the way. "I didn't really want to ask about your hair."

Warily, she lifted her head. "What, then?"

"You aren't a yoga teacher, are you?"

"What do you mean? Of course I am."

I admired her cool. "And yet you don't know the first thing about yoga. I watched you. You had to look around for child's pose, and even I know that one. Heck, Duke knows more about yoga than you."

Her eyes narrowed and she backed up. "I don't know what you're talking about. I teach at the Lazy Buddha studio in Philadelphia. Look it up."

"I did." I kept my voice low. "Sylvia Lewis is a brunette in her sixties."

Her face might as well have become a brick wall. It betrayed zero emotion. "Are you calling me a liar?"

My pulse beat double-time. "Yes."

She rose, blanket in hand. "I don't have to talk to you."

"Maybe you'd rather talk to the sheriff," I said, praying she wouldn't call my bluff.

"How are you girls doing?" Duke had managed to break away from Jean. Behind him, she gave me an "I tried" look. "Wasn't that relaxing? Say, Jean, you holding another session tomorrow night?"

I smiled blandly at Duke and threw a glance Jean's way.

She took the hint and motioned him to join her near the fire. "Duke, you have terrific form. You've done yoga before, haven't you?"

"Been following *Yoga With Priscilla* on TV for years."

I returned to Sylvia. "Who are you? Really?"

Biting her lower lip, she glanced toward the

snow dusting the stone patio, then back to the fire. "Come to the dining room."

I followed her to the dark dining room at the rear of the retreat center. Fir trees rose like an army of shadowy giants outside the floor-to-ceiling windows. The fireplace on this side was cold. We left off the lights so not to attract others, but their presence only a shout away brought me comfort.

Sylvia pulled out a chair. She kept her voice low. "You're right. I'm not a yoga teacher. You're even right that Sylvia Lewis is an alias. It's my aunt's name." She played with the checkered place mat, squeezing it and smoothing it in turns. I waited. "If I tell you," she said, "you have to promise to keep it from Cookie."

"It's the sheriff I'm thinking of. He's investigating murder, remember?"

She waved her hand in a "pshaw" gesture. "He knows."

*He knows?* "Is that so?" I said with more ice in my tone than I'd intended.

"My real name is Bobbi Williams."

"And?"

"I'm a sort of secret shopper for workshops and online courses. My aunt was kind enough to let me use her name." Sylvia raised her eyes to mine. "You won't tell anyone, will you? It's my livelihood."

The pieces began to fall into place. Being an underground consumer advocate would explain why she asked so many questions and was so attentive—plus why she was so clueless about what she'd claimed she was taking the workshop for. Still, it was too perfect an excuse.

"For what firm?" I asked.

"Keep your voice down." She craned her neck to make sure no one lingered in the doorway. "I can't tell you. It's in my contract."

"I've never heard of that kind of job. It isn't easy to get into these workshops, and they cost a lot of money."

Sylvia leaned forward. "Exactly why I'm needed. Cookie knows about it. In fact, she hired my firm. She wants our seal of approval. She just doesn't know I'm the person the firm sent."

"Cookie said you searched Marcia's room the evening she was murdered."

Sylvia leaned in. "It was murder? Are you sure?"

Shoot. I wasn't supposed to know that. "I could be wrong."

She looked at me a moment too long before relaxing again in her chair. "Cookie told you the truth. I did look in Marcia's room, but I wasn't searching it. I merely checked it against my organization's standards of excellence. We're strict about cleanliness, mattress quality, and the number of towels provided."

I pondered this. She could be legitimate. Just because I'd never heard of this kind of service didn't mean it didn't exist. "You mean, like the *Good Housekeeping* seal of approval?"

"I can't name names—also in my contract—but that's one example." Sylvia noted my hesitation. "You understand, don't you? You won't tell anyone?"

"I need to tell Jean," I said.

"I'd rather you didn't. If my cover's blown, I could lose my job."

"Sylvia—or whatever your name is—Jean's a yoga instructor. The real thing. She's on to you, anyway."

She shook her head once. "Fine. I get it. But no one else, okay?"

The lights clicked on with a brilliance that made me blink. Mug in hand, Rex ambled to the kitchen doorway and examined each of us. "What are you girls doing in here in the dark?"

"What are you here for?" I countered.

"Just getting some cocoa," he said. "For Cookie."

# CHAPTER TWENTY-ONE

The next morning, cascades of vibrato scales reverberated through the apartment. From the creak of the sofa, I knew Jean had bolted upright. In my bedroom, Rodney and I barely budged.

"You didn't tell me the Phantom of the Opera lived here," Jean said.

I rolled over and looked through the open doorway to catch a glimpse of her, flummoxed in tousled hair and flannel pajamas. "Relax. It's only Mrs. Garlington on the organ. She gives lessons on Friday mornings."

"So early?"

"They're for her son, before he goes to work as a postman. He's getting pretty good, actually."

As if in response, a creditable version of Bach's "Sheep May Safely Graze" drifted up from the mansion's former second-floor dressing room, now the music room.

With a smile, Jean tossed aside the quilts and hummed with the music.

I'd forgotten how odd my life might appear to outsiders—even to my own sister. Besides Mrs. Garlington's organ lessons, Lalena, the so-called psychic, came up from the trailer park weekly for baths in our clawfoot tub. Mona regularly brought foster animals to the library's kitchen, where she'd nurse them with a bottle while studying for her veterinary school exams. Dylan, our high school intern, kept his own index of whatever seized his imagination, usually someone from old Hollywood.

And, of course, I was a witch, and books were the source of my power. If only Jean knew. But I'd promised Mom I wouldn't tell. Besides, I didn't want to stoke any more envy. We had a good thing going now in our investigative partnership.

"Come on," I said. "I'll make breakfast."

While Jean was in the shower, I leaned over the railing and looked down on the rooms of books. "Good morning," I whispered above the Bach cantata.

"Hello, good morning," whispered the books in a cascade of voices. From deep in Language Arts, I even made out a *guten tag* from a German language primer.

"What are you doing?" Jean, toweling out her hair, stood right behind me.

I quickly straightened. "Nothing. Just babbling to myself. Oatmeal's on."

She looked at me for another few seconds, then resumed toweling her hair. "If you say so."

A few minutes later, we were at my kitchen table. Jean dipped a green tea bag into her mug of hot water. "In the shower, I was running through the suspects in my mind."

"Who could have guessed there were secret shoppers for workshops?" I said, thinking of Sylvia.

"I don't know why you're so surprised," Jean said. We'd thoroughly discussed the revelation the night before. "Given how she's been acting, it makes sense. Now I have to wonder about Rex. Remember those roses?"

I did. "He brought them for Cookie. Had to have. Did you see him gazing toward her room all night? Don't forget his threat against Marcia."

"Uh-huh," Jean said, turning her attention from her tea to the oatmeal. "He has a major thing for Cookie. Maybe he eliminated Anders and Marcia to clear his playing field."

"Sam said they found shreds of rose petals in Marcia's bedroom and rose stems in the retreat center's garbage." I paused, spoon in the air. "That would put Rex alone with Marcia in her room. It makes absolutely no sense that he'd scatter shredded rose petals, though. What if Cookie asked Rex to knock off her husband and his lover? I almost think he'd do it. He looks like he'd do anything for her."

Jean shook her head. "No. Cookie would never ask that. Rex probably found out about the affair and took matters into his own hands to protect her feelings."

I could still see Rex's tensed hands through the PO's rows of cat food cans. "While you're at the workshop, I'll see what I can dig up on his exes. Speaking of, you're due to be there in twenty minutes."

"Yes." She smiled widely. "Today we have practice coaching sessions. Cookie paired me with Bernie."

"That should be interesting. Maybe you can find out why she's taking the workshop. She seems to spend more time wandering town than attending sessions." I pushed away my empty bowl. "There's one thing I don't get, though. About Rex."

"What?"

"Why would he want to kill you?"

The organ music crashed into a crescendo and held a note that rattled the windowpanes.

"Hang on while I get my coat. I'm walking you to the retreat center."


With Jean safely at the workshop, it was time to open the library. Mrs. Garlington was occupied with a rousing version of "How Great Thou Art," and I could greet the books properly. I made my way through the old mansion, heaving open brocade curtains and flicking on lights. Salutes and snapping heels told me the sentries were still working their protective magic.

"Keep quiet on the title recommendations," I told them. "I don't want to get in trouble like I did last summer when I offered up *Parenting a Troubled Teen*." I winced at the memory of the patron's shocked expression. I later learned her son had a history of petty theft. "And I refuse to suggest any more weight loss books when I'm not asked."

A book in Self-Help tittered.

"Not funny," I said.

I unlatched the door to the foyer and marveled, as always, at its stained glass windows, then unbolted the heavy front door. A few books rested in the book return box, but no patrons waited. Finally, I crossed the atrium to open the kitchen door. Here's where most of the early-morning customers would gather, counting on a cup of coffee before they browsed the shelves. Lalena stepped in as soon as the door opened. Behind her, several members of the knitting club argued.

"Are you kidding?" one of them said. "Cabot Cove has nothing on us. In fact, we could work that into our motto. 'Compared to Wilfred, Cabot Cove is Child's Play' or 'Deadlier than St. Mary Mead.' "

"Reporting for duty," Lalena said. To generalize, librarians these days were relaxed but stylish and wore comfortable clogs, layers of clothing— the stacks could be chilly—and stylish eyeglasses. Tattoos optional. Lalena showed up to work in a getup that was more suitable to her usual job as a palm reader. She wore an old ivory lace nightgown with a petticoat over it and a chunky hand-knit sweater. "Coffee on? We have a thirsty crew here. The knitting club is holding another branding meeting."

"Couldn't make it at the café," Sherry said toting a notepad with her basket of yarn. "Not if we're working on the café's new name, too."

"All right. The stove is lit in the conservatory. I'll bring in the coffee urn in a few minutes." After the knitting club's members had filed through to the conservatory, I said, "Lalena, do you mind keeping an eye on things while I take care of some business in my office? It won't be long."

"No problem," she said, putting coffee mugs on a tray. "I thought, if you didn't mind, I might meet with Vicky later this morning."

"Boyfriend problems again?"

"Never-ending."

*The Peter Pan Syndrome* popped into my head. I ignored it. "As long as she doesn't mind being interrupted by patrons with actual library business."

"Are you kidding? She's already complained to everyone in town. She'll probably force them to take a chair and listen."

Leaving Lalena to finish the library's canteen duties, I went to my office and shut the door. Rodney was already there, lying on the heater vent, his belly almost completely covering it. He flashed me a "so what?" look and returned to his nap.

I fired up my laptop, looked up the phone number for the Lazy Buddha studio, and dialed. I wasn't going to take Sylvia's word for her story. Verify verify verify. It was three hours later in Philadelphia. I envisioned a roomful of yoga students in the warrior pose with honking taxicabs crowding past tall, gray office buildings outside the window.

"May I speak with Sylvia Lewis?" I asked. From the class schedule posted online, she should be getting ready to teach senior yoga.

The line clicked as I was thrust onto hold and serenaded with Pan flute music. Rodney shifted over the vent to heat up his other side. Senior yoga had nothing on this. Cats could stretch themselves as long as Slinkys.

"Yes?" came an East Coast–inflected voice.

"Sylvia Lewis?" I asked.

"Yes? What do you want? I have a class in just a minute." Her voice sweetened as she spoke to someone passing in the background. "Hello, Mrs. White."

I had the hunch Sylvia Lewis wouldn't mind my getting straight to the point. "Are you Bobbi Williams's aunt?"

"Who? Say what?"

"Bobbi Williams." I enunciated each syllable.

"Why? What about it? Who are you, anyway?" Then, "Straight ahead, Reggie. LeeAnn will help you with your walker."

"It's a bet. I couldn't believe she had an aunt in Pennsylvania."

"Well, she does. Is that it?"

After a brief "goodbye," I hung up the phone. So, that was that. Sylvia-slash-Bobbi was telling the truth. Assuming secret shoppers didn't include "homicide" on their list of duties, we could cross her off the list. But if the murderer wasn't Sylvia, who could it be? Only Rex, Bernie, and Desmond were left as suspects.

Before I investigated further, I thought, I'd better check on the library. After all, I did have a day job.

In the conservatory, organ lessons over, Mrs. Garlington was helping herself to a cup of coffee and chatting with the knitting club.

"As a poet, I'd prefer something more mellifluous." She dropped three sugar cubes into her mug. "Perhaps, 'Wilfred: Pastoral Delights Await.' We could name the café the Pastoral Beanery."

"Too churchy," one of the members said, feeding blue yarn onto her needles.

"*Pastoral* refers to the atmosphere of sylvan glades," Mrs. Garlington said. "Not members of the clergy."

"I still think we go with the murder theme. Killers are all the rage," Gloria said. She hadn't even

bothered to bring one of her ever-present pot holders to work on. "You can't turn on the television
without seeing a true crime story. People would
flock here by the busload if they knew about those
characters knocked off this week."

Were all knitters so bloodthirsty, or did Wilfred
specialize in them? I made my way to Circulation
to see how Lalena was getting on.

"Josie. Perfect timing. Can you suggest a new series for Lorraine? She's read every Regency romance on the shelves."

"Roz's latest should be here soon." Besides being assistant librarian, Roz wrote romance novels
as Eliza Chatterley Windsor. I relaxed to let titles
slip into my brain. "I can give you a call when it
gets here. In the meantime, let me think . . ."

*Two Weeks in Bali*, said the books. A travel guide.

*No*, I thought. *Romance novels, please.* I refused to
tell the patron she needed a vacation. It qualified
as "none of my business."

*Beach Holidays for the Busy*, the books suggested.
*Seaside Adventures for One.*

The books were not being helpful. Or were
they? "You normally read Regency romance, but
have you thought about a romance set at the
beach? It might be like having a mini-vacation."

Her face lit up. "Great idea! I've been so busy
lately, and the cold is getting me down. In the
meantime, yes, please give me a call when the new
romances come in."

Library business under control, I returned to
my office. Rodney had vanished from his station
over the heating vent, and my office was corre-
spondingly warmer.

I opened my laptop and searched Rex's name again, but this time I took a different tack. At least two of his marriages had ended suddenly. What could I find out about his wives? I returned to the obituary that mentioned him and his second wife's "sudden, tragic death." Nosing around on the internet didn't reveal anything further about the death, except its date.

I tapped my pen on my desk and considered. If Rex's wife had died under suspicious circumstances, the police would have investigated. I couldn't find any trace of that. Besides, even if Rex were somehow involved in his wife's death, what did that have to do with Anders and Marcia? Or Cookie? I returned to my laptop, this time to scroll through his latest wife's social media. She had been well loved, it seemed. She'd belonged to a cocker spaniel show organization, and several of its members had left touching messages on her feed. Not to mention photos of puppies.

Photos—that was an idea. I clicked to the gallery and unearthed more dog photos, plus a few of Rex. There they were at their wedding, once again at a country club. Rex's tan stood out against his white tuxedo. His wife's highlighted blond hair framed a Botoxed brow and plumped lips, and her mouth rounded up in a luminous smile. In fact, the women in the photo looked like they visited the same hairdresser and plastic surgeon and were copies of each other at different heights.

All of the women, except one. Bernie Stanich.

# CHAPTER TWENTY-TWO

Bernie Stanich. In Rex's wedding photo. I had a hunch why she was there—now to confirm it. I pulled the photo to my computer's desktop and typed in a reverse image search.

I had a hit right away in the country club's newsletter. The photo was grainy, but I was able to make out the names of the people in it. It was Bernie all right. Bernie Brightson Stanich. Rex's wife was Loretta Brightson. Bernie and Loretta were sisters.

This was the sister Bernie had told me about in the library yesterday, the sister who'd died not long ago. Bernie had said she'd introduced her sister to her husband. I shut the laptop. Why would she and Rex hide that they knew each other—not only that, but that they were family? If Bernie was as close to her sister as she'd claimed, she'd surely be open about knowing Rex.

Then I had another thought. Rex's wives, including Bernie's sister, seemed to appear and disappear awfully quickly. Maybe he and Bernie had teamed up to kill Marcia and Anders to make sure Cookie was both single and unencumbered by an ex drawing alimony. Then, Rex would marry Cookie, Cookie would go the way of Rex's other wives, and Cookie's assets would end up in Rex's bank account, which he'd share with Bernie. It all made sense.

Jean had told me she had a practice session with Bernie today. I grabbed my phone. Jean didn't pick up. I tapped out a text urging her to *call me ASAP*.

It should be about lunchtime at the workshop. What if Jean was wandering around on her own? It would be all too easy for Bernie to waylay her in the meadow. For a second, I considered calling Sam, but that could way too easily backfire. I grabbed my coat and hurried through the atrium. "I'm going out for a few minutes," I told Lalena, who was in Circulation examining Vicky's palm.

Lalena waved serenely. "Okay."

I took the wooded trail along the Kirby River to the retreat center. I felt no panic from Jean, I reminded myself as my feet hit the frozen ground in a pace just short of a jog. If she were in trouble, I'd know. Jean was probably engrossed in conversation, and that's why she hadn't responded to my texts and calls. Or so I told myself.

At last, I arrived at the retreat center. Without a thought about the ongoing workshop, I pushed open the door. The room was empty, except for my sister on the rug, flat on her back.

I gasped. "Jean! Are you all right?"

She popped up and smiled. "Just doing the corpse pose by the fire. Cookie taught us so much this morning. It's a lot to take in. I needed a break." She squinted. "What's with you?"

I stood for a moment, regaining my breath. "Where is everyone? Where's Bernie?"

"Lunch break. People went down to the café. As for Bernie, she skipped out on our session this morning. Typical. I have no idea where she is." Jean's attention shot to the hall overlooking the lobby. "Hi, Cookie."

"Hi, Jean, Josie. I heard voices." Cookie looked down, her hands on the banister. "Thought I'd better check, given what happened earlier this week." She returned to her room.

I drew Jean to one of the armchairs and perched on its arm. I lowered my voice. "I did some research on Rex."

Jean's eyes widened "Did he kill his wives?"

I shrugged. "He and Bernie know each other. Bernie was his sister-in-law." I sat back and let that soak in.

Jean stared at the fire. "You're joking. Although . . ."

"Although what?"

She turned to me. "Now that you mention it, it does seem like Rex intentionally ignores her. I've seen her glance toward him, and he always looks away. I thought maybe Bernie had a thing for him, and he was discouraging it since he's so infatuated with Cookie. Then again . . ."

"Then again, what?"

"Sometimes I almost get the vibe she detests him. She's hard to read."

"She might have been trying to throw the scent away from her partnership with him." I glanced toward the bedrooms upstairs to make sure no one was listening. I shook my head. "Still, too much doesn't make sense. How could either Rex or Bernie have killed Cookie's husband? Both of them were here." Outside the lobby's windows, snow fell in sparse, tight flakes. We might have been a hundred miles away in the wilderness, not a ten-minute walk across the meadow from town. "I don't like it that you're here alone. It's not safe."

"I'm not alone. Cookie's upstairs."

"That's not enough."

She nodded toward the front door. "Let's not forget the deputy posted outside."

I followed her gaze to the black SUV parked next to the shuttle bus at the front of the small lot. "What deputy? There's no one in the vehicle."

Jean stood and went to the window. "What do you mean? I saw her just a minute ago. She checked in to make sure everything was okay."

Urgent shouting from outside drew our attention.

Jean's eyes widened. "That's her. That's the deputy."

Within seconds, we were out the door, running across the stone patio, across the frost-bitten gravel, sugared with snow. The sheriff's deputy was on the levee, yelling down its rocky wall.

Facedown in the millpond was Rex.


Rex floated at least ten feet from shore among broken sheets of ice embedded with fallen leaves. There was no way to tell if he was dead or alive.

"Hang in there! We're pulling you out," I yelled.

The deputy hit the water with a splash. At the same time, a sheriff's department SUV came tearing up the meadow and halted at the levee. Rope looped over his shoulder, Sam leapt from the driver's seat. From the distance came the shriek of a siren.

"Josie," Jean whispered. "Look in the car."

Ignoring Jean, I clambered down the levee's rocks. The millpond lapped inches below me. The deputy pushed her arms in a wide motion, head above the icy water, toward Rex. "She's almost there, Rex. Stay with us!"

The deputy fastened her arms through Rex's shoulders and attempted to backstroke toward shore. She might have been treading water for all the progress she made with Rex's deadweight. Then Sam was beside me. He tossed a rope toward the deputy, and I grabbed it on our end. Inch by inch, we towed the deputy and Rex nearer.

At last, the deputy pulled Rex onto the rocks. She was soaked and shivering. He lay motionless.

"Go in to the fire." Sam pointed to the retreat center. "I've got him."

Rex's lips were blue and face gray. Sam turned his cheek to Rex's mouth and pressed fingers against his neck.

"Rex!" I said. "Say something." I grabbed his hands and warmed them between mine. "Is he still breathing?"

Sam nodded. "Barely."

Paramedics had arrived at the levee's rim surprisingly quickly, as if they'd been idling in Wilfred, waiting for the call. They lifted Rex onto a gurney and wheeled him toward the ambulance. His mylar blanket–covered body shimmered as it passed through the parking lot.

Although I was snug in my wool coat, hat, and gloves, I shivered to think of what had just happened. Hands over feet, I climbed the levee's icy boulders to the path across its ridge.

Jean tapped my shoulder and returned her arms to hug herself. Her coat was back in the retreat center, and crystals of snow as small as goose down stuck to her hair. "Look."

"You need to get inside. It's freezing out here."

"In Sam's SUV." She pointed.

In the backseat of the SUV, shielded by a metal guard, Bernie watched us.

I threw another log into the retreat center's massive fireplace while the deputy sat swaddled in blankets. Her hair fell on her face in cold, wet strips. Rex had been taken in the ambulance and another deputy had driven Bernie away. Sam, Jean, and Cookie surrounded the deputy.

Fire stoked, I returned to the arm of Jean's chair.

"Sheriff Wilfred, now that we're settled, what happened?" Cookie asked. She stood wiry and commanding, arms crossed, near the hearth.

I wanted to know, too. Sam had appeared with rope, as if knowing Rex had been pushed into the millpond. Not only that, he'd already apprehended Bernie and called for an ambulance.

"I'd like to ask you a question or two first," Sam replied. "Where are the rest of the workshop's participants?"

"We'd broken for lunch," Cookie said. "We're due to meet again in"—she glanced at the chunky Rolex on her wrist—"ten minutes."

"You're not serving lunch here?"

"No. It's good for the crumbs to leave the womb of the workshop at least daily to mingle with the rest of the world. I stayed in my room to meditate. It might surprise you, but I'm an introvert, and teaching draws a lot of energy."

"I stayed, too," Jean said. "I was supposed to meet with Bernie."

"What about everyone else?" Sam said. "Desmond, Rex, and Sylvia?"

Cookie shrugged. "I can't say. I suppose they walked to the café. I excused them a little before noon. Now, you tell me. What happened at the mill-pond?"

Jean shifted on the chair. She wanted to say something, I could tell, but thought the better of it.

Sam's gaze swept each of us—Jean next to me, Cookie, the deputy by the fire looking much better already—and seemed to decide the best strategy was to talk. "I was on my way to the retreat center to relieve the deputy, and I saw Ms. Stanich running through the meadow. She pounded on the side of the vehicle and told me to call an ambulance. I did."

Whatever I'd expected, it wasn't this. Apparently, it wasn't what Cookie had expected, either, because she gasped, then masked it as a normal breath.

"What did she want?" Cookie asked.

Sam's voice was calm. "She said she'd killed Rex."

Cookie jolted. "Say that again?"

"She told me she'd pushed him into the mill-pond, knowing he couldn't swim. She was so upset I could barely make out her words, but she demanded to be arrested. You know the rest."

"She knew Rex from before the workshop," I said. "She's his ex-sister-in-law." My working theory from the morning couldn't be right. Bernie and Rex weren't in cahoots. If anything, it was the opposite.

Sam shot me an "I'll-talk-to-you-later" look. "What happened this afternoon was unfortunate, but we're lucky in one important way."

"And that is?" Cookie asked, looking as if *disastrous* was a better descriptor than *lucky*.

"We've likely found our murderer. We'll all sleep a little better tonight."

The retreat center's front door opened, bringing with it a whoosh of snow and icy air. Sylvia stamped her feet on the doormat and Desmond shrugged the coat from his shoulders.

"Lots of action in town," Sylvia said.

Her notebook chirped from her bag. *Day five, snow. Police activity.* Odd observations for a workshop reviewer.

"Bernie tried to kill Rex," Cookie said flatly.

I almost wished we could have filmed Sylvia and Desmond's faces, the shock was so sudden and plainly drawn.

Cookie's features hardened. "That's it. I've had enough. The workshop is cancelled."

# CHAPTER TWENTY-THREE

What a relief. At last, the tension, the fear that Jean would be killed, was at an end. The murderer was in custody. Not only that, the workshop was over. It was the best possible outcome—for Jean, that is. Not Bernie. Or Rex.

Sam's vague frown told me he was happy with the news, too. He closed his notebook. "I've got to get into town for Ms. Stanich's questioning." He shook Cookie's hand. "We won't detain you. I hope you'll consider returning to Wilfred under more peaceful circumstances."

That was it, then. He considered the case closed—Bernie had murdered Anders and Marcia. But why? Bernie clearly hadn't partnered with Rex, as I'd suspected earlier. Did she loathe Rex so much that she wanted to squelch his chances for romance by plunging Cookie into grief by killing Anders? If so, that wouldn't account for Marcia's murder. Unless there was something else I didn't know.

The deputy in the armchair rose, her uniform now dry and warm from the fire. "I'll come with you."

They left and the fireplace's heat quickly subsumed the cold they'd let in. Now it was Cookie, Sylvia, Desmond, Jean, and I left in the lobby.

Cookie rested a hand on my sister's shoulder. "Jean, I'm sorry the workshop is ending early. Believe me when I say you'll make a wonderful coach. I see a little bit of myself in your profound desire to help others."

Jean glowed from the praise. Cookie had said nothing about Sylvia's potential, I noticed.

"I'll refund the workshop fees," Cookie added. "It's only right. Desmond, book us flights for tomorrow morning."

Better and better, I thought.

Sylvia clenched her jaw as if fighting an urge to say something. Desmond had disappeared up the stairwell when she gave in. "You can't leave, Cookie. You haven't found it yet."

The room's temperature seemed to plummet. The women faced each other as if they were in a boxing ring.

Cookie's eyes narrowed. "Found what?"

"You want me to spill your secrets?" Sylvia stepped forward, her voice wavering with tension.

Sam had left too quickly. "What secrets?" I asked.

Sylvia smiled, the smile of a cat who's cornered a mouse. "Ask her who tossed Marcia's room."

"Ask her what her real name is," Cookie countered.

"They know all about that," Sylvia quickly replied.

"Do they?" Cookie's own smile slowly grew.

Jean stepped to Cookie's side. "Just what are you accusing Cookie of? Don't you think she's had enough trauma lately? First her husband, then Marcia, now this. Honestly, Sylvia."

As for Sylvia, I didn't know what she insinuated, but it was impossible to ignore the swirl of anger at work in her. Merely witnessing it prickled the backs of my arms and tightened my throat.

"You won't leave until you find it, will you?" Sylvia's head jutted forward. "It wasn't in Marcia's room."

"You were in her room, not me," Cookie said. "I should report you to the sheriff."

"Why don't you?" Sylvia said with mock graciousness. "He'd have a few questions to ask, wouldn't he? Maybe you wouldn't be getting on that plane so fast."

Cookie's stare at Sylvia could have flash frozen most people. Apparently, Sylvia wasn't most people. "This is not over." With an imperious backward glance, she mounted the stairs toward her room.

I took a deep breath. "Sylvia, what are you talking about? This is about more than workshop reviews, isn't it?"

"She threatened to expose me." Sylvia lowered herself into the armchair and stared into the fire, one hand in her tote, resting on her notebook. "I lost my head. I don't know what came over me, but it won't happen again."

"You don't want to tell us?"

Ignoring my question, she seemed to emerge from her reverie. "I'm leaving. I have work to do. I'll find a hotel in Portland tonight and fly out tomorrow." She ran her palms over her face.

"Work?" I prompted. She knew something and I didn't plan to let her off the hook that easily.

"My report."

"You mentioned Cookie was looking for something. What did you mean?"

Her features composed themselves in a brittle copy of the friendly Sylvia we knew. "Did I say that? I swear, I don't even remember."

"Sylvia!" I said. "You can't leave us hanging like this."

"I have nothing more to say." She rose and made for the stairs to the bedrooms, then, hand on the rail, turned to Jean. "Except this—be careful. The sheriff may have called off the investigation, but mark my words. It's not over yet."

All the way back to the library, Jean was glum. "It's over. Just like that."

"Cookie said she'd refund your money," I said. Sylvia's parting words rang in my ears. "Watch out for that tree branch."

Snow now evenly dusted the landscape, and the trail's usual deep blue-greens and muddy brown were white against the leaden gray sky. And it was eerily quiet.

"It's not about the money. It's about my life. My dreams. I wanted to be a wellness coach."

"You can still be a wellness coach," I pointed

out. "It's not like you need a license. I bet you already have a good grasp of Ready-Set-Go."

She wouldn't look at me. "You don't understand." Her voice rose. "Why would you? You already have everything. You're running a library—your life's dream. You live in this great town where everyone loves you. Even the sheriff has a thing for you—"

"No, he doesn't," I said.

"There's something else, too. I don't know what it is, but you're different now. Stronger."

"You're strong, too."

"You have no idea what it's like to be the little sister. So cute, so helpless." She said the last words with a singsong voice.

"I don't talk like that."

"Maybe not, but you think it. Not just you, but Mom and Toni, too. You all think I'm helpless, that I'm not fit for anything but teaching yoga at the community center. I'm an adult. I have my own talents."

"Oh, Jean. We've been through this. Of course you have your own talents. Lots of them. But you have to admit that sometimes you go too far. Like back there at the retreat center, how you egged Sylvia on."

"I wasn't egging her on! She shouldn't have picked a fight with Cookie."

"Cookie can take care of herself," I said. "You don't have to fight everyone's battles."

"Don't underestimate me. Cookie believes in me."

Despite her forceful "I am woman" talk, Jean burst into tears. I cradled her against my chest, like I used to when she'd awaken with a nightmare when we were in elementary school.

She pulled away and wiped her face with her woolen gloves. "I'm sorry. I guess I'm just so disappointed. I've been dreaming about Cookie's workshop. It was my chance to make something of myself, and now it's over."

"Don't feel bad. I'm the middle sister," I said. "Remember? The dull one, the one who never lived, because she always had her nose in a book."

She kept her head low and didn't reply.

"Remember how you used to taunt me from outside the bedroom window? I'd be plowing through a Nancy Drew, and you'd walk by the window making faces."

That got a smile. She raised her eyes.

"I know what it's like to feel like an outsider," I said. "You're special. I know it and I think, deep down, you know it, too. Don't ever compare yourself to anyone else. Come on."

Snow drifting lazily around us, we continued toward the library. A trail of smoke rose from the conservatory's woodstove. The house, its Italianate tower rising proudly and dormers poking out here and there, looked like something in a fairy tale. Jean was right about one thing: Wilfred had been good to me. I was truly lucky to live here.

She was lucky, too. Bernie was in the county jail awaiting charges. Despite my reservations, I gave in to Sam's belief. She must have killed Cookie's husband and his lover. After all, what were the odds of having two murderers at the workshop?

Jean's silence and reluctance to meet my eyes told me she was still upset the workshop had ended. Of course she was. But I'd take her disappointment over her murder any day. I looked forward to a quiet evening.

At least, I could relax once I figured out what had happened at the library in my absence. Even before I put a hand on the brass doorknob, the sounds of books guffawing and gasping hinted at the mayhem inside. Worse, the shimmer of the protection spell's web over the library had vanished. I said a silent prayer and pushed open the foyer door.

In the center of the atrium was an intricate tower precariously constructed of encyclopedia volumes. Mona, from the knitting club, was on a ladder resting a colorful wildflower identification manual on top. It let out a "whee!" as it was balanced in place.

"Like this," she said. "Wilfred needs something to be remembered by, a tower of some sort. We could put it in the parking lot at Darla's." Three ducklings trotted at the ladder's base.

Jean, barely noticing the mayhem, made for the service staircase. "I'm going upstairs."

"I'll be there in a minute," I told her. Then, to the crowd milling in the atrium, "People! This is a library, not a circus show." Where was Lalena, anyway?

At the sound of my voice, Mona wavered on her perch on the ladder. She hunched to grab its top rung, and in doing so knocked the wildflower manual with her elbow and set off an avalanche of books. They thundered to the ground, sending ducklings scattering and knitters hastily backing to the atrium's edge.

"Now see what you did," Mona said.

Lalena's towel-wrapped head poked over the second-story balcony. "What's going on?"

"You're supposed to be keeping an eye on the library," I said.

"Sorry. I thought I'd squeeze in a quick bath after my palm readings. I figured you'd want the tub free tonight for your sister. But I wasn't totally lazy. I did a serious tidying up. Found books in the wrong places. Four of them. Who put *War and Peace* in Children's Literature?"

So much for the spell of protection. Could it get worse?

Another two heads peered down across the atrium, one from Natural History and one from Business and Science. "What's going on?" one person said. "I can't work on my memoirs with all this racket. I was drafting a delicate scene about my case of whooping cough."

The other head belonged to Patty of Patty's This-N-That. "I heard Sam bagged the murderer."

Good grief. Word was out already? The library's patrons—and a few ducklings—crowded the atrium, stepping over books. Lalena, wrapped in a bathrobe, toweled her hair.

"A murderer? No kidding," a high school student said. "When?" He held a history of World War II Japan. *Pew pew. Boom!* the book said.

"Great." Maureen from the knitting club folded her arms over her chest. "Cold cases were a big part of our branding strategy."

"Don't worry, Maureen," Neil said. "I bet another corpse surfaces soon."

Ignoring the morbid talk, I asked, "How did you know about Bernie's arrest?"

"I was at the shop researching starting an antiques mall—Bernie is remarkably helpful for a murderess—and I got a call from the café. Duke saw the whole thing. He said he was changing his oil when the dog groomer came tearing through the trailer park like she had hornets in her shorts. Duke called me and I stepped out of the This-N-That in time to see her flag down Sam."

"Whoa," Mona said, clutching a duckling to her chest.

"I figure it went like this," Patty said. "The first morning of the workshop, Bernie prowls the meadow, stalking Anders."

"Why?" Lalena asked.

"Who knows? Does it matter?" Lalena's concern dismissed, Patty continued. "She's looking for any excuse to get him. She follows him into the café. Lucky for her, the windows are covered over. She waits until he's comfortably seated at the counter. It only takes a second for her to grab a knife from the kitchen and let him have it in the back." She leaned back, satisfied. "Killing the other one was a cinch. Drop something in her coffee—mission accomplished."

"Why was Anders in the café in the first place?" Lalena said.

"Plus, why did Bernie leave the Ready card in Jean's bag?" I added.

"Who cares?" Patty said. "She's a lunatic. A serial killer. She probably threatened your sister as a way to draw attention away from herself."

I glanced up toward the third-floor hall over-looking the atrium. No Jean. I hoped she was find-ing some peace in my apartment. Maybe doing some yoga breathing.

All around us, books littered the floor. A duck-ling quacked from the conservatory. I hoped quacking was all he was doing.

"You know what?" I said. "I'm closing the library early." I needed to spend some time with my sister, make sure she was all right.

"Why?" Patty said. "We were just getting started. Neil thought we might rename my shop Deadly Booty."

"Tomorrow. Right now we all need time to di-gest the news." I hadn't even seen the library's in-dividual rooms, yet. There was no telling what kind of mess was up there.

"If that's how you feel, let us help clean up," Mona said.

"It's all right. I'll do it. Just collect your knitting and ducklings and go home."

After they left, I taped CLOSED UNTIL TOMORROW signs on the front and kitchen doors and let out a huge sigh. Marilyn Wilfred looked down at me from her portrait above the door. I swear she was smirking. Books littered the atrium floor. Fortu-nately, I knew a quick way to clean them up.

I glanced toward my apartment. Jean was safely out of sight.

I drew my energy back to center and closed my eyes. Breathing deeply, I let the magic readers and writers had poured into each volume resonate through me. "Books," I whispered, "Go home." I reopened my eyes.

One by one, the heavy volumes rose and formed a slow tornado before peeling off to thunk into their shelves. The wildflower identification manual left a trail of ghostlike daisies in its wake as it disappeared over the second floor's railing. The encyclopedias marched to their home in an orderly line like doctoral students at graduation. A few paperback thrillers sped through the atrium as if on a car chase and rushed to Popular Fiction in a soundtrack of explosions and gunfire.

Other than the ladder, the atrium was clear once again. I placed my hands on my hips and smiled in satisfaction. The flow of energy through me had calmed my flaring emotions and soothed me from the inside out. In a crazy day like this, what a good feeling it was to use my magic to restore order somewhere.

"Josie," came Jean's voice, wavering and unsure, from upstairs. Even from the atrium floor, I read shock on her blanched face. My skin grew hot, then froze. "Who are you?" she asked.

# CHAPTER TWENTY-FOUR

"Jean." My brain spun but couldn't gain traction. "I didn't see you up there."

"I asked you a question." She choked out the words between some kind of yoga maneuver where she alternately held and puffed out her breath.

"I'll come upstairs."

"Stop!" Jean said. "Stay where you are and answer me. I just saw a whole bunch of books flying around like in a cartoon. What is going on?"

The portrait of Marilyn Wilfred seemed to whisper in my ear. *Tell her. Do it. You'll work it out later.* Mom's words came to me, too. "Under no circumstances are you to let on that you're a witch."

"It's not what it looks like—"

"I said, answer me."

The atrium's quiet was so complete that I heard the mantle clock ticking in Circulation. *Tell her, don't tell, tell her, don't tell,* it repeated. The last thing

I wanted was make Jean feel worse than she already did. Then again, if she learned about my magic later—and surely at some point she would—she'd feel terrible.

Finally, I let the words tumble out. "I'm a witch."

"What? I couldn't hear you."

"I said, I'm a witch." My words reverberated through the atrium, and the books echoed them in a shushing *witch witch witch*.

Now what? Would Jean think it was a joke?

Even if she believed me, I had no idea how she'd take it. I'd never had to explain my magic to anyone. Mom and Toni had known—known long before I had. We already had the nightmare of Cookie's workshop driving a wedge between us. I didn't want my magic to widen that gap.

Jean vanished from behind the railing and footsteps sounded in the stairwell. In a moment, she was beside me. Rodney, somehow tuned into the situation, appeared as well and wound through my feet. Slowly, I raised my gaze to Jean's and braced myself for anger, tears—whatever might come.

Instead, she was smug. "I knew it."

I was too stunned to respond.

"I knew you had some kind of freaky power. You kept trying to hide it, but I saw." She actually laughed. "Don't try to keep anything from me, Josie."

"How did you know?"

"Little things. You always have the book you want at your fingertips, and you know titles of books you haven't even read. I mean, recommending a book of Icelandic knitting patterns for socks to Duke? You can't knit."

"I have a good memory. Maybe I saw the book and made a mental note."

She cast me a skeptical glance. "Then there's the toxicology report. Sam refused to show us, yet you somehow knew all about it. I bet you can even name the poison. What did you do, read his mind?"

I shook my head. "I can't read minds."

"Then, what?"

"Books talk to me."

Jean took a moment to digest this. She wandered to the atrium table and tipped its sole remaining book on its spine. *Folk Magic*, it read. Always on point, the books were. "I have so many questions that I don't even know where to start."

"It's like this," I said. "The women in our family each have some magic and a particular talent."

"I'm magic, too?"

I nodded. "The talent—sort of a life objective— is, in your case, to heal. Grandma and Toni are healers, too. Mom has second sight."

"You never can hide anything from her."

This was a fact. In high school, Toni used to try to sneak out at night, only to find Mom calmly reading a magazine in a chair posted by the front door.

"I need to see justice done. I'm a truth teller. Apparently, that drive comes around only every dozen generations."

"I can't make books fly around," she said.

"It's different for each of us. On top of being a truth teller, I was hit with an extra-strong dose of magic." I pulled my sweater's collar to the side, exposing my star-shaped birthmark. "This is the sign." I hesitated to tell her the next part, because

I didn't want her to make fun of me. "Rodney has it, too."

As if he could understand us, Rodney rolled to his back and showed his tummy. A chocolate brown star marked his belly, low, where his fur was thin.

"Is Rodney your familiar?" Jean asked. "I mean, isn't a black cat kind of obvious?"

"He's not my familiar," I said quickly. "He's my . . . my cat friend. I don't have a cauldron or broomstick or pointy hat, either."

"Right," Jean said.

"It's a lot to digest, I know." I shot Marilyn Wilfred's portrait a glance as I crossed to the foyer. *Satisfied?* "Come with me while I close up the library, and I'll tell you more."

I double-checked that the front door was bolted, picked up a stray glove in the entry hall to deposit in lost and found, and locked the foyer door. Rodney trailed us.

Back in the atrium, Jean said, "You told me books talk to you. How does that factor in?"

"I'm still learning about magic, but what I do know is that we're fed by what we love. I love books, so the energy invested in books by readers and their authors is what powers my magic."

"The energy?"

"Think about it. Each book is created by someone who'd spent months or years writing it, living with it in their thoughts. So, there's that source of energy. Then, each person who reads the book takes the author's words and infuses them with their own feelings and details and essentially recreates the world in their minds. That's a lot of energy. I can tap into that energy to fuel my magic."

"You're telling me that basically the library is your charging station."

"A good way to put it."

Rodney head-butted her shin, and she reached down to scratch behind his ears. We circled through Old Man Thurston's office, and I pulled the curtains and clicked off the overhead light and the lamp I kept burning on his wide oak desk. We passed through to Literature, the mansion's former drawing room. Now that I had nothing to hide, I lifted my hand toward a shelf and pushed my fingers in. Three novels a patron had pulled forward now retreated to fall in line with their neighbors.

"Whoa," Jean said.

"It does make cleanup easier," I admitted.

"So, Rodney. Does he do your beckoning? You know, put curses on people and stuff?"

"No," I said. "As if. He pretty much does whatever he wants. There's one thing, though." This was perhaps my most bizarre power. "I can slip into his body."

Jean straightened and Rodney jumped to a side table. "You must be joking."

"It's true. If I relax and he's near me, I can go where he goes and see things from inside his head." It was so nice to talk openly about my magic. It was worth it, even if it meant I had to face the music with Mom later.

"Does he then go into yours?"

I imagined the horror that could lead to. Rodney would probably drive to the store and return with a whole salmon and a pound of catnip. "Fortunately, no."

"Do it," she said. "Go into his body now."

I picked up a pen someone had dropped and set it on a side table. "I'm not going to do it now. It tires me and Rodney isn't keen on it, anyway. He likes to do his own thing. Besides, when I pop into him, I'm still around, only kind of trancelike. You wouldn't like it."

Pondering this, Jean followed me through the rest of the library, upstairs and down, as I closed curtains, shut off lights and, finally, cleaned out the coffeepot and put the kitchen in order. I whispered good night to the books, and they retreated into their worlds of Arabian deserts, sonnets, and anatomical charts. Jean couldn't hear them bid me good night, too, but she watched in fascination.

As I bolted the kitchen door, I half-listened for the clicking heels of the sentry novel. I had to remind myself that we didn't need its protection any longer. Good thing, too, since the spell had been broken.

"All this is amazing," Jean said. "I still can't get over it. A witch. What else can you do?"

"Like I said, books talk to me. They greet me, even when they're in someone else's bag. Sometimes they'll even say hello from houses I pass. Plus, I can ask them questions, and if it has to do with what the book is about, they'll answer me."

"Weird."

I nodded. There was a lot more. "Books I need to read have a habit of appearing on my nightstand. And books tell me who needs to read them."

"What do you mean?"

"Someone can come into the library looking for, say, a mystery novel, and instead a manual on treating acne will suggest itself. It's been getting me into trouble lately."

This wasn't an imagined circumstance. This exact situation had happened the week before, and the library patron had stormed out of the library in a huff. I had been too quick to listen to my inner card catalog. Now the patron wouldn't even make eye contact with me at the PO Grocery.

"That is so cool." Jean folded her arms over her chest. "Tell me. What book should I be reading now?"

"That chair you have your hand on? Check its seat." I'd seen a book's spine peeking out, and I certainly hadn't put it there. "They must sense our bond."

Jean lifted the book and showed me its cover. "Uh-oh. *The Everywoman's Guide to Self-Defense.*"

"The books aren't fortune tellers. They're good at picking up on energy, though. No doubt they sense our trouble. The knitting club's branding meetings probably haven't been helping, either." I snatched the book from her hand and hurled it into the air. Jean watched it zip from the kitchen toward its home on the shelves. I admit I was showing off. "Come on. Our last stop is the conservatory."

On winter nights I banked the coals and lowered the tile stove's damper. I turned off the lights. Only the orange flicker through the stove's tiny window illuminated the room. Through the glass windows, snow frosted the landscape. The sky had cleared and moonlight washed the garden, giving the night an eerie glow.

"Let's sit here for a moment, okay?" Jean said. "I

want to hear more about your magic. Although I knew it somehow—I feel like I've always known—I'm still taking it all in."

I pulled up a chair. Rodney settled into his favorite spot in the kindling box, where someone from the knitting club must have placed an old woolen scarf as bedding.

"I'll tell you what I can." We were going to be here a while, so I rested another log among the coals. "It started when I came to Wilfred."

"You had no inkling before?"

"None." The log in the stove popped, as if to underline my point. "On my flight over, when I crossed the Continental Divide, the spell binding my magic broke. Life got really weird."

It had been as if someone had lifted a veil or tightened a telescope to correct its focus. Colors sharpened, sounds became keener. I smelled the cottonwoods in the breeze and luxuriated in the layers of flavor in a simple cup of coffee. I marveled at how the texture of cotton sheets tickled my fingertips. And the books . . .

"Weird? Like what?"

"Mom kept having dreams that I'd be killed for being a witch, so she'd forced Grandma to cap my magic when I was only a kid. She was almost right, but the truth was more complicated. We don't have time to go into that now. Anyway, Grandma's spell was geographic. As long as I remained east of the Rockies, I was okay."

Rodney had crawled from the kindling box and stood on his hind legs to reach a paw for Jean's lap.

She leaned back to make space for him. "I was

surprised when you left DC. You'd never shown much interest in traveling. Or in life, for that matter. Even as a kid I noticed it. All you needed were books."

A book in the Humor section a room away let out a guffaw I could even hear from my apartment.

"How do you know what to do? I mean, with your magic?"

I let out a long breath. "Some of it has been by trial and error. I've made a few mistakes, and they were so terrifying that in the beginning I was tempted to shut off my magic for good. But, I'm also learning from Grandma."

"Who is dead," Jean said. "Don't tell me you talk with ghosts, too?"

I laughed. "No. Over the years she wrote me a series of sealed magic lessons. Somehow she'd known I'd need them. Remember that letter you found on my dresser? The Norwegian pen pal?"

"Sure." Her hand paused on Rodney's back. "Don't tell me that was one."

Rodney stretched out a paw to encourage her to resume petting.

"It was. She must have put a spell on the lessons so only I could read them."

Again, silence. "Mom and Toni know, don't they?" When I didn't respond at first, she said, "Don't hide it, Josie. You've always been a terrible liar."

I pretended to poke at the fire, but really I was buying time. Finally, I replaced the poker and closed the stove's door. "Yes. Yes, they know."

"But they never told me."

"If it makes you feel better, they didn't tell me, either—not until last year when I'd already figured it out myself."

Jean had undergone too much these past days. Her dream of becoming a certified life coach hadn't come true; her dream was crushed. She was on the front row to a double murder and another attempt; the murderer had been apprehended. Now, just as she was finding herself, she learned I—her life-long competition—was a witch.

We fell silent for a few minutes. From the almost complete quiet, I realized how much I'd become used to nature's sounds: the whoosh of wind in the trees, the patter of rain blowing against the windows, the hoot of an owl or a coyote's wail.

At last, Jean spoke. "Why didn't you tell me all of this when I first arrived? Why did you keep it a secret?"

What could I say? That I didn't want her to feel like an outsider? To feel worse than she already did? I punted. "Mom didn't want you to know."

She seemed to accept this, but her voice picked up urgency. "I don't want to be babied. I want to be treated as an equal, not someone who needs protection."

"I know. I'm sorry."

She leaned back, one arm cradling Rodney, her fingers in his silky chest. "If you're magic, how come you couldn't identify Bernie as the murderer and poof her into jail?"

"I'm not omnipotent," I said, grateful for the conversation's change of direction. "I can't read minds. Plus, if I don't have books to draw energy from, I'm stuck."

"You tried to help solve the murders, didn't you? You used magic to read the toxicology report."

"Yes. Sam keeps plenty of books around, and I can draw energy from them. But I couldn't read the rest of the report. It was on Sam's laptop, and computers don't give up their contents for me." I rose and adjusted the stove's damper. "Come on. It's time for dinner."

Jean nudged Rodney from her lap and followed me upstairs. From her silence, I knew she was deep in thought. Why wouldn't she be? It wasn't every day you discovered you were descended from a dynasty of witches, and your sister talked to books. Upstairs, I stood next to her to look down into the atrium. In the rooms below us, books simmered in stories and energy.

"I'm glad you know," I told Jean. "Remember, you're magic, too."

The light was dim, but I could make out the change in Jean's expression. Her curiosity had turned to sadness. "Toni is a doctor. I'm nothing, and now Cookie's workshop is over. If I'm a witch, then I've got to be the nothingest witch there ever was."

"Don't say that, Jean. There's no one like you. You can do things regular people can't. You look at people and know what they need. For instance, Mrs. Garlington. You saw her trouble with arthritis right away. You have a gift for nurturing people."

"It wasn't anything she didn't already know."

Nothing I'd say could soothe Jean now. She needed to build her own confidence as a woman and a healer. "I'll cook dinner. You'll feel better in the morning. Besides"—I couldn't help smiling at this—"at least there's no killer on the loose anymore."

"Yeah, there's that. Let me get a sweater from my bag. It's chilly."

The furnace was still chugging along, but the house was more than a hundred and fifty years old. Its walls were solid, but not insulated. I went to my kitchen to pull vegetables from the refrigerator to make a stir-fry.

"Josie!"

At the urgency in Jean's cry, my heart jammed in my throat. I rushed to the living room to find her immobile over the couch, a slip of paper in her hand.

"What is it?" I said.

"Look."

She handed it to me. It was a sheet of notebook paper ripped from a small tablet—just like the last note. "Oh, Jean."

In block letters, the note read *SET*.

# CHAPTER TWENTY-FIVE

In bone-deep shock, we looked at each other. This, on top of the emotion from revealing my magic, demolished any sense of calm I'd fostered.

"When did you last get anything from your tote bag?" I asked.

Jean stared at me, lips slightly parted. "I don't know."

"Think, Jean. Walk yourself through this afternoon. You brought your bag to the retreat center, then what?"

She stared at the bag, now slouched on the sofa. "I hung it on my shoulder before the workshop started. Then, once I'd put my lunch in the refrigerator, I set it next to my chair. I used it throughout the day for my notebook and phone."

"When was the last time you looked in your bag?"

"Just before I left the retreat center. I'd put my

gloves in it. You know how they always fall out of my coat pockets. Yes, to get my gloves." Knowing came into her eyes. "The note wasn't there then. I'm sure of it."

"Just now—the note was on top?"

She nodded, then dropped to the couch. "Someone was in here. While we were in the conservatory. Someone came upstairs."

Remembering that the protection spell had been broken, my sense of panic jumped another level. I'd locked the library doors, hadn't I? I remembered bolting the front door and latching the door to the foyer. The side door—the old entrance to the service staircase—locked automatically when it closed. The kitchen? It was usually the last part of the library I put to bed for the night, because I had coffee cups to round up and the coffeepot to clean. Had I bolted the door?

"Wait," I said. "I'll check the doors." I headed down the stairwell. Jean was right behind me. The otherworldly glow of moonlight reflecting on snow filled the kitchen. I didn't bother to turn on the light but went straight for the kitchen door. Its bolt was open.

"You locked that," Jean said.

"Did I?"

"Definitely. I remember. You glanced over to Big House. Probably looking for someone in particular."

I felt my cheeks flush. I ignored my sister and stepped outside. Unmistakable rounds of footprints led from the door, over the lawn, and toward the front road.

My breath quickened and I exchanged pan- icked looks with Jean.

I closed my eyes and filled my lungs. "Sam!"

An upstairs window flew up. Nicky's room. "Josie?" Sam called.

"Something's happened," I said.

Despite my vague reply, my voice must have be- trayed my urgency, because Sam was waiting at Big House's back entrance when we arrived. He held the door for us as we clambered up the small back porch and into his warm kitchen.

"What is it?" he asked.

My breath came in short gasps. "Someone broke into the library and left Jean"—I had to stop to catch my breath—"left Jean—"

"—this," Jean said and handed Sam the note reading *SET*. "It was in my tote bag, up in Josie's apartment."

Sam held the paper at its edges and looked to- ward the library. "You're sure it wasn't there when you left the retreat center?"

"Positive. Someone must have come into the li- brary and put it in my bag while we were dis- tracted."

"It couldn't have been Rex or Bernie. Rex is in the hospital and Bernie's in custody."

We'd thought it was over. It was not over.

Sam examined the card, then seemed to come to a decision. "You two stay here and lock the door after me. After I call into the station, I'll search the library to make sure no one is still there." He pulled the library's key from its hook and strapped on his shoulder holster. "Keep an eye on Nicky, will you? I just put him to bed. I'll be back in a few minutes."

As instructed, I bolted the door. Jean watched him cross the lawn between Big House and the library.

"He's perfect for you," she said. "I don't know why you're playing it so cool."

"Shut up." And then, "What's this?"

On the kitchen table was Sam's computer bag. A file folder peeked from the open zipper.

"Can you read it? You know, with your witch skills?" Jean asked.

"It's the toxicology report. It already told me its contents, remember?"

"Right. What about the computer? I bet it has Sam's case notes on it. Are you sure you can't read a computer?"

"Nope. It doesn't work. Besides, we shouldn't pry."

"What do you mean? It's not like you're actually opening the laptop," Jean said.

"It amounts to the same thing. It's not right. What if he has personal business on it?"

"Josie, my life is at stake. I'm not asking you to see if he has dating profiles online, I want to see what he knows about the murderer. What he might not be telling us."

Grandma's lesson asked me to discern between my business and other people's business. This was my business. Besides, Jean was right. If I could somehow narrow my search to this case alone, it wouldn't be spying.

"Okay. Let me try," I said. "Watch at the window. I don't want Sam to catch us."

Jean leaned on the kitchen windowsill and turned sideways to see both me and the expanse of lawn outside. I slipped my hand into the bag and laid a palm on the laptop's cold metal shell and closed my eyes.

"Are you getting anything?" Jean asked.

"Give me a minute."

As soon as I relaxed, words flooded my brain in a torrent of voices. The problem was that I couldn't tease one message from another. Hundreds of emails fell on me at once in an avalanche of procedures, case meetings, and office birthday celebrations. With a whoosh, the junk mail folder snowed over all those messages, and my brain was a blur of discounted sunglasses, cut-rate cruises, and questionable vitamin supplements. I yanked my hand from the laptop as if it were scalding hot.

"I can't find it. There's too much going on in there."

"You're sure?" Jean asked.

"Positive. Yikes. He should clean out his inbox."

She joined me at the table. "Heads up. He's on his way back."

When the back door opened, we were lounging nonchalantly at the other end of the table.

"Did you find anything?" Jean asked Sam.

"Nothing." He stomped the snow from his boots. "There were scratches on the dead bolt plate on the kitchen door. The lock is old. Probably a cinch to break into. I'm going to make sure all your locks are replaced first thing tomorrow."

"The trustees would have to approve that kind of expenditure," I said, my librarian's duties never far from my mind.

"It'll be my gift to the library. I'll give Duke the money and send him into town. Besides, I'm a trustee, too, remember?"

I rose from my seat and pushed the chair under the table. "I guess we're okay to go home, then."

"Oh, no," Sam said. "Someone has threatened Jean's life. Until we've found that person, you two are staying here with me."

With Sam as our bodyguard and, as his assistant, Nicky in pajamas on his hip, we gathered a few things from my apartment to get us through the night at Big House.

"Are you sure you want to put us up?" I said. "We could bolt my apartment door. That gives us two layers of safety."

"You're not staying here unless you have room for me, too. And Nicky." He pointed at the table next to the couch where Jean's suitcase lay open. "Is that where the tote bag was?"

"Yes," Jean said, stuffing a hairbrush into the duffel bag where I'd already folded a nightgown. "Since it couldn't have been Bernie or Rex who put the note in it, we're down to Sylvia and Desmond."

Socks in hand, I paused. "Why did Bernie try to kill Rex, anyway?"

Sam shifted Nicky to his other hip. The baby's

head lay on his chest, thumb in mouth. "It's not for me to tell you, but I can say that the workshop isn't the first time they met. Rex used to be married to Bernie's sister." He raised his eyes, expecting us to be shocked by this information.

Jean arranged her features into a passable imitation of surprise. "You don't say?"

"Wow. That's something," I added, less convincingly.

Sam squinted at us. "Did you already know this?"

"Rex was married to Bernie's sister, but so what?" I replied. "You don't go around trying to knock off your ex-brother-in-law." Rodney, a catnip mouse in his mouth, nudged my ankle. I dropped the mouse into the duffel.

"She had reasons," Sam said. "All I'll say is that they have nothing to do with Cookie or the workshop. The investigation is still underway."

Jean zipped the duffel closed and hoisted it over a shoulder. "All set." She grimaced at her choice of words. "You know what I mean."

We made our way down the stairs. At the kitchen door, Rodney looked up at me and meowed.

"All right, big guy." I slung him over my shoulder. Heaven forbid he should get his paws wet on the snow.

At Big House, Sam returned Nicky to bed and opened the door to his parents' former bedroom at the front of the house. "You two can sleep in here. The bed's made up, and it has its own bathroom."

I cast him a questioning glance. He didn't sleep in the master bedroom?

Answering my unspoken words, he said, "I sleep with Nicky in my old bedroom. It's easier that way if he needs me during the night. If you have everything, I'll leave you two and see you in the morning." He sneezed, no doubt because of Rodney.

"Do you want me to send the cat home?" I said, having no intention of letting him go.

"No. I'll be all right." He disappeared into the bedroom down the hall and closed the door.

Jean clicked on a bedside lamp and shut the door behind her, just as Rodney squeezed through. The large bedroom felt cold and empty, despite a four-poster bed and heavy Victorian wardrobe. In earlier days, the fireplace would have been lit and traces of talcum powder and perfume might have lingered from the mirrored vanity. I pulled down the sheets.

Jean hoisted the duffel to a chair. "If you disappear in the middle of the night, I won't ask any questions. Do you have anything nicer than that flannel number to wear to bed?"

"Hush, and keep your voice down." I set my toothbrush on the bathroom counter.

Jean appeared at the door. "Did you notice that Sam's bedroom looks out on the library? Maybe he sleeps there to keep an eye on you."

"As if." How many nights had I parted the curtains to see if the lights had gone out in Big House's kitchen and if Sam's sheriff department SUV was parked in front? I'd watched for the yellow glow of the light against the cream curtains in Nicky's room, too, but I hadn't known Sam slept there.

A few minutes later, we were in bed, plumping

the pillows and warming the cool sheets. I hadn't shared a bed with Jean since we were little girls at Grandma's house. Light as a fly, Rodney landed on the bed and padded up to curl between our pillows.

"Are you okay with Rodney here?" I asked.

"As if it would make a difference," Jean said.

"True."

Rodney purred in response and snuggled closer.

Water went on, then off in the main bathroom, then quieted. Sam must have gone to bed. The house's furnace had ceased its rush of air for the night. The whisk of snow on the windows had stopped, and now the only noise was the creaking in the wind of the big oak out front.

Who wanted to kill Jean and why? We were down to two suspects: Sylvia and Desmond. Sylvia had a secret identity, true, but it was hard to imagine her needing to manufacture a lousy evaluation by murdering people. That left Desmond. The felon.

Would he kill to protect Cookie? She didn't treat him well, and he came off as a dutiful, if not overly enthusiastic, employee. Certainly not dedicated enough to thrust a knife in someone's back for her. Perhaps prison had changed him. Besides, Cookie had told me she'd known him all her life. Their bond might go deeper than anyone suspected.

Then there was this mysterious object everyone seem to be looking for. Someone had gone through Anders's hotel room and Marcia's room had been searched twice—once by Sylvia, if what

Cookie had told me was true. Had the object been located? Why was it important?

"Josie?" Jean whispered.

"Yes?"

"Can you sleep?"

"No." At this rate, my mind would race all night.

"What do you say we sneak out of here?"

# CHAPTER TWENTY-SIX

"Sneak out?" I whispered to Jean across Rodney's furry back. "And do what?"

"Desmond's our top suspect, right?"

Between Desmond and Sylvia, Desmond was the obvious choice. "And?"

"Maybe we see what he's been doing since the workshop shut down. Check out where he's been."

I turned this over in my mind. Jean had a good point. Someone had been at the library this evening. If we knew where Desmond was at that time, we could either confirm he had the opportunity to leave the note, or, by process of elimination, pin the blame on Sylvia. Duke was the person most likely to know where Desmond had been. Right now, Duke was probably holding court on the tavern side of Darla's café.

"Come on, Josie," Jean said. "We'll be perfectly safe. The last thing the murderer will suspect is that we're wandering around Wilfred. He'll think we're holed up in your apartment with all the bolts thrown."

"Sshh." The cry of a baby sounded down the hall. Nicky must have had a nightmare. A board creaked as Sam crossed the room to comfort him. Then all was quiet.

"We'll have to be careful sneaking out of here," Jean said.

"Super-careful." I couldn't believe I was actually considering this.

"You're in, then."

"Keep your voice down." Rodney patted my cheek with a paw. "You don't know about Sam. He has this otherworldly ability to keep an eye on people. I'm not kidding."

"What do you mean?"

"When he was in the FBI, he was what they called a 'ghost.' He tracked people, followed them. He can seem to be sleeping, then snap awake, like part of his brain never leaves the person he ghosts. He said he'd keep an eye on us, and you can bet he will. He'll be on to every creak and shuffle between now and sunrise. He probably knows we're talking right now."

Jean didn't even pause. "Probably thinks it's about him, that you're confessing true love always."

I barely stifled a groan.

"We have to be smart about this. That's all. We'll use the Ready-Set-Go method."

"Good grief. Should I go find a whiteboard?"

"Knock it off." She rolled toward me and placed a hand on Rodney's belly. His purr shifted to high gear. "First, Ready. Desmond is the prime suspect. We need to know where he was today, what he was doing, if he could have left the note. To find this information, we question people who might have seen him. Like Duke."

People paid money for a workshop in this? "All right. Set."

"Set," she said. "We stuff pillows under the blankets in case Sam looks in. To minimize noise, we don't change clothes, but wear our coats and boots over our nightgowns."

"We'll freeze!"

"We don't have time for anything else. We'll just have to button up. Now for the master's touch: We create a distraction."

This was sounding worse and worse. "Yes?"

"I'll make noise by going downstairs to, say, make tea. This will lure Sam to the kitchen. I'll tell him I can't sleep. That's only natural, given everything that's happened today."

"And?"

"While Sam is distracted, you plump up the bed to look like we're asleep and gather our coats. Then, send Rodney to Sam's bedroom. He'll do what you say, right? I mean, he's your familiar and everything."

"Cat friend," I corrected.

"Whatever. Anyway, you send him in. When Sam returns to bed, thanks to his allergies, he'll be sneezing. That will give you the chance to tiptoe downstairs with our coats. In the meantime, I'll have unlatched the back door. Then, it's Go."

"How much *Scooby-Doo* do you watch, anyway?" I said, although her plan had merit. It seemed un-

likely that Sam could keep his attention every-
where at once, especially with cat dander in the
air. It just might work.

"You want to nail the killer, don't you? The one
going after me?"

"We have a sheriff to do that," I said, nodding
toward Sam's bedroom. "Besides, we're safe. That's
what's important."

"He's sleeping. Meanwhile, Cookie and Desmond
are leaving town tomorrow. No one's on the job
right now, when it counts."

The bedroom's voile curtains let in barely
enough moonlight to make out the soft curve of
Jean's cheek and her strawberry blond waves. Rodney turned his belly to her and let his tail flick her
nose.

I had to hand it to her. Most people would be
happy simply to be safe. However, this was about
more than safety. Jean had something to prove.
She wanted to show she was capable and brave and
not the youngest girl always running home to
Mom and Dad. She was playing it lightly, but this
was important to her. I owed her this.

"Okay," I said. It wasn't like I was going to sleep
anyway.

Her face relaxed into a smile.

"But we're not taking any chances. We'll go to
the café and check in with Duke. I bet he knows
where Desmond was today and when he's leaving
tomorrow. Then we come back and go to bed. In
the morning, we give Sam the info and say Lalena
called us with it. Got it? To the café, talk to Duke,
back to bed. Half an hour, tops."

Jean scooted to sitting. "You've got the plan?"

"You make tea, I prep up here and send Rodney to Sam's bedroom. When he starts sneezing, I sneak down with our coats."

"See?" Jean whispered. "So easy. What could possibly go wrong?"


"Here I go." Jean climbed from bed. She didn't muffle her footfall.

I had the sudden fear we were embarking on a Keystone Cops skit. "Maybe this isn't such a good idea."

"No chickening out now."

Before I could protest, she was out the door. Her feet sounded on the steps, creaking about halfway down. I pulled myself to sitting, disrupting Rodney, who'd crawled into my lap.

Sam's door opened. He must have floated down the stairwell, because he was absolutely silent. Seconds later, quiet voices drifted from the kitchen. So far, the plan was on track.

I placed a hand on Rodney's back and closed my eyes. *Rodney*, I willed him, *go into Sam's room. Jump up on his bed.*

Rodney yawned and looked at me.

"Seriously," I whispered. "Go."

He backed up to slink under the covers.

That's how it was going to be, was it? I took a deep breath and let myself slip into his body. Rodney reluctantly nosed out from under the blanket. Through his eyes, I saw myself sitting in bed, a dim, curly-headed silhouette in the moonlight. Now completely in his body, I leapt from the bed to land whisper-light on the bedside rug. I padded down the hall and nudged Sam's bedroom door open with a paw.

Rodney hesitated at the voices downstairs. *Keep going,* I urged. Through his eyes, I made out Nicky's crib against one wall and a twin-sized bed on the other. Sam slept on a bed that small? At Rodney's level, I made out a stupendous dust bunny under the bed. I'd have to tell Sam his housekeeper was cutting corners. On the nightstand, Raymond Chandler's *Little Sister* spouted hard-boiled phrases over the roar of the Santa Ana winds, while a biography of Maria Callas held a high note to the *bravas* of the audience.

Steps grew nearer. Sam. Rodney jumped to the still-warm mattress and curled up on Sam's pillow. Then Sam was at the doorway.

I knew I only had a moment to gather Jean's and my coats and hustle downstairs. But, through Rodney's eyes, I watched Sam shed his bathrobe to show a T-shirt and pajama bottoms, and my legs buckled. Purrs vibrated through Rodney's body, whether from my own sudden heat or the residual warmth on Sam's pillow, I couldn't tell. What I would give to see this scene tomorrow night and the next, and the night after that. Every second mattered, but neither Rodney nor I could move.

Sam leaned over the crib to check Nicky's blankets, then turned to the bed. He couldn't miss Rodney, a black cat on a white pillowcase. He opened his mouth to say something, then sneezed.

I had to get going, and quickly. I tore myself from the scene and jerked into my own body before slipping from bed. I threw our coats over one arm, grabbed our shoes, and left the bedroom door slightly ajar so Rodney would have somewhere to go when he was booted from Sam's room. As I rounded the corner on the stairwell at top speed, wincing at a creak in the stairs, I flung my fingers toward Sam's room to make the Raymond Chandler novel slip from his nightstand and distract him from any noise I made. The next two sneezes gave me cover.

At last, I arrived at the kitchen. Jean waited by the back door. "I thought you'd never get here."

I shoved a coat and shoes at her. "Let's go."

# CHAPTER TWENTY-SEVEN

The snow had stopped, thankfully. But it was still cold. And dark. We crept toward the highway and remained silent until I was sure Sam couldn't hear us.

"Do you think we got away with it?" Jean said in a low voice.

I looked back. No lights shone at Big House. In a moment, we'd be beyond the trees and out of view. "Definitely. He'd be on our tail by now if he had any idea we'd left."

"Next time, remember to bring socks."

"Maybe I should have ordered up a limo, too, huh?" I said, although she did have a point. Only an inch of snow covered the ground, but my feet, naked in my ankle boots, were freezing. Gloves and hats might have been nice, too.

"Never mind. It'll be warm in the café. We can order hot toddies."

"No, we can't," I said. "I didn't bring my purse."

"Can't you just put it on your tab?" With a finger, Jean tested an icicle on the bridge's railing.

"This isn't the 1950s, Jean. We don't have tabs. We have credit cards. Water's free, though."

Unlike the flannel "thing" mentioned earlier, Jean wore thin pajamas. She must have been chilled to the bone. In response to my comment, she buttoned her coat higher.

The diner portion of the café was closed, but the tavern side was busy. We pushed open the vinyl-padded door to a dark, narrow room with booths along both walls—and a delicious rush of warm air. The bar was at the tavern's rear, and Orson the bartender was pulling a beer. He waved us over.

"Josie, we don't see you down here often. What'll you have?"

I glanced down the rows of booths. No Desmond or Duke. A football game played silently on the TV over Orson's head.

I was just about to explain that we weren't thirsty, when Jean said, "Two hot toddies, please."

"Coming right up."

I raised my eyebrows at her, and the firm look she returned told me she'd received my message loud and clear. I shrugged.

From behind me came the voices of a few of the knitting club's members crowded into a booth with an extra chair pulled over. Mona was halfway through a sweater, but most people held notebooks, not knitting needles.

"What are they doing here?" I asked Orson.

"Branding meeting. Tonight they're working on a name for the café. From what I heard when I dropped off their basket of fries, 'Killer's Lair' and 'The Poisoned Cup' were the top contenders." He set two glass mugs of steaming amber liquid in front of us. "On your card?"

"Actually," Jean said, leaning coyly on the bar. "Could you put it on our tab?"

"You mean the one you open with your credit card?"

"I'll buy the ladies their drinks, Orson. And a cosmo for me, please." We spun to see Rex standing behind us.

"Rex!" Jean's voice sounded as shocked as I felt. "You're out of the hospital."

"How are you?" I added.

From his rosy glow and clear eyes, Rex might have spent the afternoon on the golf course instead of in the emergency room. "Not bad. Once they got me warmed up, I was fine. Shocked, maybe, but all right. Will you sit with me?"

Cocktail in hand, he led us to a booth in the corner, beyond the chatter of the knitting club, far enough from the noise of the bar that it might have been a warmer, darker extension of the snowy night outside.

"I wanted to think for a moment before I headed back to the retreat center, so I stopped in," he said. "I didn't expect to spend the afternoon in the hospital, then being questioned by the sheriff."

"You heard the workshop was cancelled, right?" Jean said.

Rex laid his hands on the table. "Poor Cookie. No, I hadn't heard. The doctors released me only an hour ago."

My fingers were beginning to thaw from the warmth of the mug. I exchanged glances with Jean. If what he said was true, Rex couldn't have tucked the *SET* note in her tote bag. "You knew Bernie from back home, didn't you?"

He looked from me to Jean and back again with his robin's-egg blue eyes, so vivid against his tan, even in dim light. "I did. I'm ashamed to say I'd forgotten about her. Forgot about her pretty quickly, in fact. I used to be married to her sister."

"No kidding?" I said at the same time Jean said, "Her sister?" Jean sounded more convincing than I did.

"My wife—her sister—died. Pancreatic cancer. We'd only been married a few years." He took a long draw from his glass. "I knew about her illness when we met. She'd come to the Tub 'N Tan to buy a Jacuzzi for relaxation. In walnut. Chose the optional corner inset lighting. I supervised the installation personally." He relaxed against the red vinyl bench. "I told her she was beautiful, made her laugh."

And she made you rich. "Bernie held that against you?"

"Loretta—that was my wife's name—was quite well-to-do. Bernie thought I married her for her money, knowing she was dying." He chugged two swallows of his cocktail, half-draining the glass. "Thing is, she was right."

I saw it all. I smelled the cedar and chlorine of the hot tub, saw Loretta's frail shoulders and frosted fingernails. I watched the scene as if it were a movie with Rex charming Loretta and offering her the emotional strength she needed to endure treatment. She'd known she might not survive, and she'd left her estate to Rex. Maybe she'd determined it a worthy trade-off.

Jean reached across the table and rested her hand on his. "I'm sorry. It sounds like you gave her a lot of comfort." She always did know what to say.

"Comfort, yes. And a kind of love. However, Bernie—she and Loretta were close."

"Maybe she didn't see you as charitably?" I ventured.

"She thought I was a money-grubbing gigolo." His hand sought his glass, but it was empty. He lifted the glass toward the bar and nodded. Orson, with his decades of keenly honed skill on picking up barfly signals, would have another in the shaker in seconds. "She wanted to kill me. In her mind, I was a part of Loretta's death."

"Grief is tricky," I whispered.

"That, it is." Rex's voice picked up passion. "I told the sheriff I won't press charges." He shook his head. "Bernie was sorry enough. Last thing I heard before I blacked out were her screams trying to save me. I know the sheriff hauled her off, but I expect she'll be back to apologize in person. Even so, it doesn't matter. Bernie did me a huge favor."

"A favor? What do you mean?" I asked.

"Falling into that pond was a sort of baptism." His fist mimicked tumbling over the piled granite boulders and flattening as it hit the water.

Orson slid a martini glass of pink liquid in front

of Rex. "Girls?" He glanced toward our mugs. I shook my head, and he took away our empties.

I hadn't needed to fear Rex would stop his story. In fact, nothing could have stopped him now. He needed witnesses to whatever transformation had occurred today.

"It was a full twenty-four hours before I realized Bernie was Bernie. That's how little I knew her, even though Loretta was always on the phone with her, always telling me stories. Bernie was at the wedding, of course—and the funeral. I suppose she knew quite a bit about me, including the fact that I can't swim."

The owner of Tub 'N Tan couldn't swim?

"I'm a damned good tennis player," he added as an aside. Perhaps that had helped him bag wives number one through three. "I hit that water this afternoon and it wiped my head clean. When I regained consciousness in the ambulance, my world had done a one-eighty. Money? As long as you have enough to put food on the table, it doesn't matter." He shook his head as if he couldn't believe it himself. He leaned forward. "You know what does matter?"

It was if Rex had undergone a religious conversion, and tonight's cocktail was his sacrament. "What?" I asked. "What matters?" I had a hunch it wasn't Ready-Set-Go.

"Love," he replied.

It hadn't been love that had led him down the aisle with his last wife. Perhaps with none of them.

"Love," Jean repeated.

"I came here with one goal." With the back of a hand, Rex pushed his nearly full glass to the table's edge. Again, he shook his head. "Hell, I'm a new person. It's crazy. I don't mind telling you that I don't give a fig about life coaching. I came here to meet Cookie." He looked at us as if we'd be surprised.

"To marry her?" I said, since he seemed to wait for the prompt.

"Yes. I'd met her after one of her motivational speeches, and I saw an opportunity to pad my bank account. Shocked?" Fortunately, he didn't wait for a reply. "Here's the clincher. I don't want Cookie's money anymore. Fact is, I have plenty of money of my own. I came here to woo her for cash, and I fell in love." He leaned back and tapped the table for emphasis. "That's what matters. I love that woman's passion to make this a better world."

"Yes," Jean said. "Her ability to see what needs strengthening in us and to make it grow."

"She's a gal in a million," Rex said. "I'm not playing any more games. First thing tomorrow, I'm going to come clean with her. We're meant to be together—her husband's death was fate. I can help her be even more of herself. I can support her as she spreads her vision."

Jean nodded enthusiastically. Soon they'd be circulating through the bar, handing out memberships to the Cookie Masterson fan club.

"Seriously, it's all about love," he said with the ardor of the newly converted. "Don't wait for it to come to you. You see it, you grab it, ladies. I don't regret easing Loretta through her hard times, but I'll never forgive myself for not understanding what real wealth is. L-O-V-E."

Orson must listen to this kind of talk all the time, I realized. I hoped the tips were worth it. The tavern door opened to a burst of frosty air, and for a second I panicked that it might be Sam. Fortunately, it was Duke and Desmond, deep in conversation. They passed us to take a booth nearer the bar.

"Rex, I'm so happy you're feeling better," I said.

"Cookie is a wonderful woman," Jean added. "I hope you spend many happy years together."

I slipped out of the booth. "If you'll excuse us, we have someone else to see."

# CHAPTER TWENTY-EIGHT

Desmond and Duke appeared oblivious to the world, as if all that mattered was the oily chunk of machinery on the table between them. Duke was tidy enough to have laid newspaper under it, but it wafted diesel.

"You see, Desi, rebuilding a piston, you don't want to take shortcuts. It's all about the quality of the components." He looked up, startled to see us. "Hi, girls. You still up?"

"We couldn't sleep. Jean"—I glanced at her, getting her unspoken permission to continue—"got another note."

"SET," Desmond said in his gravelly voice. "Oh, no."

"I see," Duke replied. "Pull up a chair to Dr. Duke's couch and tell me about it. You informed Sam, I take it?"

"Oh, yes." I pictured Sam, deep in dreamland,

up at Big House. If I hadn't been in my nightgown, I would have unbuttoned my coat to cool off.

"And he's letting you run around alone?" Duke shook his head. "Never mind. You two look warm in those coats. You can hang them right there. Thank goodness Darla got the heating right in the remodel." He pointed toward the coat hooks at the end of each booth. Besides the lack of rips in the vinyl seats and the smell of fresh carpet, the new tavern was identical to the old one. Surprise, surprise.

"No, thank you," I said demurely.

"I'll keep mine on, too, thank you," Jean said.

Duke raised an eyebrow. "Suit yourself."

We settled into the benches, one on each side. From the knitters, a comment drifted over about how it was too bad Wilfred didn't have a music store, or it could be called "Blunt Instrument."

"Not just killers roaming Wilfred," Duke said, "But thieves. Keep an eye on your valuables."

"Why?" I asked.

"Someone lifted Desmond's knife."

Desmond swatted the air. "Oh, it'll turn up sooner or later."

"How's that? It was snapped onto your belt. Those things don't go walking off on their own." Duke tapped the table. "You girls had better be careful. I have half a mind to call Sam right now and roust him from bed. Letting the both of you wander town while there's a murderer about. Honestly."

"Don't do that," I said quickly. Then smiled. "I mean, we're here with you, right? We're safe." I averted my eyes from Desmond.

"Bet your sister didn't know when she came to

Wilfred she was walking into a death trap," Duke said. "I tell you what. Two murders, then another one attempted this afternoon. Woo-wee."

His talk cut a bit too close to home. I flashed him a sour smile.

"Desmond, what's your take on all this?" Jean asked sweetly. "As an outsider, you should have an interesting perspective."

Orson delivered a basket of fries, a pint of beer for Duke, and a Coke for Desmond. He didn't look twice at the engine pieces.

Poor Duke. He and Desmond had clearly hit it off, and I had no doubt he hadn't a clue about Desmond's criminal past. As irritating as Duke could be—he was crude to a degree that would have Emily Post spinning in her casket—at heart he was a good man. I hated to think of him bonding with a murderer.

"I'd like to know, too, Desmond. Especially as you're a felon and all," Duke said, as if he were commenting on the weather or the state of the tavern's fries. "Being in the joint, you see all sorts." He punctuated this comment with a long sip of beer.

So much for my concern.

One hand grasping the Coke, Desmond examined us. He gave no hint of what was going on behind those hard gray eyes and craggy skin. Finally, he said, "I could machine you a part for your starter."

Voices drifted from the table of knitters. "The This-N-That might specialize in true crime books. Patty could decorate with ice picks and nooses."

"Fix the starter?" Duke said, Desmond's opinion

on the murders forgotten. "Finding parts for a 1952 Nash is impossible."

"Used to do some machining. I don't reckon it would be a problem."

Duke pulled a pair of reading glasses from his shirt pocket and was turning in his hand the greasy object on the table. We weren't going to get anything from them. Not as long as there were engine parts to ponder. No, I had a better idea. I glanced at Jean to see if she'd caught my drift. She had.

"We were just leaving," I said.

Taking my cue, Jean scooted from the bench and I followed. In the parking lot, we buttoned our coats to the top. An icy wind whooshed over the quiet street, whisking feather-light pellets of snow.

"It's desolate out here," Jean said.

It was near midnight, and other than the tavern's inhabitants and Mrs. Garlington, who famously suffered from insomnia, Wilfredians were tucked under eiderdowns and lost to the sandman. I glanced toward the bluff. Through the trees, both the library and Big House were dark.

"What do you say?"

Jean didn't need to ask what I suggested. Our sisterly understanding told her everything she needed to know.

She shoved her hands in her sleeves, making a sort of muff of them. "We'd better get to it now, while Desmond is busy with Duke."

"Isn't it strange that Desmond wouldn't give any opinion about the murders? Nothing at all? It was like we never even mentioned them. I thought when Duke spilled the beans about his time in prison, he'd have something to say."

"He knows something," Jean said.

"It could have been Desmond who searched Marcia's room. And Anders's hotel room. Maybe on Cookie's behalf."

"No," Jean said. "Cookie had nothing to do with this. Desmond has his own motivation for getting involved."

We turned toward the path through the trailer park to the meadow, and eventually to the retreat center. It was going to be viciously cold. "Hurry. If we're going to figure it out, we don't have long."

The cedar trees flanking the entrance to the Magnolia Rolling Estates were shingled with snow that reflected in sparkles under the single mercury light illuminating the drive. We moved quickly, partly because of time and partly to keep warm.

I kept my voice low. "How much time do we have? He might be right behind us."

"Duke will keep him for at least a beer's worth of conversation. Come on."

The short rows of trailers on both sides of the central drive were quiet. Roz's was dark, of course, since she was on her honeymoon. Rose vines, scrawny with winter, grew up Lalena's mail post and over her sign advertising palm reading. Darla and Montgomery's suite of two trailers joined by a yard were also dark. A porch light shone outside Duke's double-wide, illuminating his tidy gravel pad and evenly trimmed lawn, tonight smooth with snow.

Beyond the trailer park, the meadow path plunged into darkness. I glanced behind us. We were alone.

"My feet are freezing," Jean said.

"My everything is freezing. You were the one who wanted to do this," I pointed out. "We could be warm in bed right now."

"Or you could have brought socks."

Thick woolen socks. Socks from toes to knees. I nearly swooned at the thought, not that I would admit it. "Socks wouldn't help much in this cold, anyway. But I wouldn't mind a flashlight." Alternating glances at the barely visible path and the distant yellow patio light at the retreat center, we arrived at the path over the levee where the Kirby River met the millpond.

"Don't look down," I told Jean. "Keep going."

Ignoring me, she paused a moment to gaze down the rocky barrier to the millpond. Only that afternoon, Rex had been pulled from its bone-chilling water. I looped my arm under her sleeve and pulled her forward.

The deputy sent to guard the retreat center was long gone now that Bernie had been apprehended. But that was before Jean had received her second death threat.

We mounted the patio and tried the front door. Locked. Without speaking, we edged to the center's rear, being more careful here since the guest rooms faced this direction. All the rooms were dark. Sylvia had left town. Only Cookie would be in now, and she would be asleep.

We tried the kitchen door and met with success. Desmond must have left it open so he could re-

turn. Inside, the retreat center was almost oppres-
sively warm. Heaven. The light over the stove gave
us enough illumination to see by.

"Which room is Desmond's?" I whispered.

"The one next to Cookie's." She started toward
the stairway.

The retreat was solidly constructed, and its
strong wooden floors were silent as we crept upstairs. The hall light was off, but the floor-to-ceiling
windows in the main room shed enough light that
once our eyes adjusted, we were fine. Jean glanced
at me, then tried Desmond's door. The knob
turned, but the door remained closed

"Shoot," she whispered. "Too bad I don't have
my phone, or we could look up lock-picking online."

"I might be able to help. Hang on."

In the landing's mini-library, surely one of the
crime novels had a lock-picking scene that could
instruct us. We returned to the landing, and I motioned for Jean to take a chair.

I centered my energy and cleared my mind.
*Books, show me how to break into a room.*

At once, the books trembled with life. A sparkle
of white light shot off some of them. Two thrillers,
three cozies, and a Mickey Spillane mystery flew to
the end table next to the armchair.

Jean's mouth fell open. "That's so cool."

The thriller, a hardback, opened to a scene with
a jewel heist. The protagonist and his team were
circumventing a museum's high-tech alarm system. Too sophisticated for us. I tapped that book,
and it flew back to the shelf to slip between two
other novels. Jean watched with bald amazement.

Next, the Mickey Spillane. I placed my palm on its cover. A rough voice with a deep Brooklyn accent recited a break-in thrumming with suspense. I jolted as the novel's hero kicked in a door. Nope. Not for us, either. I flicked my fingers at it, and it shot to its shelf.

Cozies ran the gamut, I knew. Some were more accurate and detailed than others. I closed my eyes and ran my hands over them, all too aware that Desmond or Rex might return at any moment. One cozy described breaking into a room secured with a skeleton key in an old lock, like we had at the library.

"It's not a skeleton key lock, is it?" I whispered to Jean. "If it is, it's a cinch. Push out the key from the inside onto a sheet of paper. Pull the sheet under the door, and use the key to open from inside the door."

"No," Jean said. "The building's too new. Besides, we want to break in, not out."

"Right." I focused again on the books.

Bingo! My hand stopped at a bedroom break-in. Sure, the book featured a bed-and-breakfast in Cape Cod, but the situation was the same. The scent of warm blueberry muffins rose from the pages. The narrator was a sassy woman about my age, a burned-out caterer from the big city who'd unexpectedly inherited a charming Queen Anne cottage from her aunt. She described cracking a simple doorknob lock.

"I've got it," I said, slipping the book into my coat pocket. "We need two butter knives from the kitchen."

"Wait here." Light as a cat, Jean disappeared

down the stairs and returned moments later with the knives.

Following Jean, I padded down the hall. She stopped in front of Desmond's door and looked at me before trying the knob again. Still locked.

"Hold this," I whispered. I set the book in Jean's hands.

"It's warm," she said in surprise. "The book is."

"Too hot?"

"No. I like it. It's almost as good as gloves."

"Just hold it and let me concentrate."

I half-closed my eyes and let the novel's words guide me. Instantly, the rush of a seaboard storm filled my head. The heroine, Brittany, was in the attic of a remote cabin, struggling to free her bound-and-gagged neighbor from a locked bedroom while a murderer stalked the grounds.

> *Hands shaking, Brittany drew the old butter knife from her pocket. "Hang on, Mrs. Goldblum," she whispered. "I'm coming."*
> *Muffled groans reached her ears.*
> *Quickly, but with a precision borne of years of icing petits fours, Brittany inserted the knives into the doorframe, one above and one below the handle mechanism. She jiggled them with swift but sure motions.*

My motions weren't particularly swift nor sure, and the knives simply didn't fit into the doorframe. Damn it. Duke had been foreman for the retreat center's construction. The man was too much of a perfectionist to set a door that didn't seal tightly.

*The storm raged. A slate roof tile grated as it
tumbled from the roof and shattered on the
ground, but its crash was a mere accent to the old
house howling and creaking around them.*

*At last, the bedroom door popped ajar, and
Brittany rushed in to loosen Mrs. Goldblum's gag.
The older woman spat, then said, "Careful,
Brittany, he's still out there."*

"You're doing that all wrong."

I jumped, flattening myself against the wall.
Jean and I had been so intent on breaking into
Desmond's room that we hadn't heard him arrive.
"Him" being Desmond. He stood impassive before
us, his coat unzipped as if the winter outside were
a mild breeze.

My breath came too quickly for me to squeeze
out words. Jean's eyes had widened to the size of
Brittany's famed chocolate chip cookies, the rec-
ipe for which, the cozy informed me, was at the
back of the book.

"Give me that." He extracted one of the knives
from my grip. "You go like this. Gently." With a
deft twist, the knob clicked and door sprang open.

"Thanks," Jean said. "We'd better go now. It's
getting late."

Still unable to speak, I nodded rapidly in agree-
ment.

"There's something you wanted, wasn't there?
Now that the door is open, why not come in and
check it out?"

He pushed the door all the way open and motioned in. Jean glanced at me in sheer panic. We

didn't have a choice but to follow his instructions. He stood between us and the stairwell. On our other side was one more bedroom—Cookie's.

"Cookie!" I shouted.

"She won't hear you," Desmond said. "She takes a pill to sleep."

"Sylvia?" My voice, still loud, was less sure.

"She left for Portland, remember? Anyway, don't be so jumpy. I'm not keeping you here." He picked up the mystery novel, now askew on the floor. "You girls reading? I'm not much into books. Duke says *Peaceful Cove Dead and Breakfast*, is pretty good, though."

He stepped aside, giving us the chance to run, if we wanted. I was more than happy to take him up on the invitation, but Jean grabbed my sleeve.

"Someone has threatened my life, and it can't be Bernie or Rex," she said. "I know you don't want to talk about it, but we're worried."

I gaped at Jean. She was blowing our chance to escape. "Jean," I warned.

"Shut up, Josie. We need Desmond. You'll help us, won't you?"

He shrugged. "If I can. I've met a few men in for manslaughter, and they weren't real nice. Well, one of them was." His smile indicated a pleasant memory. "Anyway. How can I help?"

I looked at him in amazement. He seemed sincere, not at all like a homicidal maniac.

"Is that why you're here?" he said. "You think I might be the murderer?"

"No, but we had to be sure," Jean said. "You understand."

I looked at her with admiration. My little sister had more presence of mind than I'd given her credit for. I began to relax.

"The thing is, someone might have hidden something in your room. To implicate you," Jean said. "We thought while you were at the café, we'd have a look around."

"You didn't need to be sneaky about it," he said. "You could have asked me."

Jean looked up in full "sweet, forlorn me" mode. This look had garnered her no end of peanut butter cups—her favorite—as a child. "It's my life at stake. Besides, didn't you lose your knife? Someone might be trying to frame you."

Desmond bought it. He stepped into the bedroom and turned on the overhead light. "Come on in. Let's search this place. What are we looking for?"

# CHAPTER TWENTY-NINE

"Truth is," I told Desmond and Jean, "I'm not entirely sure what we're looking for, but I'm guessing it's legal documents." I had a working theory. "Whatever it is, we're not the only people who want to find it. To keep it safe, someone may have hidden it in your room while you were out."

In Desmond's room, a double bed, made with military precision, stood to our left as we entered. A modest closet and coat hooks were on the wall to the right, the wall the room shared with Cookie's suite. Straight ahead was a window with a view of the forest—or it would, if the shades were open. To the left, beyond the bed, sat a nightstand with a lamp and, along the adjacent wall, a short bookcase, desk, and chair.

In short, there wasn't much room to hide anything, and if Desmond's tidiness was any indicator, he would have found it.

"Do you mind if I look in here?" Jean pointed to the closet.

"Fine with me." Desmond lowered himself to the bedside rug and plunged an arm between the mattress and foundation.

We looked like a couple of chumps, bare-legged in our coats with our hair all over the place. Jean couldn't help but still be adorable, but I knew I could double as a Halloween lawn ornament.

Naturally, I directed my search to the bookshelf. As I approached, I heard one of the books gagging. What genre could that be? I ran my fingers lightly over the dozen or so spines, feeling for a burst of energy.

"Nothing hidden in or under the bed," Desmond said.

The gagging noise became louder and erupted into a cough. I didn't remember choosing medical manuals for guest reading. My fingers tingled as they landed upon a bird identification guide. Mrs. Littlewood had donated one for every room in the retreat. The book let out an especially dramatic gag.

I glanced behind me. Desmond was meticulously examining the items in his suitcase while Jean, standing on the chair she'd pulled over from the desk, felt around the closet's top shelf.

We still didn't know with 100 percent certainty that Desmond was innocent. I pulled the bird identification book from the shelf. A document of half a dozen pages or so fell from it. *Book*, I asked it silently, *did Desmond stuff this in you?*

*Not a chance*, the book said and let out a few chirps. The image of Desmond, his back to the bookshelves, came to mind. *He doesn't read,* another book said. *Not a page. Nothing,* a thriller added above the faint sound of squealing brakes and an explosion. *He just lies there and looks at the ceiling. Like he's been captured by rebel soldiers,* a biography of Abraham Lincoln added in a professorial tone.

Someone, then, had hidden these papers in Desmond's room. Someone was indeed framing him—or simply wanted the papers out of the way. Who?

I turned to Desmond and Jean to show them the still-folded document and came face-to-face with Sam, looming from the doorway, hands on hips. From the broad smile on his lips, it was clear he was not happy. Seriously not happy. Sam had generously taken us into his home to protect us and we'd snuck out. He'd warned me against becoming involved in the investigation, and I was rifling through a murder suspect's room. I froze, heart pounding, and prepared for a major dressing down.

"I brought these for you." He thrust out a hand with two pairs of wool socks in it.

The realization plowed into me like a train on a track. At that moment, I knew with every micron of blood surging through my body, I was deeply, madly, irrevocably in love with Sam. If I were a cartoon, hearts would be flooding from my eyes. Maybe it was my conversation with Jean, or maybe Rex's story, but seeing Sam barely able to contain his anger, holding two pairs of wool socks, I knew it: This man was for me. This was no mere infatuation and I was finished denying it.

Furthermore, I knew something else: He loved me, too. He might not know it, but he was hooked. This certainty set off a flash flood of happiness like I'd never experienced.

At the sound of Sam's voice, both Desmond and Jean swiveled. Desmond simply stood, dumbstruck, but after a few curious glances at me, Jean regained her composure.

"Why, thank you. How thoughtful." She snatched a pair of socks and unrolled them.

Without thinking, I slipped the papers into my coat pocket. "You found us."

"I heard you leave. Nice trick, sneaking Rodney into my room."

"Why didn't you come after us? What took you so long?" I asked.

"I had to find someone to watch Nicky. I got in touch with the tavern and Orson told me you were there, safe. Then I got a call from the sheriff's office. After I'd phoned in Jean's note, they sent a detective to the airport hotel to question Sylvia. She isn't who she claims to be. As of now, Sylvia Lewis is being held on suspicion of homicide."

"Sylvia?" Desmond said.

"That's what she calls herself, anyway. She had extensive notes about the murders. On top of that, we found a third note with *GO* on it."

"But we already know Sylvia is someone else," I said, barely able to keep my brain on the murders, not with Sam anywhere nearby.

"Bobbi Williams," Jean said, looking cozier now with her legs covered. "Workshop reviewer."

"Nope. That was her story to us, too, but that identity didn't hold. There is no Bobbi Williams who reviews workshops. We couldn't even find a firm that hires the kind of workshop evaluators Sylvia claims she is."

"Then who is she?" I asked. *Sylvia Lewis*. Chills ran down my neck and the backs of my arms, and it wasn't from the night's cold, either.

"We don't know. She refuses to talk without an attorney. He's flying out from New York and won't be here until sometime tomorrow."

My brain was a miasma of fear for Jean, curiosity about Sylvia, and love for this smart, brave, handsome, eccentric man. "We thought something was up with her," was all I could mutter.

"She didn't know downward dog from a napping beagle," Jean said. "She was a phony, but the Bobbi Williams story seemed all right."

"That was her plan." Sam nodded toward the room. "By the way, I could have saved you tonight's trouble. We spent the afternoon searching the guest rooms."

"Desmond, you knew this? You didn't say anything," I said.

"You girls seemed determined," he replied.

"Why?" I asked. "Why would Sylvia—or whoever she is—kill Cookie's husband and Marcia? I don't get it."

"You don't have to get it. That's my job. Come on, I'm taking you home."

The night's adventure, panic, and open questions faded under the warmth of my emotion for Sam. I tucked my arm into his, earning a glance of surprise, and said, "Come on, Jean. Time for bed."

# CHAPTER THIRTY

Now that Sylvia—or Bobbi or whatever she called herself—was in custody, Sam allowed us to return to my apartment.

Rodney, happy to be home, curled up on the sofa. The books murmured welcome and the library's furnace chugged along with a low, comforting waft of heat. Something about the books' chatter was different tonight, but I didn't have the mental space to deal with it. My head was full of Sam.

"Sylvia," Jean said. "Who would have known? I totally bought the workshop evaluator story. And all this time I thought she liked me."

"Hmm," I said, barely listening.

I tossed my coat over the chair by the fireplace. Now that Sylvia was in jail, I could let go of thoughts of murder and open up to the emotion that threatened to fritz my nervous system. I loved Sam. Truly and completely. Seeing him standing in Desmond's doorway with my socks in his hands had ripped my heart wide open. I loved him, and there was no going back.

"Sure." Jean crumpled paper to start a fire. "She didn't know yoga, but I thought she was simply a wannabe."

"Oh." I wandered to the window. Pale light burned behind the curtains in Sam's window. He was awake, no doubt going over the day's happenings. I sighed. He'd brought me socks. He'd thought I might be cold.

A book at my elbow was trying to get my attention. It must have selected itself for bedtime reading. I half-smiled, sure it was a book about relationships. Instead, I picked up *Due or Die,* a murder mystery set in a library. I tossed it aside. The books must not be up to date on the investigation.

Meanwhile, Jean continued to process the evening. "You'd be surprised how many fake yoga teachers are out there. They squeeze into some expensive leggings, fill a to-go cup with green juice, and pretend they're Zen. Yoga is about so much more than that."

"No kidding." I flattened my palm against the cold windowpane.

The light went out at Sam's. I remembered his body heat, the warmth I'd felt when Rodney had curled up on his pillow. That's where Sam was now, in his boyhood room, with a Raymond Chandler novel on the bedstand next to a Persian cookbook and a biography of Maria Callas. Could he be thinking of me? Did he know yet that he loved me? As soon as dawn broke, I planned to find out.

"I compare yoga to a pig ballet. The hard part is getting them in toe shoes. Once you do that, they plié like it's nobody's business."

I sighed. "Huh."

"Josie, pay attention. I'm talking to you. You haven't heard a thing I've said."

I forced myself to turn away from the window, toward the fire. "What? I'm listening."

"No, you're not. You're planning your wedding with Sheriff Dreamboat across the way. Ever since he tracked us down at the retreat center, you've acted like you're drugged. What happened?"

I sat next to Jean on the couch. "Honestly, I don't know. I looked at him, and one thought hit me like a falling piano. I knew he was for me. You're right. I'm so stuck on Sam, I can't think straight. This might sound crazy, but I think he loves me, too."

Jean took a moment to study me. I could feel our connection as her pale blue eyes locked on mine. "Haven't I been telling you so?"

"I think I've been afraid to open the floodgates. I mean, what if it doesn't work out? What if Sam refuses to tune into his feelings for me?"

"You told me yourself he's a recent widower. Plus, the baby takes up a lot of his brain space."

My heart headed south and landed with a thud somewhere near my appendix. "You don't think he'll ever come around romantically?"

"I didn't say that, Josie. Like you, he hasn't been

ready to acknowledge it." She shrugged. "He'll either shake loose his feelings, or—"

"Or what?"

"Or not. You'll have to wait to see." She scrunched her lips. "And if he does, you'll have to figure out how to tell him you're a witch. I'd like to see that."

The windows rattled with the winter wind and I shivered, more from emotion than cold. I rose to get my bathrobe, hanging on the corner of my bedroom door. In its pocket, I found two vintage crime novels: *She Shall Have Murder* by Delano Ames and *Beginning With a Bash* by Alice Tilton. I tossed them on the side table.

Jean pointed to the paperbacks. "What are those?"

"Volunteers. The books do that sometimes. They probably slipped into my pockets when we were in danger." I'd have expected romance novels by now.

"Maybe they have a point," she said, "Sylvia is a fraud. Okay, I get that. Still, it's not coming together for me."

I wrenched my thoughts from Big House and Sam inside it. "In what way?"

"Well, for one, she couldn't have killed Anders. She was with us at the retreat center when he was stabbed. Plus, she couldn't have left *SET* in my tote. She'd left town after her fight with Cookie. Would she have had time to break in here, put the card in my bag, then drive to Portland?"

I shrugged. "Maybe if she hurried. You don't think Sylvia's the murderer?"

Jean folded her arms. "I don't see it."

"Then who is she? She isn't Sylvia and she isn't Bobbi, and she keeps a New York lawyer on the hook."

"She takes a lot of notes, questions people, and searches rooms."

"But she isn't law enforcement," I said, "Or Sam would know. If the murderer isn't Sylvia . . ." Wind rattled through the chimney, causing the fire to flame and spark.

Jean pulled up her quilt. "Are you sure you locked all the doors?"

"I bolted the kitchen door after Sam"—ah, Sam. My body warmed and tingled—"and we locked the upstairs door, too. We're safe." I put more conviction in my words than I felt.

"Back to the matter at hand, Josie. No googly eyes."

"All right. Who else could it be? We've ruled out everyone else—even Desmond." Then I remembered. "Wait. I found papers in a book in Desmond's room. The books said he didn't put them there, that he never even cracked one of them. He's no reader." In two steps, I was at the armchair, rifling through my coat pockets.

"You forgot about suspicious papers? Really?" She shook her head. "I thought the sheriff's office searched all the rooms."

"I don't know how they missed them." Here they were. Barely intelligible legalese droned from the folded packet. "Sam. He hijacked my brain." I smoothed open the documents. "It's a divorce settlement." I flipped to the end, then back to the beginning. "Signed by Anders, but not Cookie. 'On this day, blah blah blah.'" Still reading the papers, I lowered myself next to Jean. "Anders wanted a lot of money." I set the draft settlement on my lap. "Money and the Ready-Set-Go trademark. This document claims Anders rightfully owns it."

At that moment, the furnace let out a boom and silenced. Jean and I looked at each other.

"I'll reset the furnace. It won't take a second."

"Josie," Jean said, her voice low. "Are you nuts? Don't be an idiot. Two people have died. It's the middle of a winter's night. You're proposing to go into a dark basement? In a movie, this is where the axe murderer ambushes you." She cupped her ear with a hand and narrowed her eyes, mimicking listening intently. "Could that be scary music I hear in the background?"

I couldn't help but laugh. "Seriously. It's cold tonight. The books need to be kept at a stable temperature. Plus, Lyndon would never forgive me if I let his orchids die. Two minutes, and the furnace will be back up and running."

A few taps resonated through the vents. New noises for the furnace. Eyebrows raised, I looked at Jean, then rose to bolt my living room door. "I guess it's okay to wait until morning. The conservatory stove is probably still making enough heat to get by."

"Good. Come sit," Jean said, "What about the papers? What do you think they mean?"

Once again, I dropped to the couch. I drew the papers closer and this time I read them through carefully. "Other than what I said, Cookie's husband—through his attorney—claims he's entitled to half their assets, plus a hefty monthly allowance."

"He must not have intended to marry Marcia," Jean said. "Or his alimony would have been cut off."

I tapped the papers. "The big thing here is that he claims to have invented Ready-Set-Go and is entitled to its trademark. He doesn't even offer to let her buy him out."

"Which would put Cookie's career under his control."

We pondered this a moment. The night's chill began to permeate the old mansion's walls.

"We already cleared Cookie," I said. "Maybe—just maybe—she could have poisoned Marcia. But there's no possible way she could have stabbed her husband. Too many witnesses put her at the retreat center when he was murdered. Besides, why would Marcia have to die? Anders—I get it. He was trying to steal her livelihood. Who else could it have been?"

"He was sleeping with her student, Josie. She'd have a grudge against her." Jean pulled up a blanket. "Not that it makes her a murderer."

I tucked the blanket's other end over my knees. I really should have reset the furnace. "Despite what she says, she didn't seem very attached to her husband. Look at her marketing materials. She was busy dating all sorts of men. Maybe Cookie's ego was hurt, but she doesn't seem rash enough to knock off her husband's girlfriend. In fact, I'd say she was hyperrational." I shook my head. "Although if anything could make her a killer, it would be losing Ready-Set-Go."

"Where does that leave Sylvia? Why was she threatening to kill me?"

My head hurt. Besides that, I was cold. "I don't know." I tossed the divorce papers on the coffee table and poked at the fire. "Sam should have these. Should we call him? Time might be important."

"You just want to see him again." She glanced at her phone. "It's two in the morning, Josie. You really want to wake him now?"

I parted the curtains. "Big House is dark. Sam's in bed." Jean was right—I did want to see him again. And again and again. But this was an important piece of evidence and Sylvia was in custody, possibly being questioned at this very moment. I turned to Jean, who'd pulled the blanket all the way up to her neck. "We should call him. He'd want us to."

My purse was on a side table. I dialed Sam's number, going to the window to see if his light switched on. It remained dark, and the call went straight to voice mail. "He has his phone on silent."

"That's his personal number, right? What about his sheriff's phone?"

"I don't have that number programmed." Not that it would be too hard to find. My imagination drifted toward Sam, sleeping after a long day. "You know what? Let's leave it until morning. These papers aren't going anywhere. There is one thing I'm going to do, though, and that's reset the furnace. It's colder than I thought."

Jean had slouched into the couch, but now she sat up. "No, Josie. I know it's silly, but I feel like we should stay close."

"You think the killer would get me?" Despite my joking tone, I was half serious.

"Stay here. I really don't feel good about you poking around in the basement. I have plenty of blankets."

I rested a hand on my bedroom doorknob. "Okay. No basement. I'll see you in the morning."

Before I made it all the way into the room, someone grabbed my nightgown by the collar.

It was Cookie Masterson, and she had a knife.

# CHAPTER THIRTY-ONE

The knife's blade glinted in the light of the nearby lamp. The bone handle, thick blade—I knew that knife. It was Desmond's. Cookie was planning to kill us and blame it on Desmond.

"What?" was all I could say.

From the confusion on Jean's face, she hadn't seen this coming, either.

Cookie pushed me toward Jean and kept the knife's razor tip at throat level. She circled toward the living room's door, our only exit, now bolted shut.

Mom had known Cookie was bad news. She had no idea just how bad.

"Josie," Cookie said. "Give me those papers."

"Why?" Jean said. "Why are you doing this?"

She looked at us incredulously. "I'd thought you, of anyone, would understand, Jean."

In the blink of an eye, Jean's face underwent a

series of emotions, from bewilderment to pain to an eerie calm. She nodded slowly. "You mean, you're needed."

Shocked, I stared at Jean. What was she thinking? For once, our sisterly connection had frazzled.

"Needed?" Cookie replied before Jean's words were even finished. "I'm essential. Without me, Ready-Set-Go are empty words. I took the concept and made it into something that has transformed countless lives." Her voice climbed in pitch. "You don't get it, do you?"

I couldn't do anything but swallow and stare, wide-eyed.

"So many people look up to you," Jean said.

"Every day I receive scores of emails from people thanking me because I helped them achieve their dreams. Then they, in turn, help other people. I save lives."

My gaze dropped to the knife, then returned to her face. If she had her way, our lives wouldn't be among them.

"Anders would have put an end to it all," Cookie said. "What's one life compared to the tens of thousands I help?"

"How's that?" Jean asked.

She shook her head. "Stop playing for time and give me the papers."

"What papers?" I wracked my brain, trying to think of a way out of this.

"The divorce papers." Her gaze drifted to the fire.

I didn't need her trademarked program to figure out her plans for the divorce settlement. "Why would you need divorce papers?" I asked. "Your husband's dead." I instantly regretted my choice of words.

"Stop being coy. I heard you talking about them. You knew Anders planned to steal Ready-Set-Go." She snorted. "Claiming he'd thought of it. So what? So he had the outline of an idea after a few beers. He's not the one who built and nurtured the program. Without me, the idea would have been forgotten by the time he brushed his teeth for bed. He couldn't steal my program." Rage had overtaken reason, and her hands trembled. She lifted the knife higher.

"I don't know what you're talking about," I said.

Whatever Cookie had done, whatever she said, murder didn't come easily to her. Her confident I-can-manage-this attitude had frayed, and her eyes darted around the room. I couldn't imagine her plunging a knife into Anders's back.

"Fortunately," she said, her voice cracking, "GO isn't simply the execution of SET's plan. It incorporates room for last-minute changes. Expect the unexpected."

"Just like you taught us," Jean said with reverence.

Cookie had lost her mind, but Jean's worshipful attitude concerned me even more.

"Because the successful creator understands she has control only over her own actions and not the universe, no matter how well she has planned," Jean said, as if reciting a lesson plan.

"That's right." A fraction of Cookie's calm returned. Keeping an eye on us, she lifted a flask from her coat pocket and set it on the end table next to the bust of Emily Dickinson. "Of course, you'll want a nip of something warm before bed. This will really help you sleep."

A knife and now poison? One thing I had to say for Cookie: When she prepared for a murder, she really prepared.

I scooted closer to Jean and squeezed her hand. Rodney leapt to the side table with the flask.

There's no way Cookie could have stabbed Anders. Judging from her shakiness now, she didn't have the stomach for it. She was running on pure panic. I could imagine her slipping something into Marcia's morning coffee. That was an indirect action. Sure, she would have been responsible for what happened, but Marcia would have drunk it herself, just as Cookie was clearly planning for one of us to do. Anders's death was something else completely.

How had she pulled that off? She was charismatic, sure. Persuasive, yes. *Persuasive.* With a sudden and sure conviction, I knew how it had happened. I finally understood. It had been ingenious, a superb execution of the Ready-Set-Go model.

I calmed my breathing so I could speak. "You persuaded Marcia to kill Anders, didn't you? You gave her an overdose of sleeping pills—something that would muddy her thinking, but need time to take effect—then somehow convinced her to murder Anders. Or maybe you convinced Anders to poison her. It wouldn't have been difficult. Not for you." I remembered the pill bottles I'd seen in her husband's luggage when we'd talked in her room. "Yes, that's what you did."

She watched me, but didn't respond.

"Marcia worshipped you," I said. "That's why she was attracted to Anders in the first place. She would have believed anything you told her. For instance, that Anders wasn't planning to leave you, that she was being used. You might have even shown her the roses Rex gave you, saying they were from your husband." It was a guess, but a good one. From the look of satisfaction that spread over her face, I knew it had hit home. Cookie had persuaded Marcia to kill Anders.

Behind Cookie, Rodney nosed the flask. *Keep at it,* I willed him. He raised his head to look at me.

"He wasn't getting any money out of me," Cookie said.

"You killed them both," I said. "By having them kill each other."

Rodney head-butted the flask. It didn't budge. *Good work, kitty,* I told him. *Don't give up.*

"You're right—I let Anders kill her. You think Marcia was easy to convince? Anders rolled over instantly. All I had to do was call him with a story about how Marcia and I had a partnership to grow the life coaching institute, and he went ballistic. Tried to hide it, of course. Anders already took sleeping medication. All he had to do was quadruple the dose for Marcia. I gave them plenty of time to meet before the workshop started and let them take care of the rest themselves."

It had been a cold morning. I pictured Marcia hurrying through the frost-tinged meadow to meet Anders behind the café. That way, they'd be out of sight of anyone coming and going at the PO Grocery across the street. She'd filled her to-go mug with coffee. The café's side door was unlocked, and with the paper over the windows, they thought they'd be safe. An unexpected bonus. When Marcia's back was turned, Anders put drugs in her travel mug. They argued. Marcia waved the roses Rex had given Cookie, thinking they were a gift of love from Anders to his wife and evidence of betrayal. In anger, she ripped the red petals. And stabbed Anders. Then she returned to the retreat center to die.

"The papers," Cookie said. "Put them in the fire."

Those papers were proof of Cookie's motive to kill Anders and she knew it. I couldn't destroy them.

Rodney patted at the flask, but it was too heavy to knock off the table. Not only that, its cap was screwed on tightly. He let out a mournful meow. Cookie knocked him to the ground with her elbow without once letting the knife drop. He slinked toward the door, but it was shut. And bolted.

"Why?" I asked. "They're not divorce papers. Or whatever. Look." Grandma had put a spell on my lessons so that only I could read them. She'd been able to change the text in the mind of the reader. Surely I could do that, too, but adrenaline had shattered my focus. I silently called on the books' energy, funneling it in my mind into a concentrated beam of energy. Slowly and firmly, I willed the text to morph. "It's a knitting pattern. The knitting club leaves them all over the place."

To read in the dim light, she had to switch focus from the knife to the papers.

Jaw set, eyes unwavering, Jean stared at me. Her thoughts were clear. *Let me handle this*, they said.

"No," I mouthed.

Jean spoke up anyway. "I've followed you for a long time, Cookie, and I've dreamed of becoming a crumb. At last, this week, I achieved my dream. Hand me the flask. I know what you mean to the world, and I'm ready to sacrifice myself for it. Just don't make Josie pay."

Sacrifice herself for it? "You'll do no such thing."

"Leave me alone. I make my own decisions about my life."

I couldn't let this happen. She was willing to drink poison so I could escape, yet Cookie would kill me, too. She couldn't let me live. Not now. Besides, Jean was not a planner. Whatever she had in mind would go wrong, as it always had.

"Jean, she's going to kill you. She'll make you drink poison, stab you with Desmond's knife, and pin it on him."

"It's for the greater good." Jean fixed me with a steely gaze. *Trust me*, it said. "In the scheme of things, I don't matter. Cookie does. She's a thousand times more important to the world than I am. If I can help Cookie continue, I'll willingly do it."

I couldn't speak. Jean had asked me to do the impossible. She wanted me to leave her in the hands of a murderer. I shook my head. There was no freaking way I was going to let her get herself killed.

"No," I said. "Forget it."

"Cookie, take Josie outside and tie her to the banister." Jean pulled the sash from her bathrobe and handed it over. "Here. I'll go in the bedroom and drink from the flask."

This was insanity. If I ran at Cookie, she'd stab me, sure, but maybe it wouldn't kill me. Then Jean could get away, dart across the lawn and bang on Sam's door. But would Jean run? Or would she stay and fall in with Cookie's plan?

Jean stared at me with a conviction I'd never witnessed in her. Could I trust her to make the right decision?

"Okay." The word wrenched from my mouth.

Cookie's confidence had returned, and she looked more like the Mistress of the Universe I was used to seeing. "Good thinking, Jean. I'm gratified that you believe in me. But I'm not leaving you alone in here while I take care of your sister."

"Lock me in the bedroom. Then you won't have to worry I'll change my mind," Jean said.

Knife still trained on us, Cookie looked from Jean to the head of the skeleton key in the lock. A smile spread over her face. "You really do understand. I'm proud of you. You won't die in vain, I promise."

Moving slowly, Jean crossed the room and picked up the flask. She closed the bedroom door behind her.

My heart ached. "Jean! No."

With a solid click, Cookie turned the key in the lock. She waved the knife toward the living room door.

"You. Outside. You're going to have an accident in a moment."

Rodney mewed and slipped out behind her. All around us, books moaned and sighed and hummed at a deafening pitch. To Cookie, the library would be dead silent, but to me it was a torrent of raw energy I fought to keep under control. I relaxed my shoulders and slowed my breathing in an attempt to rein it in. The library's lights, off for hours, flickered like faraway lightning.

She backed me to the banister overlooking the atrium. "You'll fall, unfortunately, and break your neck. I'll make sure of that." She set down the knife to tie my hands behind my back.

This was my moment. I thrust a knee into her belly, and she deftly knocked it aside, grasping me by the wrists.

"Don't try that again." Cookie pushed me to the banister, this time face forward. The floor, two stories below, almost vanished in the night. If I were somehow able to walk after the fall, there's no way I could open doors and run for help. If I survived, that is.

Rodney crept behind her and nudged the heavy knife, moving it a fraction of an inch.

"Your sister understands," Cookie said, tightening the sash into a tourniquet.

I refused to give her the satisfaction of crying out, but sweat moistened my forehead.

"Jean might change her mind about drinking the poison. She will, though. Eventually." Satisfaction reverberated in her tone. "As you deduced, I'm very persuasive."

I closed my eyes and felt the library's energy roar through me, nearly obliterating my senses. *Books*, I said silently, *Are you ready?*

"Lean over the rail. Do it," Cookie said.

I kept my eyes closed and took a deep breath.

"No." The star-shaped birthmark on my shoulder burned as if pierced by a fire-torched skewer.

She crouched to snatch the knife just as it was about to fall between the railing. "Damned cat." She attempted to kick Rodney, but he raced toward the cat door. Over the books' torrent of moans and cries, I barely heard the flap thunk after him.

She pressed the knife's cold tip to the back of my neck. "Jump."

I only hesitated a moment as energy screamed through me. Then I did it. I put a leg over the railing and let myself fall. My blood raced with adrenaline—and magic. As the books' cries reached a crescendo, they shot from their shelves almost too quickly to see; large, flat hardbound books on the bottom, pulpy paperbacks on the top, and cushioned my fall better than any mattress. On my raft of books, I hovered at the level of the second floor.

Cookie's shriek from above me echoed through the library. She vanished a moment, then reappeared holding the marble bust of Emily Dickinson.

Stunned, I struggled to free my wrists. Could I cocoon myself with books and, if so, would they shield me from the bust's deadly weight?

I had no time to find out. Cookie leaned over the balcony and, with both hands, lifted the bust. I closed my eyes against the impact I expected to shatter my bones, but it didn't come.

I opened my eyes. Standing behind her was Jean, the light from the living room outlining her silhouette, a lamp raised above her head. She swung and Cookie fell.

# CHAPTER THIRTY-TWO

The raft of books gently lowered me to the atrium floor. Drained and trembling, I rolled to my side and sat up, a paperback tumbling from my chest.

"I'm locking her in the bedroom," Jean yelled from upstairs. Cookie slowly disappeared as Jean pulled her, feet first, into my apartment.

Rodney sauntered in and head-butted my leg. Behind him, Sam, in pajamas and a robe, hurried from the kitchen. "Rodney got into the house again and—" He took in the disaster of books and pulled me to my feet. "Josie! Are you all right?"

I couldn't take any more drama. I burst into tears, leaning into Sam's chest, my wrists still tightly bound. Jean's head poked over the railing, then drew back. She gave me a thumbs-up. Cookie must be safely locked away.

"What's going on?" Sam pulled at the bathrobe

sash binding my wrists. "Rodney woke me, and I saw that you'd called. How did these books get down here?"

Hands now free, I wiped my face with my sleeve and took a deep breath. Freak-out over. "Sorry. I needed to offload some emotion."

"That's okay." Could that have been tenderness in his voice? "What happened? Is Jean all right?"

"I love you." I hadn't planned to confess it now, but the words came flying from my mouth on a magic carpet of emotion: intense longing, the adrenaline dregs of a near-death experience, exhaustion from having summoned so much magic so quickly, and, finally, relief. Relief that I was alive. Relief that Sam knew how I felt.

I hid my face against his chest. It smelled like all the best things I could imagine: the ocean's salt, the crook of a neck, long mornings in bed. Now he knew how I felt. He could do with it whatever he wanted. Maybe he kissed the top of my head, but I couldn't tell for sure.

"For crissakes," came a man's voice. Toolbox in hand, Duke and Desmond stood at the entrance to the atrium. The furnace once again rumbled below us. "What happened?"

Dazed, I lifted my head. "What are you doing here?"

"I asked you first."

"Long story," I said. Then, to Sam, "Upstairs. Cookie tried to kill us. Jean's got her locked in my bedroom."

Sam ran to the side stairwell, and from the sound of his feet on the tread, he took the stairs

two at a time. Duke and Desmond were right behind him. I sat again among the books. Rodney
sauntered over and crawled in my lap. "Thanks for
waking Sam. I know, buddy. Not the best timing
for proclamations of love."

I felt no need to rush to my apartment. As she'd
signaled, Jean had the situation well at hand. I
sensed it clearly. After rubbing my wrists and a taking a long look at the books I'd have to clean up, I
went to the kitchen to make coffee. The sheriff's
crew might want some when they arrived. Getting
pushed off a third-floor landing, confessions of
love with no response, sister single-handedly detaining a murderer—all in a day's work as Wilfred's
librarian.

After a few minutes, Duke and Desmond joined
me in the kitchen. "Sam has it under control,"
Duke said.

"I repeat, what are you doing here, anyway?" I
asked.

"After you and your sister left the retreat center,
I couldn't sleep, so I wandered back to the café to
chat some more with Duke. They kicked us out at
closing time," Desmond said.

"Since it was Desi's last day in town, we thought
we'd hang out and fix the furnace. We were trying
to be quiet. Turns out we could have been holding
cannon practice, and it wouldn't have mattered."

I looked from man to man. The two were on a
prolonged handyman's spree. Ready-Set-Go and
Cookie's plan to kill us and frame Desmond hadn't
accounted for this.

At the sound of crunching gravel, I peeked out

the kitchen window to see two sheriff's office SUVs pull into the driveway. Behind them, an ambulance rolled to a stop.

"We have company," I said.

"You might want to change." Duke rose to pull a coffee mug from the cupboard. "And do something with your hair. It's a real rat's nest."

Four deputies entered, one with a suitcase, and one holding the door open for the EMTs.

"Upstairs," I told them and took a seat at the kitchen table. I smoothed my hair, but it was no use trying to put on proper clothing, not with an apartment full of sheriff's deputies. Soon, I knew, someone would be downstairs to interview me. Right now, Jean could take the spotlight. Besides, there wouldn't be any more threat from Cookie. I knew it.

A few minutes later, Sam came downstairs, alone. He took the seat across from me.

"Coffee?" I said.

He frowned—a sign of happiness—then smiled slightly. "Don't you want to know what's going on upstairs?"

He was as rumpled as I was, and it gave me comfort. His hair stuck out in crazy directions and stubble spread over his jaw. He ran his fingers along his chin. The love that saturated me was so intoxicating and powerful, it could only be magic's sister. He was my Sam, no matter what. He had something to tell me, I saw it in his eyes.

"She drank it, didn't she?" I asked.

He nodded. "Cookie's dead."

# CHAPTER THIRTY-THREE

L ater that afternoon, when I—Jean behind me—
pushed open the door to Darla's café, every
seat was taken, and the air was warm with the fra-
grance of patty melts and jambalaya. Once the
sheriff's office had left the library, taking Cookie's
body with them, Jean and I had slept for four
hours straight in Sam's guest bed. As soon as I'd
risen, I ordered a new mattress, despite Lalena's
offer to sage the bedroom.

We'd awoken hungry. Now it looked like the
café didn't have room for us, and we'd have to return to the library and fry up some eggs.

"Josie!" called a voice from a corner booth.
Duke stood and waved, Desmond beside him.
"Come sit with us. In a minute, Darla's going to an-
nounce the winner of the café naming contest."

I scanned the room for Sam, but didn't see him.
Jean had told me he was probably busy with the in-

vestigation, but I couldn't help but wonder if his absence was by design. I sat next to Desmond, momentarily flustered. "You heard—about Cookie?"

Desmond nodded and speared a piece of sausage. "A shame. But maybe for the best."

"That woman was downright cruel to Desmond," Duke said with enough feeling that he might have been talking about the unexpected breakdown of the Tohlers' tractor. "If you ask me, justice was served."

"Oh, Duke, she wasn't all bad. She made a lot of people happy with that Ready-Set-Go nonsense," Desmond said.

"She wasn't kind to you, Desi. She had you by the neck, she did. Treated you like an indentured servant. No more of that."

"I'd always wondered why you stayed with her," I said. "You didn't seem like the traditional assistant to an entrepreneur and social media star." He didn't seem to be in mourning, either, I noted.

"She had me over a barrel," Desmond said. "She knew about my record and threatened to expose it anywhere I applied for work if I didn't stay on as her unpaid assistant. She's always been like that."

"Made him work for room and board only." Duke shook his head in disgust. "Not that it matters now. He's rich. Or, he will be soon."

"No kidding?" Jean said.

"Sure," Duke said. "Didn't you know? Desmond, tell them."

Desmond laid his fork on the table. "It's okay to talk now, I guess. Cookie was my sister. Since Anders is dead, I inherit."

Looking at Desmond, I was surprised I hadn't

marked the resemblance sooner. Both he and Cookie had eyes an unusual shade of gray, and both were built small and lean. It was their different situations in the world—Cookie, the prosperous, charismatic leader, and Desmond, the haunted underdog—that had set them apart.

I barely had time to digest this nugget of information when Darla, relaxed despite the full house, poured coffee. "I heard there was quite a to-do up at the library last night."

"Sam told you?" I asked. "Has he come in?" I longed to see him, yet dreaded it. The more hours that passed without seeing him, the more I doubted he returned my feelings.

"Haven't seen him, but Mrs. Garlington has the baby. I imagine he has quite the workload after this week."

I glanced across the room to see Helen Garlington bouncing Nicky on her knee.

"I'll have your food up in a jiffy," Darla added. "We're busy. You're getting waffles this afternoon. We're out of everything else."

"I love waffles," Jean said.

After Darla passed on to another table, Duke turned to me. "What a week, huh? We figured out most of what happened the night Cookie died. She hid in your bedroom?"

I explained how Cookie had convinced Anders to kill Marcia and vice versa. "Remember those shredded rose petals in the café and the rest in the retreat center's garbage?"

"A waste of good roses," Duke said.

"Rex gave them to Cookie. I'm almost certain Cookie told Marcia they were from Anders, that he'd promised he'd never leave her and was using Marcia." Rex's gift had played into her hands beautifully. "Marcia brought one of the rosebuds to her meeting with Anders and shredded it in front of him. Then she took a knife from the kitchen and stabbed him in the back."

"And Anders poisoned Marcia," Desmond said.

I nodded. "With his sleeping pills. I saw the bottle in Cookie's room when Anders's suitcases were returned to her. Cookie had each of them so riled up that they wouldn't stop to talk to each other."

"What about last night? How did you escape?" Duke asked.

"When Cookie had a plan, it was almost always a sure thing it concluded her way," Desmond added.

"That was Jean," I said. Trusting her had been the hardest thing I'd ever done, but it had paid off—not only with my life, but with her self-confidence. "Jean, you tell them."

"Josie said"—she shifted her gaze toward me while she found words that wouldn't betray my magic— "Josie had inadvertently let on how to break out of a room locked with a skeleton key, as long as the key was still in the lock."

"The old sheet-of-paper-under-the-door trick?" Desmond asked.

Jean nodded. "Josie has books all over the place. I ripped a page out of one of them to use to slide the key into the bedroom. Sorry about that."

"Which book?" Funny I hadn't noticed.

"Something by Anthony Horowitz. *Skeleton Key*, I think it was called. Anyway, Cookie's one weakness was her ego. Yes, Josie, I recognized that," she said quickly before I could get in an incredulous word.

"I convinced her I was willing to sacrifice myself so she wouldn't be convicted for the murders. I told her to lock me in the bedroom, that I'd drink the poison."

"Jean is the real heroine here," I said.

"She was going to pin the murders on Desmond, wasn't she?" Duke said with indignation.

"She had Desmond's knife. My guess is she was going to stab Jean with it once she was dead and tell the sheriff Jean had killed Anders—remember, Jean was the only crumb besides Marcia not at the retreat center when he died—and Desmond was seeking justice." Darla slid plates of waffles in front of us, and I buttered mine lavishly before continuing. The break gave me a moment to condense timing to gloss over my rescue by the books. "She took me to the hall to push me over the railing, and Jean broke out and knocked her on the head with a lamp."

"Then I dragged her to Josie's bedroom and locked her in. And"—Jean raised her fork for emphasis—"unlike Cookie, I took the key out of the lock."

We'd spent a good part of the morning talking about Cookie. Jean was disappointed, sure, but as Jean had put it, she'd learned more from Cookie than Cookie could have ever realized. She'd learned to trust herself and she'd proven she was capable. All of this was infinitely more important than Ready-Set-Go.

I turned to Desmond. "Now that Cookie is gone, what will you do?"

"I'm staying in Wilfred," Desmond said, his tone softening. "It's a fine town."

"Yep," Duke said. "There's opportunity here for him. Patty needs help converting the This-N-That to an antiques mall. Darla said he can have the guest trailer for a while. We're going to open a business together."

Before I could congratulate them, Darla silenced the crowd by tapping a water glass with a spoon. Montgomery's whistle shut down the remaining chatter.

Darla climbed onto a chair. "Attention, everyone. Thank you for coming. It's time to announce the café's new name."

Chairs squeaked against the linoleum as the crowd, including a table of knitters, swiveled toward her.

"We've had so many good suggestions. I want to thank each of you who participated." She smiled toward the crowd.

Not a fork budged, nor coffee mug lifted. Every one of us waited to hear the new name.

"And the new name is—honey, are you ready?"

Montgomery emerged from the kitchen, drying his hands on a towel. "I'm here."

"The new name is—get ready." She lifted her chin. "Darla's Café."

We sat in silence a moment.

"Come again?" asked Maureen from the knitting club.

"Darla's Café is what we're naming it. That's what folks call it, anyway, and I didn't see any reason to change. Shouldn't be hard to remember. We're having new menus printed and a sign made in town."

"Why print new menus?" Maureen asked, clearly still stupefied.

"Why, we'll need a capital 'C' now on *café*," Darla replied. With a hand on Montgomery's arm, she stepped down from the chair.

"You've got to be joking," Mona said. "This is robbery."

"We should have seen this coming," I told Jean.

Grumbling arose from the knitters' tables, but stopped when the cafe's front door opened. Was it Sam? I turned to look.

Rex, dark circles smudging his eyes even through his tan, stood uncertainly inside the door.

Jean rose and dragged over the chair Darla had just stood on. "Come sit with us, Rex." Then, to Darla, "Could we have another place setting?"

He tossed the day's issue of the *New York Times* on the table. "I'm not hungry."

"You'll want a cup of coffee, at least," Jean said. "Maybe a small serving of protein, too. You'll thank me later."

The paper's headline caught my eye. LIFE COACH IN DEATH MATCH, it read. "What's this?"

"Sylvia Lewis, that fink. Turns out she's really Evangeline Philbin, an investigative reporter," Rex said. "This is the concluding piece in her series on life coaches. Cookie deserves better. Maybe she wasn't perfect, but she was a hell of a woman."

I glanced at Jean. The pieces clicked in place for both of us. "All those notes. Asking questions. Mom even mentioned the series, come to think of it."

"Sylvia was researching Cookie the whole time," Jean said.

"Wow." Duke drained his coffee mug. "Did she ever bag a story."

"She doesn't understand Cookie," Rex said with sudden passion. "She was a good woman. Trying to help people achieve their dreams. What's wrong with that?"

My heart went out to him. I knew just how he felt. Now, maybe for the first time, he was actually in love. Maybe he'd first pursued Cookie out of greed, but he'd fallen for her. Hard. And it was too late.

I touched his forearm. "I'm sorry. You had a special bond with her, didn't you? I get it."

"But she was a coldhearted murderer," Duke added with his usual lack of diplomacy.

Rex ran his fingers over the gray stubble on his jaw. "One good thing that came of it is I fixed things up with Bernie. We had a long talk this morning. I'm going to sign over the country house to her. She always loved it there, and it's where Loretta died. Bernie deserves it."

"I wonder what will become of her?" Jean asked.

"Back to dog grooming, I guess," I said.

"No, actually." Rex leaned back as Darla filled his coffee cup. "She plans to become a coach. A grief coach. With therapy dogs."

She'd be a good one, too. I remembered her gentle talk with Patty about her late husband earlier this week.

"Darla." Duke raised his mug. "Refill, please." He shook his head. "What a crazy life this is."

\*    \*    \*

The next day, Jean and I walked down the hill to Wilfred. It hadn't even been a week, but it might have been a year ago that I'd waited here for her in the middle of the night. This afternoon was only marginally brighter. Leaden clouds promised more snow.

"Did you remember everything?" I asked, more to cover my sadness at her departure than to make sure she hadn't forgotten her toothbrush. We stopped at the café's parking lot, and Jean set down her duffel bag.

Rodney jumped on top of it and she scratched his ears. "I'm good."

The shuttle bus, Duke behind the wheel, idled in the café's parking lot. Desmond sat in the seat behind him, and they both waved pieces of a ratchet set as if discussing their relative merits. Rex was slumped toward the rear. Sylvia—or Evangeline, as I was coming to think of her—was long gone. Bernie had also left town once the sheriff's department had released her.

"Jean." I carried her duffel to the shuttle bus door. "I'm going to miss you. I'm sorry I didn't trust you. I won't make that mistake again."

"Are you coming up or not?" Duke shouted from the driver's seat. "You have a plane to catch."

Jean gave me one last squeeze. "I'll call when I get home." She raised her head a moment, looked past my shoulder and smiled widely, then quickly said, "Got to go. Bye!"

I didn't have time to get in another word before the bus door closed. The shuttle bus rolled from the parking lot, and I waved until it was only a spot on the horizon.

I turned to see Sam, in uniform, standing at the parking lot's edge. He walked toward me. My heart pounded with every step. Here it came, the "I love you but I'm not in love with you" speech. I steeled myself.

"Josie," he said, his breath clouding the winter's cold.

I'd watched for Sam the night before, seen his bedroom illuminate briefly near midnight, then darken. But he hadn't visited, hadn't even texted. This was my chance to take back my proclamations of love. I could chalk them up to the hysteria of fear. I could laugh them off. I could say anything. I remained silent.

Sam pulled my gloved hands from my coat pockets and held them in his. He opened his mouth, then closed it. Was he smiling—or frowning? I didn't know this expression.

"Josie," he said again. Then he pulled me in.